ALSO BY ISABELLA THORNE

CONTENTS

WINNING LADY JANE

Winning

Lady Jane

A Christmas Regency Romance

The Ladies of Bath

Isabella Thorne

Winning Lady Jane
A Christmas Regency Romance

Winning Lady Jane © 2019 by Isabella Thorne
Cover Art by Mary Lepiane

2019 Mikita Associates Publishing

Published in the United States of America.

www.isabellathorne.com

Part 1

Merriment & Mistletoe

1

---

*T*he sun was shining on a cold December morning, and the day was full of possibilities. Miss Jane Bellevue fastened her last button and smoothed her travel frock, thinking about how unlikely it was that she would be dressing herself again anytime soon.

Fancier dresses took more care than her simple robe. Jane took pride in the task today, reminding herself that she was not noble, but neither was she helpless. No matter how exciting her trip, nor how esteemed her new companions, she would not allow her head to be turned by such things as servants performing simple tasks for her.

Jane found it a satisfying pleasure to see a task well done, not at all like some ladies who could do nothing without a ladies' maid or a man to hold their hand. After her mother died in a carriage accident, Jane's father had taken her into his confidence. He had relied upon her in her mother's absence, and Jane saw the advantages of his tutelage. He had taught her sums and shared all manner of his business practices, ensuring that his daughter grew into a clever and capable young woman. Jane had to laugh at herself for even considering that perhaps a servant would be undertaking mundane tasks for her in the future. She was having grand designs again.

Her family was not of noble birth, but she loved them all the same. Jane knew that neither money, property, nor even a title, could provide a guarantee of a gentle nature. Her father was simply Mr. Bellevue, the second son of the second son of a viscount. Jane loved him dearly, and her little sister Julia was a joy. So what if Jane's family was not the *crème de le crème* of the *Beau Monde Ton*? They were hers.

If truth be told, her extended family did possess some gems. Not that Jane had ever spent much time with her more esteemed relatives. She had met briefly with several, but there was no love lost between them. Although she sometimes envied the bustle of her friends' houses, her father and Julia were enough family for Jane.

Still, I should have seen my cousins in Bath, she thought. *I should have made connections as Father wished.* The viscount still had a house there, as did Jane's father. For some time now, she had been certain their paths would cross naturally.

Jane would not insinuate herself into higher circles simply to find a match. Such actions seemed disingenuous, so she had left the matter to fate. Surely serendipity would strike, and her more noble relatives would invite her to join their number, but Jane and her esteemed cousins had missed one another at every turn.

No matter, Jane told herself. They were likely in London for the season now; not that she would see them there either. The expense of a season was too great for one such as plain Jane Bellevue.

Although her father affectionately called her Lady Jane in jest when she was feeling particularly high-minded, the truth was she was only a simple miss. Mr. Bellevue was no pauper, but neither was he overly wealthy. Jane knew she must be temperate in her desires.

She had known there would be no London season from the time she was old enough to consider it. The dresses alone would be a terrible expense, one she knew her father could not bear, despite his wish to give his daughters everything. Still, luck had been with Jane this summer past, and now, who knew where her new friendships would take her?

Perhaps she would find love. The thought made her giddy, and she hoped that it would be true. Jane was not yet considered a spinster, but time was ominously ticking by. Her task as eldest daughter was to marry, and to marry well. She knew this and did not mind it, but she wished for someone she could get on with.

She was looking for a friend and true life companion. A good match would provide her younger sister, Julia, with greater opportunities than were afforded to Jane herself.

Jane examined her face in the glass. She was no great beauty, but neither was she unappealing. She was on the petite side, with a full and bountiful figure. She had dark hair and dark eyes, which were not the current fashion. Blondes were more likely to be viewed with approval.

Still, Jane looked carefully and could find no sign of wrinkles about her eyes or forehead.

She still looked young and fresh, not at all like a spinster. Surely, there was some gentleman who wanted a woman of real substance, rather than one possessing mere monetary gain and pale fragile beauty. She had met no such man.

Jane stood back from the glass and shook her head to clear such thoughts. She surveyed her bedchamber critically, wondering at the person she would be when she next returned. Would she be changed by noble association? This summer past, she had left this room carrying high hopes. She had thought, surely, she would return a lady spoken for. She had not.

She had met no gentleman to her liking in Bath, although she had met several ladies of quality. She knew Lady Charity Abernathy, the daughter of the Earl of Shalace, from their shared association with the Poppy family. Lady Charity visited Bath often when her father came to take the waters.

Last summer she met Lady Charlotte Keening, younger sister to the Earl of Keegain. Lady Charlotte was outgoing, friendly, and did not seem to mind Jane's lower birth. Jane had enjoyed Lady Charlotte's company ever since she had quite literally run into the young lady upon the streets of Bath.

Lady Charlotte admitted that her family did not often summer in Bath, preferring Brighton, but a potential suitor had convinced Lady Charlotte to reconsider her travel plans; with Charlotte's persuasion, the family had decided to let a house in Bath instead of Brighton for their summer holiday.

Jane took it upon herself to show Lady Charlotte all of the best shops in Bath. In turn, Charlotte introduced Jane to some of her London friends who regularly summered in the city.

In addition to Lady Charity, there was Lady Patience Beatram, the redheaded daughter of the Earl of Battonsbury. Lady Patience was sweet and welcoming. Her friend, Lady Amelia Atherton, the only daughter of the Duke of Ely, was a bit more detached.

Lady Amelia was blonde, coolly disaffected and unutterably beautiful. Lady Amelia thought it her task to bring all her companions up to her high standard, which both Lady Charity and Lady Charlotte eschewed with much amusement.

Jane, however, did not argue that she could use a bit more polish, and she was grateful to the duke's daughter for her assistance. Lady Amelia was sometimes abrasive with her opinions, but Jane thought she meant well, and officiousness was somewhat expected of one so highborn. Jane did not take offense to Lady Amelia's candor.

Jane had not found a husband while society progressed in Bath, but she had made friends, and that was certainly a step in the right direction. Lady Amelia, Lady Charlotte, and most especially Lady Patience did not look down upon Jane for her humble beginnings, and nor did Lady Charity. Jane was grateful to be accepted into their circle of friends.

Still, Jane was not sure how she felt about being in the

company of ladies of such renown. At summer's end, when Lady Charlotte promised she would invite Jane to visit her at her country home, Jane had tried not to be overly excited. Jane did not know the ladies well and, although she had enjoyed their summer together immensely, she had a sinking feeling that Lady Charlotte would forget all about her plain companion once she returned home.

Jane was overjoyed when Lady Charlotte had remembered her promise and invited Jane to celebrate the Christmas season with her family at their country manor, Kennett Park. She had hesitated at the thought of spending Christmas away from home, but Charlotte spoke of a visit to London afterwards once the weather cleared, if Jane so wished. It was a taste of a true London season, and Jane could not refuse. She would rejoin her Father and sister before long.

The trip had now captured Jane's utmost attention. She whirled around the room, searching for any small item left unpacked, but nothing was out of place. Jane would have hated to leave a mess behind for their elderly maid, and she liked having everything in proper order. She checked once more to be sure that the small gifts she had chosen for Lady Charlotte and her sisters were all wrapped and ready.

The yuletide celebrations were fast approaching. Jane would miss the celebration with her family, but she had a quiet farewell dinner last evening with Julia and their father and celebrated in their own way. Still, she felt neglectful leaving her little sister at home. She fretted about Julia having a solemn Christmas alone.

Julia was four years her junior, and since their mother

had died, Jane had felt that the girl was her charge. To ease her mind, Father had promised to take Julia to the Poppy home for their yuletide frivolity. Julia could not feel alone amongst such a large and welcoming family. Jane was headed for greater things, which in the long run would benefit Julia too, but right now, the thought of traveling was both exhilarating and unnerving.

Jane was excited to join Lady Charlotte along with Charlotte's sisters and elder brother for the Christmas season. Of course, she would be properly chaperoned by Lady Charlotte's mother, the Dowager Lady Keegain, but Jane had never met the woman. Most of all, she was nervous about the carriage ride to the Keegain estate, but she would not allow her fear of travel to stop her. This trip was too important.

Jane reminded herself she had no guarantee of a noble husband, although her company did increase her chances. She felt a little giddy with the thought, and then a bit guilty for her joy. She would enjoy the experience, husband or no husband. After all, when again would she get the opportunity to attend such events as Lady Charlotte frequented?

She knew she was being obsessive, but she bent to examine the contents of her trunk more closely, tucking in a stray ribbon that fluttered over the edge in danger of being crushed. Her gowns were not grandiose, but they were appealing and well made. She thought an understated elegance suited her better than frills anyway.

She had put careful consideration into every gown that had been packed, every accessory, bonnet, and even the multiple pairs of gloves she would need. It was so easy to soil them; she wanted to have extras and not to have to ask one of the maids to wash them for her too often. She did not want to be a bother.

Tucked into the side of her largest trunk, tied into the fabric, was her mother's pearl necklace. She reached in and felt the pearls underneath her fingers, reassured to feel them there. She may be making this adventure alone, but she would have her mother's spirit with her. *Wish me luck, Mother*, she thought as she fingered the necklace. *I will make you proud.*

2

———

*J*ane took a deep breath, and closed the trunk as her little sister Julia bounced into the room with a spot of paint on her nose.

"Oh, Jane, I shall miss you terribly!" Julia flung herself at her older sister and hugged her fiercely.

Jane returned the hug. "And I you," Jane said holding her sister close and stroking her dark hair. It was the only feature the two girls shared. Julia was tall and stately while Jane was short and buxom. Already, Julia was nearly a head taller than her elder sister.

"You are up early," Jane noted.

"I wanted to paint the sunrise," Julia said with a shrug. "The clouds are so perfect. I have been awake for hours awaiting the dawn."

"Oh," Jane said, and could not help but smile; it was so like Julia to do as she pleased. "And will you sleep the afternoon away?" she teased.

"Perhaps," Julia said with a shrug and a yawn. "Oh, I shan't know what to do without you here, Jane. I know it is a great honor to have this visit with all the fine ladies, but I shall miss you terribly, especially on Christmas." Julia stuck her lip out in a pout.

"Father has said you are to visit the Poppys in a fortnight. There are so many sisters there, you shall not miss me."

"I shall. The Poppys are not you." Jane gave her sister another hug, and a melancholy pout.

"If the weather holds, perhaps Connie will ride with you," Jane said. "Tell her I said she must."

Julia wrinkled her nose. Jane knew her younger sister would much rather be inside with her paints than out of doors. Still, Jane's friend, Constance Poppy, was an excellent horsewoman and had taught Jane all she knew about horses. The Poppys were good friends.

"You know that my connections will benefit you too. Soon enough, you will be preparing for your own season," Jane said, pushing down Julia's mass of tangled hair, fighting the urge to fix it for her. Julia would not appreciate Jane's fussing. "I shall miss you as well, but we shall be back together soon enough."

Julia bounced on the bed, messing the coverlet, and ran a hand through her hair, pulling some of the tangles out with her fingers. "Are you nervous?" she asked.

"Just a bit," Jane said handing Julia her own hairbrush from the tray in the top of the trunk. "But it is only a short trip."

"No. I meant because you shall be with fine ladies attending fancy balls. I would probably cast up my accounts." Julia paused, the hairbrush caught in her tangles.

"You would not," Jane assured her sister.

"You are braver than I," Julia said with a shudder. She held the brush suspended above her head as she worked loose the tangles. "But Father said we can return to Bath before Easter, and meet you here, if not in London. I shall miss you so. We shall be apart so long!"

"Time shall fly," Jane said.

"For you, no doubt," Julia pouted. She pulled on the brush to no avail. It was stuck fast within her curls.

Jane could stand it no longer. She reached for the hairbrush. "Let me," she offered, thinking it would be the last time she would brush her little sister's hair for quite a while.

"The winter shall be interminable," Julia continued. "But Father says that next summer, I might join the picnics in Bath if I am very proper and well-behaved." She brightened somewhat as she said this.

"Then I am sure you shall be proper," Jane replied, as she turned her sister away from her so she could see her hair properly. It was a complete rat's nest. "What have you been doing with this hair? Never mind. Give me that." She took the hairbrush from her sister and carefully began to separate the curls.

"I wish I was going to London," Julia said, sighing wistfully. "I would imagine there would be so much to paint."

Jane laughed. "And you do not have enough to paint here?"

"I suppose," Julia said.

"Do you not remember London?" Jane asked. "We went there as children." *When Mother was alive,* Jane thought, but she did not mention their mother. There was no use to bring up such sadness. Julia had been only a child when she passed. Jane knew Julia hardly remembered their mother. Even Jane's memories were starting to fade, which was why she kept Mother's pearls with her always; so she would never forget.

Julia attempted to glance over her shoulder as Jane brushed her hair. "I do remember a bit of London." She wrinkled her nose. "I remember the smell," she said, and Jane laughed.

"All the more reason to summer in Bath," Jane said with a wistful smile, thinking that maybe it would be this year that she would find a husband of her own.

"Oh, Jane," Julia said, twisting to look at her while Jane continued to attempt to brush her thick mop of hair. "I do hope you find a handsome beau. How can you do otherwise with Lady Charlotte and Lady Amelia?" Julia sighed.

"I am afraid I shall be quite out of my depth," Jane admitted, surprised that her sister had followed her thoughts so well. "They are both ladies and I..." Jane paused to untangle a particularly stubborn hank of hair, trying to think how to put into words her thoughts when they were as unruly as her sister's curls.

"You will be beautiful and charming," Julia said, reaching up to help. "I know you shall. You shall find the most handsome husband of them all."

"Looks are not everything, Julia," Jane said swatting her sister's hands away as Julia was only making the tangles worse. "I only wish to enjoy the company of my newfound friends. If I were to encounter a suitor, I would hope to find a kind and gentle man. If he has but a fraction of Father's integrity, then I shall be most lucky." Jane finished her sister's hair and tied the curls with a blue ribbon from her own store.

"And if he's handsome, luckier still," Julia added, reaching up to feel the ribbon and breaking into a wide smile. "Thank you. That feels much better."

"You must remember to braid your hair at night," Jane said, "then it will not be so tangled in the morning."

"I shall," Julia said, hugging her sister again.

Jane laughed at her little sister's enthusiasm as Julia turned toward the door, likely going back to her painting.

"Do not forget," Jane admonished.

"I won't." Julia paused to look back at her. "And *you* must remember what Mother always said," she admonished.

"What is that?" Jane asked, her face a question. She did not think Julia remembered much about Mother.

"Trust your heart and you shall never be unhappy," Julia said.

Jane shook her head and smiled at her little sister. "I shall," she promised.

"And please, Jane, tell me when you are ready to leave. I shall want to say goodbye."

"Is that not what we are doing now?" Jane teased.

"Well, yes. But I shall want to say goodbye again. I shall be frightfully lonely without you." Julia's face knotted in a frown and she looked about ready to cry. If she started, Jane was sure she would follow. This was not a sad occasion, it was a happy one, but right now, it was difficult.

Jane put a smile on her face. She needed to hold her emotions together and be strong for Julia. "I shall write to you, and we will be back together before you know it," she said. "And if you plan to come down to the sitting room to say goodbye, you should wash your face. You have a bit of paint, just there." Jane touched her sister on the nose. "If you get paint on the dress Father just had made for you, he will be cross."

"He shan't mind." Julia giggled.

Perhaps not, Jane thought. Their father always indulged Julia's painting.

"*I* shall be cross then." Jane amended.

"I shall change directly, Lady Jane," Julia teased with a mocking curtsey. In the next moment, she had skipped out of the room, leaving her sister smiling and shaking her head as she watched her go.

Jane sat down in front of the glass and tidied her own long brown hair into a snug braid that would be comfortable for traveling. Although Jane had risen early, she was running out of time to join her family in the dining room for breakfast.

Mrs. Carron had been Mother's maid, and the elder woman had stiff fingers in the morning. Jane had wanted to save her the trouble of fixing her hair when it would be covered by a bonnet throughout her trip, but if Jane did not hurry, Mrs. Carron would probably take over anyway. She wanted Mrs. Carron to be surprised to see Jane all prepared for the day without any assistance. Besides, the action helped to calm her. She liked to be busy when she was nervous.

Relax, Jane, She reassured herself. *People travel in*

carriages every day without mishap. There is nothing to fear.
Even in her thoughts, the words lacked conviction.
Terrible things could happen. They had to her mother.

Jane's most beautiful mother had been alive one
moment, and in the next, her carriage had overturned
and claimed her life along with Jane's unborn baby
brother. Jane wished more than anything for the actual
journey to be over with, and she had not yet even left her
own room. She took a breath and tried to put her anxiety
out of her mind.

Most carriages did not crash. She would be safe. Her
father had chosen the best horses and the best driver to
take her to Kennett Park, and she knew Mrs. Poppy well.
The elder woman was to travel with Jane to the Keegain
estate, and then on to London to visit her eldest son,
Michael, and do some shopping in Town before she
returned to her own home for Christmas.

Mrs. Poppy was well known to Jane as a chaperone
and companion. She traveled with her own daughters
quite often and without fail. Besides, it was less than a
day's ride. Jane wished Constance Poppy was traveling
with her mother. She and Connie had always gotten on,
and Jane would appreciate the companionship to calm
her nerves.

Everything would be fine, Jane told herself, but she
could not quite dismiss the anxiety that plagued her
whenever she embarked upon a journey. She would not
sit easy until she reached her destination.

She would actually rather ride. Connie was an
excellent horsewoman and always gave Jane such good
tips to keep her seat. Jane enjoyed riding. She was not the

horsewoman the women of the Poppy family were, but she was competent. When she was in control of her horse, travel did not seem so nerve-wracking, but ladies could not ride horseback across the countryside. Jane had to put herself in the hands of the driver and his wretched wheeled box.

Jane could hear the service bells ringing down the hallway as she finished braiding her hair. If her father was not already awake and downstairs, he soon would be. Jane knew she couldn't hide in her room forever. She couldn't prevent what was about to happen even if she wanted to, which she did not.

As much as she looked forward to the experience, she never wanted to go anywhere at all that required a carriage ride.

"It would be much easier if they would come here, instead of my having to go to them," she muttered as she rose, shaking out her skirts and trying to ignore the nervous flutters in the pit of her stomach.

She reminded herself that this was a wonderful opportunity that the Dowager Lady Keegain was offering her. Especially given that she did not know the family well, only Lady Charlotte. Her sisters Jane knew only in passing. She knew Lady Charlotte had an older brother as well, Randolph Keening, the Earl of Keegain, but Jane had not met him either.

She rather wished Mrs. Carron were coming with her, just to have a familiar face nearby, but the maid was elderly. The Dowager Keegain would have someone to do Jane's hair and help her with dressing. Mrs. Carron would not be needed, nor would she have wished to go on the trip. The elderly maid would be happier here in her own home with Father and Julia.

With another deep breath, Jane smoothed her light brown traveling dress a final time, thinking that it would be comfortable enough in the carriage: one small blessing in what was sure to be a difficult day.

She looked at herself in the glass one last time. "It shall be an adventure," she told herself firmly. Then, with one last appraising look at her appearance, she strode purposely out of the room.

3

$\mathcal{T}$he trip was mercifully uneventful, and Mrs.
Poppy was dozing in the corner of the
carriage. Jane stared out the window at the light misting
of snow dusting the ground in the failing light. She was
thankful that they were almost there.

The roads were not yet slick, but she had worried lest
they should become so. Riding in a carriage was bad
enough; riding in the snow was another thing altogether.
At least most of the guests planned to stay at the manor
at the earl's invitation. Jane would not need to travel
anywhere again until it was time to leave.

Satisfied that she had indeed made the trip safely
after all, Jane allowed herself to feel the excitement of
what was to come. This *was* an adventure, a delightful
one filled with all manner of possibilities.

Next to her, Mrs. Poppy awoke with a start.

"We are almost there," she told the older woman.

They both peered out the window of the carriage.

"Isn't it grand?" Mrs. Poppy said with a voice of awe.

Jane had to agree. There, in the distance, she kept catching glimpses through the trees of a massive stone house. As they came around a sharp bend, the carriage left the wood behind, and there was Kennett Park in all its glory. What Jane saw left her absolutely mesmerized. The vast beauty of the manor house robbed her of speech.

The manor was rectangular in shape, with four floors and several outbuildings. From the lane she could see the stable and glimpse the lake beyond the fields, tucked behind the house. Was that a boathouse? She imagined the view from the upper floors of the manor would be spectacular.

Jane and Mrs. Poppy rode up a drive of round river stones, which made the carriage rattle noisily as they reached the front of the house. The horses clip-clopped up the long curved drive, coming to a halt just shy of the front steps. They stood, pawing the ground eagerly, awaiting the grooms who appeared to take the tired animals to their warm stalls.

Jane craned her neck to see balconies dotting the front of the manor house, denoting the larger, finer rooms where important guests stayed. The spaces between the balconies showed plainer windows, indicating rooms for regular visitors or relatives on the outer fringes of the family. This would likely be where she would stay. Stately rooms would be reserved for distinguished guests. After all, she was only a casual acquaintance of the earl's younger sister, Lady Charlotte.

As the footman handed her out of the carriage, Jane stood transfixed by the elegant estate. Griffins stood watch over the ornate stone doorway, their cold stone eyes surveying everything and everyone who approached. They were fierce and should have been frightening, she realized, but Jane was strangely pleased with them. They seemed to be keeping watch. It really was a grand old house with a stately charm.

In that moment, Lady Charlotte appeared under the arch of the doorway, her face lighting up with pleasure as she saw Jane. Charlotte squealed and rushed to hug her friend, catching her hands and sizing up her person.

"Oh, Jane! I'm so glad you could come. Helen and I said we would wait up for you if you were late, but Mother forbade it. She said we needed our beauty sleep."

Helen, Jane remembered, was one of Charlotte's sisters.

"Well, you do," said a slender girl who came up behind Lady Charlotte. In the moment, Jane could not remember which sister she was, Helen or Alice.

"I simply cannot wait for the ball," Charlotte gushed. "Everyone will be here, absolutely everyone. Oh, Jane, I could just die with the anticipation."

The other girl turned up her nose and Jane realized that she was Lady Alice, the younger sister, who was not yet out. To have such a party in one's own home and not be allowed to attend, must be quite trying, Jane thought. She resolved to be especially kind to the younger girl.

Without stopping to think about it, Jane stood on tiptoes to take one of the cases being handed down by the carriage driver when another set of arms reached up and took it for her, right over her head. She turned, expecting to find a servant, only to have her first sight of the Earl of Keegain. It was surely he.

Jane saw the family resemblance to Lady Charlotte immediately, as surely no servant would wear such fine garments. His overcoat was crafted from the finest gray wool. Her breath caught in her throat. Lord Keegain was not much taller than she was, which was surprising, since Jane was certainly not a tall woman. They were so much the same height that she could look directly into his beautiful hazel eyes. He had the longest lashes she had ever seen, except of course for Lady Charlotte. His cheerful smile drew her instantly.

The earl was not as she had been led to believe by his sisters. It occurred to Jane belatedly that siblings were not always accurate in their estimations of their brothers and sisters. By Lady Charlotte's descriptions, Lord Keegain was dowdy and slow. Jane had taken that to mean he would not likely be handsome, and yet she found him endearingly so.

She wondered what other details Charlotte had omitted, or appraised entirely wrong. She caught her breath, stepping out of his way, watching as the earl took her case and handed it to the footman, who said, quietly, "I will take that, my lord."

Jane realized she had already made a social gaffe. She should have allowed the footman to do his job, but she could not be concerned with that, not when such a gentleman stood by her side.

Lord Keegain was several years older than his sisters, Jane remembered, though he did not look it. What else had Lady Charlotte said... that he kept to himself, with his books and figures? His young sister said that Lord Keegain was quite the dullard, but how could Jane trust such outlandish statements when the earl was obviously not dowdy, nor particularly slow? There was a spark in his eyes that belayed the sharp mind behind them.

The earl caught her staring and smiled, sending a warm thrill through her. He returned her gaze, studying her as if he were taking an investigation for the Crown. Jane blushed and turned away, though she could still feel his eyes upon her as if they could somehow touch her very soul.

"Jane, you must meet my brother," Lady Charlotte said, turning to make introductions.

Jane curtseyed, positive that her cheeks were flaming crimson as the earl bent over her gloved hand. It was impossible of course, but she could swear she felt his kiss sear her through the soft leather of her kid gloves. For a moment, she couldn't breathe and had to look away, though the warmth of his hand lingered long after he released her fingers.

Her face still felt warm, the remnants of the blush continuing. Perhaps he would just think her cheeks were red from the cold.

"Welcome to Kennett Park, Miss Bellevue. I do hope you enjoy your stay," the earl said smoothly.

His voice was everything she had expected, deep with silken tones that washed over her, leaving her insides melting. Perfection. He was perfection. How had Lady Charlotte not told her so?

Their gaze caught and held. Jane's heart was racing. She knew in that moment that she most certainly would enjoy her visit. In fact, if he would have her, she would marry this man. She grinned at the thought.

The earl turned away, speaking briefly to the footman about which rooms they would occupy. How silly she must appear to convey such emotion so openly upon their first meeting. She attempted to gather her wits, but her face simply would not co-operate. Surely, Lady Charlotte would understand and be glad for her.

Jane turned to share these things with her friend, and saw for the first time, the second figure upon the step beside Lady Alice. The tall blonde woman projected an air of elegance and refinement; her expression cool and implacable.

"Dearest, do come in out of the cold," she said.

Her words were addressed to Lord Keegain, but Jane's heart dropped as Lady Charlotte hurried into the house with Jane in tow. She turned to introduce the unknown lady, for a lady she most certainly was. "Jane, this is Lady Margret Fairfax, my brother's intended," Lady Charlotte said.

There it was. In the space of less than a dozen words, Jane's world had ended. Her smile faltered. Somehow she managed to curtsey properly, but all the words of welcome became a buzz in her ears as the earl took the arm of his betrothed and led her into the house, leaving Jane feeling bereft.

Whatever Charlotte said as she drew her into the house, Jane never so much as heard. How could she, when in the space of mere minutes she had found the very thing that had made her world complete, only to lose him in the next instant?

Jane forced a smile. She could not be rude. It did not matter that the most interesting gentleman she had ever laid eyes upon was already engaged, and his bride-to-be was looking daggers at her. She let Lady Charlotte lead her into the house, with Mrs. Poppy following chatting animatedly with the footmen and the ladies alike. There would be other gentlemen, Jane promised herself, but it was an empty promise. She felt entirely hollow.

4

---

*B*y the time Jane was shown to her room, she found that her trunk had been brought up and was already partially unpacked. She marveled at the efficiency of the household. Her chamber was nearly double the size of her bedroom at home and had an adjoining sitting room.

The maid curtseyed to her as if she were a person of importance.

"I am Jacqueline Toussand," she said with a thick French accent. "Welcome, *mademoiselle*. I thought the emerald dress, but if you should choose another for dinner…"

"Oh, no," Jane said. "The green one is fine."

"*Tres bon*," the maid said as she laid the dress out on the bed. "It is lovely. The bodice…" She waved an excited hand and switched to French. "*Accentuez votre cou et vos épaules.*"

Accentuate your neck and shoulders, Jane translated

mentally. She could not have cared less about her neck or shoulders, except that she wanted to lay them both upon a pillow. She felt bruised and tired from the journey. She was drained from the anxious carriage ride and the revelation of the earl and Lady Margret.

Still, Jane was hungry after the long trip. The repast along the way had not sustained her, and she was glad that the earl had held dinner for them. She wanted more than a supper of bread, meats, and cheeses, and was happy to expect warm food.

Jane allowed Jacqueline to assist her in dressing. She let her hands slide down the front of her dress as she meticulously straightened the gown. It was not as mussed as she expected it to be.

"It seems being packed in a trunk has not wrinkled the gown unduly," she commented, and Jacqueline shook her head.

"*Non, mademoiselle*, I only had time to air out the one frock, but I can have another done for you in a moment if you have decided differently," she said. Jane opened her mouth in astonishment. The household was even more efficient than she had thought.

"No," she stammered. "This is perfect. Thank you."

"*Vous êtes les bienvenus, mademoiselle.* You are most welcome, mademoiselle," Jacqueline said with a bright smile for Jane. "*Dois-je épingler vos cheveux?*" She asked, and Jane nodded accepting the offer to do her hair.

Plaits were not the height of fashion and would not do for dinner, even a casual one. She wondered if those so esteemed as the earl and his family were ever truly casual.

"Thank you," Jane said to the maid who complemented her on her hair with a strange mixture of English and French. After a few moments, they both fell silent, Jane musing absently in her fatigue. "I am afraid I am not much company," she said into the stillness.

"*Non, mademoiselle*, you do not have to be company for me."

Jane was glad for the peace as she closed her eyes and allowed the French maid to brush her hair. The smooth strokes felt unaccountably relaxing. She did not know when someone besides herself had brushed her hair. This was quite the life, Jane thought. She attempted to remind herself that she should not come to expect such pampering, but found she could not muster protest. In fact, Jane was in danger of falling asleep before she even ate.

She let out a long sigh as her thoughts once again turned to her path in life. Right now, all she had to do was get through dinner, and then she could fall into bed.

"*Magnifique*," Jacqueline announced, having finished her pinning.

Jane looked this way and that, craning her head side to side to get a good look at her hair in the glass. It did look quite magnificent, considering that just moments ago, it was straggling from her braids. Jacqueline was skilled in her work.

"Yes. Thank you, I do feel quite lovely," Jane offered. She wondered for a moment if she should wait for Mrs. Poppy, but she was unsure where they had placed her, so she asked Jacqueline to show her to the dining room. "I am afraid I will get lost on the way," she told the maid, and the young woman nodded.

"The manor is quite large," she said. "I shall be happy to show you." But at that moment, Lady Charlotte knocked upon the door.

"Are you ready for dinner?" she inquired. "Your traveling companion has decided to retire early. She asked for a tray to be sent up since she is leaving for London at dawn."

That was understandable. Jane herself was exhausted from bouncing about in the carriage. Mrs. Poppy was far older in years and would be fatigued from the journey, although the woman had always appeared quite spry.

Jane thanked Jacqueline again and allowed Lady Charlotte to help her find her way to the dining room. The manor was a maze of turns, and Jane thought she would become lost within the large edifice. She was glad to follow Lady Charlotte as she chatted amicably.

~~~∞⊲⊳∞~~~

JANE HAD PROMISED herself that she would put the thought of Lord Keegain aside, but it was difficult with the earl and his intended bride seated right there at the table. Jane was here to visit with Lady Charlotte and her sisters. Jane promised herself she would have a good time. She had not seen Lady Charlotte since the summer, and they had much catching up to do. She would keep her attention on Charlotte.

Introductions were made all around, and Jane remembered Lady Helen and young Alice, both of whom she had met at a picnic in Bath. Jane was glad Lady Charlotte remade the introductions, because although she had met Charlotte's sisters, she could not remember which girl was which. Now, she concentrated on their names.

Lady Alice had large honey brown eyes and lighter hair than her elder sisters. It was still styled in braids as befitting a younger girl. Her long arms and legs gave her a young coltish appearance, but it was clear that she would grow into a golden-haired beauty. Lady Helen was the elder sister, a stately lady with wavy blonde hair, though it was not as curly as Lady Charlotte's.

Lord Keegain introduced his two gentlemen friends, Mr. Edgar Fitzwilliam and Mr. Theodore Reynolds, both of whom were visiting. As the gentlemen seated the ladies, the earl commented. "Mr. White was afraid that fowl would dry out waiting upon your arrival, so we decided on simpler fare. I hope you do not mind," Lord Keegain said, drawing Jane's attention back to him.

The table did not look simple to Jane, but she shook her head. "Oh no, I do not mind at all," she replied with sincerity. "I am glad for warm food. I was expecting meats and cheese."

"I would not leave a lady hungry," the earl said, and Jane blushed. He must know she was not a lady, only a miss, but she could not think enough to speak at all, much less disavow him of the notion that she was of a higher class.

Soon the meal was served, and Jane, who found herself quite hungry after the long ride, applied herself to her food while the sisters discussed their Christmas holiday plans. Jane found that the earl did not stand on ceremony.

His sisters occupied one end of the table with their mother, and Lord Keegain the other with his fiancée and friends. He sat proudly at the head of the table, with Lady Margret seated to his right, and then Mr. Reynolds. Jane was seated between Mr. Fitzwilliam and Lady Charlotte.

Jane could barely keep her eyes from Lord Keegain and Lady Margret. Determined to ignore them, she spoke to Charlotte. After all, Charlotte was the lady she was here to visit.

"Will your other sister, Lady Sophia, be arriving soon?" Jane asked, and Lady Charlotte launched into a diatribe about why Sophia was too busy to come until the last minute.

"She is a guest now, you see," Lady Charlotte huffed.

"Well, she is," Lady Helen added as she paused in cutting her venison, which was prepared in a rich wine sauce. "She is married and has her own house."

"This will always be my house," Lady Alice said.

"Well, that would depend upon Randolph and his bride-to-be, shan't it?" Charlotte said with a glance down the table towards Lady Margret, who was laughing prettily at something the gentlemen had said.

Jane's eyes went back to the couple. Lady Margret had her hand on the earl's arm. Jane looked back at Charlotte, resolved to ignore their joviality.

"Have you heard from Lord Marley?" Jane asked Charlotte about her suitor from Bath. The gentleman had been quite persistent last summer. Too late, Jane remembered that Lady Charlotte had spurned the man.

"No, and if I never do it will be too soon," Charlotte said sitting her glass down with a clunk. "The cad."

"He married Miss Church just last month," Lady Helen supplied. "Quite a rushed affair if rumor can be believed. Some say that is why he invited our sister to Bath in the first place."

"Helen, rumor cannot ever be believed," the Dowager Keegain said, directing her daughter away from gossip. "Rumor is not truth."

"And that is truth," Jane added softly, thinking of the rumors that abounded about her own mother and how hurtful they were.

"But Mama, the man left our sister heartbroken," Lady Helen said, with a solidarity that Jane admired although she was not sure it was so.

"Were you really heartbroken?" Jane inquired of Lady Charlotte. "As I remember you had dismissed him before a week of summer had passed, and yet he still followed you determined to call upon you. Were you in love with him, Lady Charlotte?"

"I suppose not," Charlotte sighed. "But he was so attentive and quite handsome."

"Handsome is as handsome does," the dowager said in a no-nonsense tone. "You are well rid of him, my dear." She reached out to pat Charlotte's hand, as if her daughter needed consoling.

Jane knew that the romance was far gone now. "He was a philanderer with his eyes only on your money."

"And some other skirt," Alice added.

"Alice," the dowager said sharply.

"What? Ruddy says it." Alice pouted.

The sound of his youngest sister's nickname for him must have drawn the earl's attention to their end of the table. Jane realized that Lord Keegain was looking in their direction and his friends had stopped their conversation.

"I shall have to have a sit down with your brother then," the dowager said with a look to her son. She then turned to Jane and apologized. "Alice is barely out of the school room and has some rough edges to smooth before her season. In fact, if she does not watch her manners, I shall think she is not ready for polite society, and we shall have to wait another year," the dowager said with an edge to her voice.

"Oh no, Mama," Alice cried. "Please, have a care."

"Oh, I do not mind frank speech," Jane soothed. "I appreciate her honesty. Lady Alice and my sister Julia must be of an age."

"Mother would have sent her to finishing school, but she cried to Randolph, and he let her stay home," Lady Charlotte confessed.

"I never went to finishing school either," Jane admitted to Lady Alice.

"That much is obvious," Lady Margret spoke into her glass of wine, and Jane realized the lady had been privy to their conversation all along. Jane blushed with embarrassment.

"I am sure your manners are without reproach, Jane," Lady Charlotte said, defending her.

Jane sent a grateful smile to her friend.

The dowager put down her fork and spoke. "I suppose I was less inclined to send my younger girls," she said thoughtfully. "No matter that it would have been good for them. I wanted them close."

After the death of their father, Jane assumed, but she did not voice her thought, she simply sipped her own wine. With her lack of sleep the night before, the alcohol went straight to her head. She put down the glass and buttered a slice of bread.

"I am sure you regret it, Miss Bellevue," Lady Margret said coolly. "I consider finishing school a necessity for any lady of quality." She spoke as if the matter were decided.

Lady Alice looked quite pale.

Jane considered her answer as she laid her knife aside on her bread plate. The comment made Jane think of her own manners. Were they in some way lacking that Lady Margret would comment upon them?

The Lady Margret went right on talking without waiting for an answer. She smiled thinly at Alice. "We shall have to get your brother to reconsider. I made some wonderful friends at school, and I'm sure you will as well," she said with finality, as she leaned on Lord Keegain's arm and beamed up at him. "Is that not right?"

"We shall see," the earl said noncommittally, returning to his discussion with Mr. Fitzwilliam.

The earl's other friend Mr. Reynolds had a pained look on his face, and Jane wondered if he would jump to Lady Alice's defense, but he only applied himself to his plate.

"I already know how to play the piano and paint," Lady Alice complained in a sulky voice.

"That is not the entirety of finishing school," Lady

Margret said. "There is a question of manners and deportment."

"Your own manner is impeccable, Lady Margret," Reynolds commented.

"It shan't be so bad," Mr. Fitzwilliam consoled Alice, proving that he, too, was a close friend of the family.

"I shall not go," Alice insisted, muttering under her breath. "Never have I slept the night in a bed not my own. I am sure I would not get a wink."

"You shall have need to sleep in another's bed sooner or later," Charlotte said in a low voice that only Jane and her sisters could hear.

"Oh, I do doubt it," Lady Helen whispered back. "Who would have our wild little sister?"

Charlotte restrained a most unladylike snigger.

"It shall be later rather than sooner, I do suppose," Lady Charlotte added.

"I tell you I should not get a wink of sleep!" Alice insisted, her voice growing loud over her sister's whispers. Her protest caused the two older girls to dissolve in mirth although Lady Helen tried to pass her laughter off as a cough.

Jane had to smile, but decorum kept her from outright laughter.

"Pray tell, what are you two giggling about now?" the earl asked. "It will not do for you to be keeping secrets, Charlotte. The last secret you harbored nearly had you married to that clout, Marley."

"Oh, you would have never made me marry him, Brother," Lady Charlotte insisted. "You are not so cruel."

"All the same, out with it," the earl insisted.

Lady Charlotte frowned, unable to reveal the suggestive conversation, and Lady Helen came to her rescue with some alacrity.

"Charlotte was only speculating on the type of gentleman whom Alice might catch," Lady Helen said, her voice amazingly steady, her mirth hidden behind a stern mask of indifference.

"You should be thinking of catching your own gentleman, Charlotte. After that ruckus with Lord Marley, the *Ton* will have its eye on you," the Dowager Keegain warned. "You must be above reproach."

"Yes, Mother," Lady Charlotte said dutifully. She picked up her fork and applied herself to her dinner.

Jane could see from the worried look in the dowager's eye that she was concerned about her daughter's prospects, but that concern was tempered with love. It was a sentiment much like what her own father had given her on occasion, and yet there was a softer side of femininity to her scolding. Jane thought this must be what it was like to have a mother's love. The thought gave her a warm feeling.

"Never fear, little sister. You will find a true gentleman who will earn your love and respect," Lord Keegain said kindly to Charlotte, who just wrinkled her nose.

It was the perfect thing to say to ease the situation, and Jane's estimation of the earl rose even further.

"Yes," Lady Helen agreed, raising her glass. "Let us toast to all true gentlemen this holiday season."

Jane's eyes fell for a moment on Lord Keegain. "And ladies," Jane added softly. Her eyes accidentally met Lady

Margret's and she saw a spark of animosity smoldering there.

"And ladies," Lady Margret echoed, but Jane thought her understanding of the sentiment was much different than her own.

5

---

*R*andolph Keening, the Earl of Keegain, stood at the entrance to the manor, watching Lady Margret direct his servants. She had brought half of her household with her and now was taking them home again.

No matter that she would be back in a fortnight for the Christmas ball. To Keegain, all this packing and unpacking seemed like a monumental waste of time and manpower, since Margret would be bringing her own household staff permanently when they married.

The thought did not bring him pleasure. He sighed and shook off the unwelcome feeling. It would be good for Margret to have the company of her own lady's maids and companions; it would help to ease the transition. Still, he watched the bustle in the courtyard and did not feel easy.

He did not know what he expected. His marriage would be like many amongst the *Ton*. Lady Margret and himself were of the same social background, their families had known each other all their lives, and they were both hale and hearty. They were a good match.

Lady Margret was a beautiful woman. She would be an impeccable hostess for his balls and a stunning addition on his arm. She would maintain his household and bear his heirs. She was perfect, but he feared that she would upend his life. He was not a man for complication or conflict, and Lady Margret thrived on such encounters.

Lord Keegain tried to convince himself that opposites attract. If so, then they should be the perfect match. His position would give her security. She would have children to fill her life with purpose...and what would he have?

He was certain there should be something more. Lady Margret was beautiful, poised, and of good family. She was all he could want, but she did not heat his blood. She did not inspire him to passion. Still, he could not overthrow Lady Margret for something so sentimental as a lack of sentiment.

Reason told him that passion was not a necessity to marriage. He knew many men kept a wife in the country and a mistress in Town, but keeping a mistress at all went against his sensibilities. Did the marriage vows not say to forsake all others?

Lord Keegain was not a man to break a vow. Aside from this fact, living such a double life seemed to elicit a monumental amount of stress and bother. No, a vow once made must be kept. The thought should not have left him cold.

The grey light of dawn had just broken, and the day promised clear skies. Lady Margret would have good weather for travel. He had insisted that she leave early so she would be home well before dark, but the minutes were ticking by and she still fussed with her belongings, much to his footmen's dismay. Keegain stayed out of the fray. He reminded himself that one day, this woman would be the lady of his house. He would not countermand her. He let her direct the servants as she wished.

Mr. Theodore Reynolds appeared at the door with sleepy eyes and a cup of coffee held in his hand.

"You are up early, Ted," Keegain observed. Usually, his friend was not an early riser.

"Humph," Reynolds hummed, taking a sip of the coffee. The two of them had developed a taste for the bitter liquid while traveling when they were young men, Keegain for his grand tour, and Reynolds upon his work for the Crown. Keegain's trip had been aborted when his father passed, but the two remained good friends and Ted visited often.

"I came to see off Lady Margret. You are not escorting her?" Reynolds asked. The man was a worrier, forever solicitous of a lady's needs. "Even with the threat of highwaymen?"

Keegain considered. It was not only highwaymen. He had heard various rumors, but he did not give credence to rumor alone. Lord Beresford had sent him a letter hinting of some trouble, but all that bother was much closer to London. It was only a day's trip to Lady Margret's country home, and not upon the London road.

"She insists upon going, and I must stay," Lord Keegain said. "Guests for the Christmas Ball will be arriving forthwith."

"Women do not always know they need protecting. It is up to a gentleman to provide it," Reynolds urged.

Keegain brushed away his friend's over-apprehension. Reynolds was a King's man, and saw danger around every corner. It was his job to do so. Keegain had the safety of his intended well in hand.

"Lady Margret will be home safe well before nightfall," he said, comforting himself with the thought. He did not know the specifics of the duke's concern, which was why he insisted that Margret leave early and sent with her his best protection.

"I am sending several trusted footmen to accompany her on the journey," Keegain said. "Much to her chagrin, and theirs." He could not help but smile. Lady Margret was a demanding woman. "No harm will befall her."

Reynolds nodded, although he inquired after which footmen, and Keegain supplied the men's names.

"I am so glad they meet with the approval of the Crown," Keegain teased. "Where is Fitz?"

"Still abed, no doubt, like any respectable gentleman," Reynolds said, yawning.

When at last the luggage was placed to her satisfaction, Keegain moved to help Margret into the carriage and bid her farewell. He held her hand for the briefest of moments.

"Safe journey, Lady Margret," Reynolds said over his shoulder.

"I wish you had deigned to stay," Keegain added, although they had already had this conversation, and she repeated her previous comment.

"I shall be back before you shall miss me," Lady

Margret said, turning her cheek for a kiss, which he dutifully supplied.

Keegain shut the carriage door, and they were on their way.

Reynolds still stood upon the front steps with an unreadable expression.

"Come," Keegain said, after the carriage had moved down the lane. "Shall I fleece you in a game of cards?"

"You can try," Reynolds said, laughing. "You forget; I have sharper eyes than you."

"Ah, but I have deeper pockets."

"Indeed you do. Are we playing for pence, then?" Reynolds asked.

"I think so. I can ill afford more."

"Ah you are untruthful," Reynolds said, with a gesture to the grand grounds. There was no envy in his voice, only a calm matter-of-factness.

"Very well then," Keegain agreed. "*You* can ill afford more."

"Ah, but I do not intend to lose," Reynolds retorted, and Keegain laughed.

"No one ever does."

He knew that Reynolds had been bemoaning his lack of funds, which in the absence of a title kept him from marrying the lady of his choosing. Keegain had tried to wheedle the news from the man, but Reynolds would not divulge the lady's name. He was a remarkably close-lipped man. Keegain supposed it came from hiding secrets for the Crown.

"Come, you shall win my assets a penny at a time,"

Keegain teased as he slapped his friend upon the back and led him towards the parlor.

"It is no penny I wish to win from you." Reynolds replied with a more serious air, although their game was friendly. Keegain would not beggar the man.

For a while, there was only the clink of coin and the sound of the cards being shuffled and dealt as each man held his own musings.

"I've had a letter from Percival Beresford," Lord Keegain said at last.

"Then the rumors are true?"

Lord Keegain shook his head. "He did not say as much," the earl admitted. "I am sure he did not want to spill secrets upon paper."

Reynolds nodded and put his cards aside. "What would he have us do?"

"Do?" Keegain lifted a shoulder. "Nothing at the moment. The Duke of Ely will be here by the end of the week. We will know more once he arrives. In any case, the trouble was based in London. I doubt it will touch us here."

Reynolds picked up his cards again, moving one card in his hand, and then another. Keegain could see the worry on his friend's face.

"Put aside your concerns," Lord Keegain urged. "It is Christmas. What trouble could befall us here?"

"I am sure you are right," Reynolds said. "I shall attempt to be of good cheer." He put a smile upon his face, but it did not reach his eyes. "We should not want to upset the ladies."

"Certainly not," the earl agreed.

6

———

The pale light of the winter sun was streaming through the window into Jane's borrowed chamber. She had been awake since dawn, but had not wanted to disturb anyone, so she waited until she heard the house stirring before getting out of bed.

Peering out her window, she saw Lady Margret take her leave. The earl's goodbye to his intended had left Jane sulking. She reminded herself that she had no right to the man. She was only a guest of his sister. Still, the kiss the earl had left upon Lady Margret's cheek stung.

Jane realized she had no idea what time it was, and although she often dressed herself, she hesitated a moment before pulling the servant's call bell. She needed someone to guide her downstairs. If she got lost and missed breakfast entirely, that would be terribly embarrassing.

She expected Jacqueline or some other maid to return, but instead, Lady Charlotte herself greeted her, coming into the room with a smile and a hug. "Oh, Jane, I cannot wait for Christmas and the ball. Are you not just bursting with excitement?" she said.

"It is weeks away," Jane said, but Charlotte's bubbling enthusiasm quickly dispelled Jane's melancholy, and she was grateful for the distraction.

"The day will be here before we know it," Lady Charlotte continued.

Jane noted that Lady Charlotte was already dressed for the day in a cream and rose day dress. Was the whole household awake? She did not want to be a bother, and told Charlotte so.

"Oh, nonsense," Lady Charlotte said with a wave of her hand. "Alice bullies our maids on a regular basis."

"She is the youngest of you, correct?" Jane asked.

"Yes." Charlotte sighed as she looked at herself in the glass and fussed with a curl of reddish-blonde hair that had come loose from her chignon. Charlotte's hair was nearly as curly as Julia's, Jane thought, as she smiled at her friend.

"Surely Lady Alice would act appropriately," Jane said as a servant brought in a tray of tea and biscuits with setting for four.

Lady Charlotte chuckled at Jane's look of outrage. "My little sister can be very gracious. She is just...rather spoiled. It comes from being the youngest, you know. Randolph lavishes his love upon her."

"Is that not what an elder brother should do?" Jane asked softly once again, thinking of the earl.

"I suppose so, but I hate to think of the merry chase upon which Alice will lead a gentleman when she has her season. Mother thinks her beauty will make her a diamond of the first water, but do not tell her so. Her head is big enough already." Charlotte nodded towards the tea service. "I ordered tea for us, or would you rather have chocolate?"

"Tea would be wonderful," Jane said as she pulled on her dressing gown.

"I can barely open my eyes at all without my tea," Lady Charlotte said. "Sophia has taken to drinking coffee like Randolph. I think she is just being pretentious."

Jane remembered that Lady Sophia was Charlotte's eldest sister. The others were younger than Charlotte, although Helen acted as if she were older.

"Have you ever tasted coffee?" Lady Charlotte continued. "Ugh. It is disgustingly bitter. I cannot imagine why anyone would drink the stuff." She shuddered. "Ruddy says it is an acquired taste."

"I wouldn't know," Jane said. "I have never tasted coffee."

"Give me a good English tea any day." Charlotte grinned at her and practically shivered with excitement. "Oh Jane! Are you not just overflowing with delight? Our first season!"

"It is not the season yet," Jane reminded her.

"Yes, but balls and soirées. Oh Jane, I am so tired of being relegated to the back of the room with the children, or worse yet, upstairs. Shan't it be wonderful to dance the night away?" Lady Charlotte picked up a pillow from Jane's bed and twirled in imitation of a courtly dance.

"You needn't lord it over me," said a voice from the doorway.

"Oh, come in, Alice," Lady Charlotte ordered,

reacquainting Jane with her youngest sister. "Helen shall share our season, but Mother says Alice must wait until she is sixteen."

Lady Alice grimaced, crinkling her pert nose. She reached across the tea tray to snag a biscuit, and Charlotte slapped her hand. "Wait until we are ready for tea!"

"I'm ready," Alice said with a pout.

"Shall I pour?" the maid asked, gesturing to the waiting tray.

"No, no. I shall." Charlotte waved the maid away so the girls could talk. "See," Charlotte said. "Everyone spoils Alice."

"They do not," Alice protested.

"Shall we wait for Helen, then?" Charlotte asked.

"If you wish," Jane replied.

"She will be hours and hours," Alice protested. "We shall all perish of thirst."

Jane grinned at her friend as Lady Charlotte sat in the armchair of the small sitting room and poured tea for them, proving that Lady Alice did get her way.

"Where is Lady Helen?" Jane inquired.

"She is still sound asleep." Lady Charlotte said, stirring sugar into her tea. "But that is what comes from staying up half the night reading. Alice is right; we should perish from hunger if we waited upon Helen."

Another maid asked for entrance to the dressing room, and Jane recognized her as Miss Jacqueline from the night before.

In her accented English, she asked Jane, "Do you have a preference for this morning?" She held up Jane's blue morning frock. "*Une belle robe,*" she said admiringly, although the dress was simple. "*Cette robe, peut-être?*"

Jane nodded. "Yes. I shall wear that one, thank you."

"I have several pressed for you if you would like another," Jacqueline explained.

"The blue dress will be fine," Jane said, choosing the dress the maid held. It was one of her favorites, trimmed around the front and shoulders with tiny bows.

"That dress is pretty," Lady Alice said. "I like the bows. Very feminine." She took a bite of a crumpet and closed her eyes in bliss.

The crumpets were excellent, crispy on the edges and buttery inside. "These are wonderful," Jane commented.

"Yes. Mrs. Muir, our cook, is a wonder with pastries," Lady Charlotte said.

For a while they discussed various dressmakers, while Jacqueline helped Jane to dress. Jacqueline asked if she could do Jane's hair, and when Jane nodded, began pulling it into a simple style.

Charlotte sighed and bemoaned her own hair. Lady Charlotte's hair was curly as a lamb's wool. It escaped its pins on a regular basis, but since it was so early in the day, it seemed to be tamed this morning. Charlotte had told Jane in a hushed voice in Bath that she thought the very air of the city conspired against her, the moisture turning her locks into an unruly mess just when she wanted to look her best.

"Actually, Charlotte, I think your hair is very becoming," Jane said. "It is curly and a lovely shade of strawberry blonde, unlike my own, which is just plain brown."

Lady Charlotte gave her a look. "It's nearly ginger," she said, aghast.

"It is not. I wish I had your distinctive shade and your height. I've always wished to be taller," Jane added. "You have to admit your gentleman would be able to find you in a crowd."

Charlotte laughed at Jane's joke. "When I find a gentleman, I do hope he is tall. Oh, it is just so exciting. We must find the very best dresses for the ball. Everyone will be here. I cannot wait. Randolph invited the Duke of Ely and his daughter, Lady Amelia, of course."

"And the Beatrams," Lady Alice added. "You know Lady Patience?"

Jane nodded.

"Lady Patience is a true ginger," Jane commented to Charlotte.

"And a dear friend," Lady Charlotte said. "Patience is kindness itself to everyone."

Jane's hair was nearly finished when Lady Helen joined them in the sitting room.

Lady Helen was also taller than Jane, but not as tall as Charlotte. Her hair was like spun gold and her eyes were the color of honey, only a little darker than Alice's.

Only the earl had brown hair. All of his sisters were varying shades of blonde. Jane felt like the odd brown goose amongst the blonde beauties, but they laughed and shared crumpets and tea while the young French maid finished her hair.

Miss Jacqueline held a glass before her face, and Jane was amazed that her dark brown locks were in such order this morning. She was not used to such pampering.

"*Magnifique*," Miss Jacqueline pronounced, and Jane had to agree.

"Thank you," Jane said as the maid finished. "You are quite talented, Jacqueline."

She curtseyed and left the girls to their own devices. Jane had servants at home, but Mrs. Carron was sometimes forgetful, and her fingers were certainly not as deft as Miss Jacqueline's. It seemed strange to have someone pressing her clothing before she even thought of it.

"Lady Margret thinks we should not have Jacqueline in our house," Lady Charlotte confided over her teacup.

"Why ever not?" Jane asked.

Lady Charlotte gave a shrug. "Because of the war and the fact that she is French; as if Jacqueline might be a spy for Bonaparte." She sniffed. "The very notion is ridiculous."

"Oh. I never thought of that." Jane wondered if it could be true. Jacqueline seemed so kind. It could not be so.

"Well, it does not bear thinking on at all," Lady Helen said, sipping her tea. "Condemning the poor girl on nothing but her accent and country of birth. She fled from the trouble in France and her family was killed for it. Jacqueline has more reason than most to hate Bonaparte. She could never be a spy. Margret is only being cruel."

"I am glad you are sure," Jane said. "I quite like the girl."

"Oh, I do, too," Lady Charlotte agreed. "Margret and Ruddy had a terrible row about it. He said he would not leave the daughter of an associate of our father destitute and Margret refused to allow Jacqueline to touch her."

Lady Charlotte bit her biscuit and shrugged. "I find I do not understand Margret anymore. We used to be quite good friends. All of us rode together when we were young, before father died, and Margret went off to finishing school."

"Which is why I shall never go," Lady Alice announced loudly. "I shall not be *finished* into an entirely different person."

"It is true," Helen added. "When Lady Margret returned, she was not the same. She is the daughter of a marquess, but you would think she is a princess related to the Regent himself with the way she puts on airs. She acts as though she is above us all because she will one day be the Lady Keegain."

Jane was not sure what to say. She was sure she did not wish to discuss her opinion of Lady Margret.

"You must not let her attitude bother you," Lady Charlotte said.

Jane nodded, but that was easier said than done.

"Shall we ride, today?" Lady Charlotte asked, rising and turning to the window. A frown creased her face as she pulled back the heavy draperies. "Drat. It is raining."

"Perhaps we shall have snow by Christmas," Jane offered as she came up beside her friend and peered out.

"Perhaps," Charlotte agreed. "That would be grand."

The rain continued, and the ladies spent the morning sharing stories. Afterwards, Lady Charlotte took it upon herself to show Jane around Kennett.

Jane paid careful attention so as to not lose her way

within the grand house as they turned this way and that. Lady Charlotte showed Jane a looking-glass as tall as she was, which she explained was imported by her grandfather.

"It is made of Venetian mirrored glass," she said. "An artisan came with it to put it together. It used to be downstairs, but Randolph had it moved up here."

Jane thought it strange to see the entirety of one's self in a looking glass. It seemed to be the height of pretentiousness. Uncharitably, she thought Lady Margret would love it.

Other rooms held silk-covered chairs and velvet draperies. She saw elaborate console tables set between windows which looked out on the expansive grounds, and several guest chambers with beds so large Jane thought whole families could sleep in them.

Lady Charlotte paused, and gestured. "That way, of course, is the servants' stairs and their wing. There is an exceedingly large amount of rooms on that side of the house, but none are as beautiful as these," she explained as they turned in the opposite direction.

"How many servants live here?" Jane wondered, thinking she and her family got by with a butler, a cook, a kitchen maid, a housemaid, her father's valet and Mrs. Carron.

Lady Charlotte considered, and then she began counting on her fingers. "Well, there is Mr. Davies the House Steward, Mr. Hughes the Butler, Mrs. Price, Mrs. Muir and the Kitchen Clerk, Mr. White, the Stable master Mr. Griswold, all the maids and footmen..." She trailed off. "Oh, I'm certain I do not know." She laughed. "Over a hundred, I suppose," she said off-handedly.

Jane's eyes widened at the number.

The corridor they traversed was wide, and the end of the hall opened into a sweeping foyer with a balustrade which was carved with an intricate scrollwork of fruits, flowers, and leaves crawling across the dark wood. The walls above the grand staircase were lined with paintings from masters, done in a majestic scale with gilded frames.

Jane thought of her sister Julia as she looked at the paintings. Julia would no doubt know the names of the artists, but Jane did not. She was simply impressed with the amount of gold on the frames, never mind the paintings themselves.

"I am getting hungry," Lady Charlotte commented. "It must be coming on towards time for dinner. Shall we go back to our rooms to dress?"

Jane nodded. It had taken much of the day to simply walk through the house. She was quite overwhelmed with her friend's wealth. Jane had known that they were not of the same social status, but it had never been quite so clear as when she was walking through the magnificent corridors. Her father's home was nice, beautiful even, but it was probably less ostentatious than the servants' quarters here.

As they walked on, Jane wondered if she would be seated near the earl at dinner. The thought gave her butterflies.

"I do hope the weather clears tomorrow," Lady Charlotte commented. "Then we may ride, and I could show you around the grounds as well."

"It will still be muddy," Jane said. "I would not want one of your horses to slip and be injured."

Lady Charlotte waved a nonchalant hand. "The higher paths will be clear as long as it is not pouring, and we needn't push our mounts; or would you rather not go riding even in a light mist?" she inquired. "You shan't mind, would you?" She sounded hopeful.

"Oh no," Jane said, and told of the time when she and Connie Poppy were drenched by a sudden summer shower while out riding. "It was actually quite exhilarating," Jane admitted.

"We shan't let a little bit of rain stop us," Lady Charlotte declared.

The ladies dressed for dinner while sharing equestrian tales.

7

————

When Jane and Lady Charlotte descended for the evening meal, Jane was quite sure that the earl was waiting for her at the stair. He gave her a curt bow.

"May I escort you to dinner, Miss Bellevue?"

Jane's heart did a small flip flop.

"So formal, Randolph," Lady Charlotte teased, but Jane couldn't contain her own smile as she nodded her approval and took Lord Keegain's arm.

"Would you have me leave our guest unescorted?" The earl asked his sister, and Jane remembered that he was only being polite. His taking her hand meant nothing. The thought saddened her.

Still, she noticed the strength in his arm as she clasped her hand over his. His hands were large with strong, blunt fingers. She blushed slightly as she allowed Lord Keegain to lead her toward the dining room, inhaling sharply as his deep earthy scent struck her senses. Her blush deepened. *He's engaged*, she reminded herself. *And to a proper lady. Nothing can come of these thoughts.*

Still, Jane was perfectly prepared to spend the remainder of the evening close to Lord Keegain, enjoying, hopefully, a pleasant conversation through the course of the meal as he placed her next to his own seat at the head of the table, opposite of his mother. Helen and Alice were seated further down the table, chatting pleasantly with Mr. Fitzwilliam.

The gentleman rose from his seat at Jane and Lady Charlotte's entrance with the earl.

"Keegain. Ladies," Fitzwilliam said pleasantly as they seated themselves.

It would be awkward to speak to include Helen and Alice in their conversation at this distance, but Jane supposed they would converse on the morrow. She sat next to Lord Keegain on the one side and Mr. Theodore Reynolds sat on the other. She was glad to have Lady Charlotte on the other side of Mr. Reynolds. Jane had been introduced to the man previously in Bath; she could not remember when, but she greeted him kindly.

"Lady Charlotte; Miss Bellevue," he said with a small smile and a nod, retaking his seat. Mr. Reynolds seemed the sort of man who could jump from joy to melancholia in a moment. Last night he was smiling, but today, as he conversed with Keegain, he had a very serious look upon his face. Jane could appreciate that he was handsome, but when she looked at him, she felt none of the flutter she experienced when she gazed upon the earl.

Mr. Reynolds seemed somewhat sad this evening

though Jane could not put her finger on a particular reason. He seemed to keep everyone at bay, as if he held some secret. But then again, Jane chided herself, didn't everyone? Such thoughts were uncharitable at this holy season, and it was clear that Lord Keegain liked and trusted the man.

Lady Charlotte had said that Mr. Reynolds was looking for a wife, and Jane was aware she was closer to Mr. Reynold's social station than the earl's, but she was not drawn to the man. Not as much as she was drawn to Lord Keegain. *It does not matter*, she chided herself again. *The earl is engaged.*

Jane gave Mr. Reynolds a genuine smile, which he returned. She was actually curious about his presence. He did not seem to be the type to run in high circles, and yet, he was here, as was she. *How did he come to be friends with an earl?* she wondered.

"Good evening, Miss Bellevue," Mr. Theodore Reynolds said to Jane. "You are looking most lovely tonight."

"Thank you. It is good to see you again. I was surprised to find you here," Jane confessed, certain her confusion was also painted on her face. "I visited with your mother when she was in Bath. How is she, your mother?"

"Irritable as always," he said.

"I see you are acquainted," the earl said. "I am glad. Mr. Reynolds is one of my oldest and dearest friends, Miss Bellevue." That explained why he was here in this esteemed company.

"Yes, that's because he couldn't abide my brother,

stick up...in the mud that he is," Reynolds commented with a smile on his face.

Jane's lips twitched, aware that was not what Reynolds would have said if they were not in mixed company. Still, she was at a bit of a loss. Although she was acquainted with Mr. Reynolds, she did not know he had a brother and said so.

"Ah, yes, I understand completely. Thomas is very forgettable," Mr. Reynolds joked.

"Ted's elder brother, Thomas, is the Baron Wortingham," Lord Keegain explained.

"Worts if you ask me," Mr. Reynolds said with a smile in his voice. "The sort that is quite difficult to rid one's self."

The words were harsh, but there was no malice in his tone. The earl smiled at the comment, so Jane thought it must be in jest. Still, she was surprised Mr. Reynolds would speak so of his brother, especially when the man was not here to defend himself.

"Surely not," Jane said, lightly thinking of the love she bore her own sister.

"You know my brother," Reynolds said tossing a look at Lord Keegain.

"I do," Keegain said with a chuckle and a conciliatory nod.

Did the earl approve of the brother or the jest? Jane wondered, but Mr. Reynolds explained.

"Do not fret, Miss Bellevue. Worts is like a warm woolen sock on a cold winter night, quite comfortable, but not the height of fashion. He is well aware of this fact and does not attempt to alter it."

Lady Charlotte chuckled. "You are so droll, Mr. Reynolds," she said. "Lady Margret is right. You have a quick wit."

Mr. Reynold's eyes brightened at her compliment, and continued. "Thomas is a kind-hearted and thoughtful brother, as well as a conscientious and hardworking baron, but in some circles, let us say, it is not always fashionable to love one's elder brother."

"Surely fashion has nothing to do with love," Jane said, trying to form a picture in her mind of the fellow. She must know him. After all, she knew Mr. Reynolds.

Jane finally dredged up the memory of the Baron Wortingham. "He looks nothing like you," she commented, and that was true. "I never would have taken you for brothers."

"Yes, he got the title, but I got the looks," Reynolds explained with a wicked grin, taking a moment to sip from his wine glass and appearing quite pleased with himself.

Indeed, that was true. Reynolds was tall, blond and virile. His brother was shorter, perhaps even shorter than Keegain, and he had his father's ruddy complexion and unassuming brown hair.

"Wortingham will be at the ball," Lord Keegain added.

"Yes," Reynolds said. "And he is a good man in a pinch, Keegain, but not at all a dancer. Ladies, I would suggest you beg off if he asks you."

"Oh yes," Lady Charlotte laughed. "I may still have bruises on my toes. Jane, simply tell the man you have a thirst and decline dancing. Your feet shall thank you."

"Perhaps I shall," Jane said. "If the occasion arises."

"Then you must save a dance for me, Miss Bellevue," Lord Keegain said.

Jane's heart did another flip flop at his request. She was certain that the earl would not tread upon her toes. She nodded shyly, peering at Lord Keegain from beneath her lashes.

"And me also," Mr. Reynolds added. "Both of you fine ladies."

Jane and Lady Charlotte agreed, while Alice went into a sulk at the thought of balls and parties which she could not attend.

Jane turned to the food as the first course was served then: a light soup of creamed asparagus that looked very appetizing to Jane, but she hesitated before tucking in with gusto.

That would not be ladylike, and the earl was doubtless used to Lady Margret's impeccable manner and ladylike appetite, but Jane was near starved. Breakfast had been hours ago, and the girls had only had a simple tea sent up while they went through their toilette.

When the earl set in on his food, so did Jane, savoring the lovely cream soup. In a few moments, her appetite somewhat sated, and her bowl empty, she focused her attention back on Lord Keegain.

"I have met three of your sisters," she said, "but Lady Charlotte tells me there is a fourth."

"Yes, Sophia. You will meet her at the Christmas party." Lord Keegain's smile warmed her heart and relaxed her nerves as his eyes fell on hers. "She was wed this past year to the love of her life."

"How charming," Mr. Reynolds said. "And you Keegain, when will you wed the love of your life?"

Jane felt as if she had been doused in cold water. She had relaxed too much into the conversation and forgot the man was engaged to be married.

"Yes," she said stiffly. "You also have upcoming nuptials, my lord." She could not quite bring herself to offer congratulations.

"I do," he said.

"That's the word," Reynolds teased.

"I believe that is two words," Lord Keegain corrected, and Jane fell to eating the next course, uncertain of what to say to the sudden tension in the room.

"So you have met my other sisters, Miss Bellevue?" the earl asked, at last, shifting the conversation from his absent fiancée and back to his family. "And not just Charlotte?"

"Jane met Helen and Alice in Bath," Lady Charlotte added. "She and Lady Charity were ever so helpful in showing us the town."

"I did not have the pleasure of meeting Lady Sophia," Jane said, "but I did enjoy spending time with Lady Charlotte and Lady Helen. I do not know Lady Alice well."

He nodded. "Because she is not yet out," he surmised. "Do you have any siblings?" he asked.

"I am blessed with just one, my younger sister, Julia. Although she keeps me quite busy; I can hardly fathom having four sisters to look after," Jane said as she sniffed the savory smell of the next course. "I think it would be a great task to keep up with all of them."

"We are no bother," Lady Charlotte protested from further down the table.

Lord Keegain chuckled as he said, "A task, yes, but never a burden."

Jane nodded; she felt the same about Julia. "You must have wanted a brother though, to share manly things with."

"Strangely, I believe, Charlotte has filled that need," Lord Keegain said with a chuckle.

Lady Charlotte, who had been speaking down the other end of the table turned and called out in a most unladylike manner, "What have I done now, brother?"

"Only that you ride and shoot as well as any man," he answered her in the same loud voice. "But I cannot speak to your table manners." Laughter erupted from the other end of the table, and Jane relaxed into the casual family atmosphere.

"Indeed," the Dowager Keegain spoke. "What will our guest think of us?"

Jane only smiled and thought she loved the camaraderie of the family. She remembered when she was young, she had wished for a house full of brothers and sisters, but Mother had died after only her and Julia.

The earl paused with a forkful of food and put it down, addressing Jane again. "I suppose there was a time when I longed for a brother, and the feeling increased every time my dear mother produced another sister. But as time has gone on, I would not trade my sisters for anything in the world. I am sure they have all taught me to have a kinder heart, and for that I am grateful."

"How humble," Jane offered in return.

"No. Just truth," he said.

"I am sure there are many things my sister has taught me, but they escape me at the moment," Jane replied.

The earl chuckled.

"I suppose Julia has taught me how to paint," Jane mused. "Or at least, she did try."

"Paint?" Keegain repeated.

"Yes, my sister Julia is quite the artist." Jane shook her head with mock sadness. "I have no talent for it at all."

"I am sure you have other talents, Miss Bellevue," he said softly, and Jane blushed at the compliment, although she could not think of a single talent to which she could lay claim. She busied herself with her food when the next course of boiled potatoes, beef, and venison was brought into the dining room and the soup plates were taken away.

"Do you have a deer park?" Jane asked at the sight of the venison.

"We do. It is beyond the lake. Sophia and I often rode at dawn as youngsters. I suppose I shall have to rouse Charlotte from her sleep to accompany me, now that Sophia has married."

Jane thought of the quiet at that time of the morning, and wondered that he did not say he rode with his fiancée.

"Lady Margret does not ride?" Jane asked.

Lord Keegain sighed. "Only if she can see or be seen,"

he said. "She prefers Hyde Park, which is a far cry from our little deer park."

Little? thought Jane. The property was expansive.

"There is nothing to see but the wildlife in a deer park," the earl continued.

"Oh, there is wild life to see in Hyde Park if you know where to look," Mr. Reynolds interjected.

"Quite," Lord Keegain said.

"Come now, Keegain," Reynolds continued. "Do not tell me that you are not appreciative of the sights in Hyde Park, especially when the lovely Lady Margret accompanies you."

"Town is a wonder, it is true," the earl conceded, "but there is something most magical about riding through the wood in the pre-dawn hours. You can see the deer so clearly. While on horseback, you can walk right up to them."

"And then shoot them," Mr. Reynolds said gaily.

Jane laid her fork aside, the bite of venison now dry in her mouth.

"Is the venison not to your taste?" Mr. Reynolds asked.

"Less so now," Jane answered coolly.

"I am sorry," he said, "but that *is* the purpose of a deer park, you know."

Jane did know that, but perhaps discussing the subject at the dinner table was not the best idea.

"I hardly think your comments are good for digestion," Lord Keegain said, dryly censuring his friend.

"You are getting old, Keegain. Digestion problems, indeed?"

"And you are getting more uncouth as each day passes. Why, just the other day, Lady Margret was saying – "

"She spoke of me?"

"Only to say what a scoundrel you are."

Jane did not want to speak of Lady Margret. Tapping her lips with her napkin, she smiled at Keegain and attempted to bring the conversation back to the subject of his lands.

"I would love to see the deer, whether on the hoof or on the plate," she said, sending a defiant glare at Mr. Reynolds.

"Ho!" Keegain chuckled. "I commend you, Miss Bellevue. You see, Ted, she is not so easily riled."

Jane turned back to the earl, who continued to tell her of the wildlife on the estate. "As I was saying, the deer amble along with their young in the spring," he continued. "They come to drink at the lake, or the river, but that is a bit more of a ride."

Jane blinked. That meant that the lands were even more vast than she had first imagined. She could just picture riding with him through the morning mist along a wooded trail, his presence a solid warmth at her side.

Oh, what was she thinking? Lord Keegain was only being kind. She could not consider a ride with him. He was an earl and engaged to another. She could not consider him at all.

"Do you like to ride, Miss Bellevue?" Lord Keegain asked, unaware of her musing.

"I do," Jane said shortly, "but I should hardly consider

myself an expert horsewoman." Best to keep herself out of temptation, she thought.

"Nonsense," Mr. Reynolds interjected from the other side of her. "She and Miss Constance Poppy left me in the dust last time we had a hunt. Wort and James Poppy teased me relentlessly for ending up on the ground whilst trying to keep up with the ladies."

That was where she met Mr. Reynolds, Jane realised. The moment was coming back to her now. Her lips twitched in a smile. "Neither of them caught the fox," she remembered.

The earl took his wine glass and raised it towards her. "Then let us drink to fun, family and free foxes," he offered.

Jane laughed. "And to a joyous yuletide," she added, clinking her glass against his before taking a small sip. She knew if she drank too much wine, she would soon be asleep at the table.

Keegain sipped his wine. "Will your mother and father spend Christmas in the country?" he asked. "Or will they return to London?"

"My father and sister shall spend the holiday in the country. With friends." Jane took a deep breath as she looked at Lord Keegain. "My mother loved Christmastide, but she passed away many years ago. She was a wonderful woman, active in many charities, and is dearly missed by all who knew her." Jane explained all this with the least emotion she could. She did not want to seem morose.

Lord Keegain's face softened as he lightly placed his hand on top of hers and gave it a gentle squeeze. Shivers ran through Jane at the feeling of his bare hand on top of hers, and she found herself staring at his large blunt fingers. His hand nearly covered hers completely.

"I am sure she is missed most of all by her family," Lord Keegain said. "Unfortunately, I know how you feel." His words and his touch were meant to be comforting, and while Jane did feel some measure of comfort, she mostly felt a wild well of excitement boil up in her at the intimacy of his touch.

She found her own words at last. "I appreciate the gesture, and wish I could offer up some words of comfort in return. But it seems that no matter how much time has passed, I shall always miss my mother, most especially at Christmas." She hoped she did not sound too dreary.

"Then we shall be two upon the face of this earth who feel the same in this season," the earl said with kind eyes. "I miss my father most at Christmas. I have fond childhood memories of the celebrations. I feel the lack of his presence most keenly, but I also feel closest to him at this time. We shall celebrate the Lord's birth for the both of them, your lost parent and mine. Although, surely the celebration they both enjoy in heaven must outshine anything we could offer here on earth."

Jane couldn't contain the smile that spread across her lips at such a statement. Lord Keegain had dispelled the melancholy and brought back the Christmas joy. She could imagine her mother seated at a vast feast amongst the clouds, surrounded by the heavenly host.

She nodded her head before placing her focus back on her food, but sensed that he was still watching her. Jane's cheeks burned as she felt the full force of his gaze upon her. They had known each other only a few short hours, and yet he understood her. Never before had she had such a rapport with a person she had only just met, certainly not a gentleman. Never before had she felt both a comfort and a wild expectation unleashed by his mere presence, or by a simple touch of hands. It was most confusing.

8

$\mathcal{J}$ ane rose early and dressed herself. Poor Jacqueline had been entirely appalled to learn later that Jane quite often did this. Jane had learned to do the job at thirteen, when she put aside her childhood clothing and began to dress like a lady. Father, wrapped up in grief at Mother's death, had not noticed. When he had realized the lack, Jane protested that Mrs. Carron would do just fine.

The sky had lightened to a rosy hue and the clouds looked like snow, or at least a bit of rain. Jane went back to the small desk in the room. When at home, Jane would have loitered over breakfast with a book, but here, she did not know what to do with herself. She had already read the novel she had brought with her, and written a letter to Julia. She thought she would love a cup of tea, but surely it would be poor manners to go roaming about the house before the family was awake, and the servants must have other tasks besides running after her. At last, she pulled the bell and requested tea.

Once Lady Charlotte realized that Jane was awake at dawn and sitting in her room awaiting the beginning of the day, she promised to be a better hostess.

"Oh, no," Jane said. "I shall just stay abed."

Lady Charlotte told Jane that she did not mind Jane's early rising, and no one in the house would mind either. Jane learned later that it was Jacqueline who told Lady Charlotte she was an early riser.

"You need not stay in your room," Lady Charlotte chided Jane, "but I must warn you, I shan't be up before nine at least." She stretched luxuriously and smiled at Jane. "As Helen says, I need my beauty sleep."

Jane laughed as Lady Charlotte took her hand and led her down the back stairs to the kitchen to meet Mrs. Muir, the cook, in her own domain. "As children, all of us snuck sweets from Mrs. Muir," Charlotte confided. "You must do the same. You shall be one of the family."

Mrs. Muir was busy directing the staff, but when the girls peeked into the room, she waved them into the warm kitchen. Lady Charlotte introduced Jane one by one to the staff as they entered and exited the kitchen rushing about their duties. She learned that Mr. White was the kitchen clerk, and that it was actually his kitchen to manage. He kept the accounts, while Mrs. Muir did most of the cooking.

Lady Charlotte pointed out all manner of maids, footmen and hall boys, and Jane was soon lost in a flurry of names.

It was all very cozy as they sat near the fire and chatted while Mrs. Muir fed them hot chocolate and cinnamon rolls fresh from the oven. Once again, Jane had never tasted the like and exclaimed, "These would melt in your mouth."

"The cinnamon, among other things, has become dreadfully hard to come by due to the war. Randolph has a special supplier who imports it," Lady Charlotte confided. "My brother was cross for a month when the shipment didn't come in. The rolls are his favorite."

Jane could not imagine the earl cross. He seemed a very easy-going sort of man. Still, she could see why these were the earl's favorite. They were quite delightful. Jane was tempted to take a few morsels for a snack later, but she refrained, thinking that squirreling away treats would be quite improper behavior.

"Jane may come down in the mornings before I am awake," Lady Charlotte warned Mrs. Muir. "Now, you must promise to put her to work as you used to do for us."

"Oh, my lady, I couldn't," Mrs. Muir said, shaking her head. "That was when you were children."

Lady Charlotte lapsed into a story of when she and her sisters and Lord Keegain sat in the kitchen with Mrs. Muir and ate an entire tray of biscuits which were baked for some social event or other. "Mother was furious, and Mrs. Muir never breathed a word of our antics. Eventually, Randolph's conscience got the better of him and he confessed," Lady Charlotte said with a laugh as she finished the tale. "Miss Bellevue is my friend," She told Mrs. Muir firmly. "You must treat her as one of the family."

"I shall, Lady Charlotte," Mrs. Muir said. "Whenever you wish to visit, you are most welcome, Miss Bellevue."

The girls smiled and waved goodbye, allowing Mrs. Muir to get back to work.

After they left the kitchen, Charlotte suggested a ride, but once again it looked likely to rain all day, so they postponed it. Instead, the women worked on needlepoint. They discussed their favorite novels as they sewed and chatted about Christmas plans. Lady Helen was very secretive about the gifts she had thought to give her sisters, and Lady Alice was determined to wheedle the news from her.

Several days passed with Alice becoming more and more determined to learn what gifts were bought and which were made.

"Now, Alice, it shan't be a surprise if you know what the gift is," her mother said finally. "Besides, Christmas is not about gifts. You know that." She raised an eyebrow in a soft but unmistakable correction.

Jane remembered her own mother telling her much the same thing when she was a child. The sentiment brought back warm memories.

"Yes, Mother," Alice said dutifully, but as soon as her mother's eyes were back on her sewing she stuck her tongue out at her sister, Helen.

"I might just keep your gift," Lady Helen said teasingly as she rethreaded her needle.

"You wouldn't," Alice accused.

Jane smiled at their antics.

When the conversation strayed to people that Jane did not know, her mind conjured the earl's face. She had not seen Lord Keegain all day and felt the loss. She hoped to see him at dinner, but he was as absent as he had been earlier in the day. Jane wondered where he had gone, but it would not do to express her curiosity. Instead, she shared the evening with the ladies, sewing and discussing Christmas gifts, giving little hints to one another that could not possibly allow the other to guess.

Hours later, Lady Alice, bored with the game, tossed her sewing aside and declared she was for bed. Her sisters laughed and teased her.

By the light of the fire in her room, Jane recorded much of the day in another letter to Julia, but she left out the most important part: her confused feelings about the earl.

9

A week passed at Kennett Park. The winter weather had set in, but it had yet to snow. Jane hoped for snow for Christmas, if only a light dusting.

Once again Jane awoke early. Charlotte was still abed, but a routine had been established in the household. Jane always rose just after dawn and she would take the back stairs down to the kitchen to have a cup of tea with Mrs. Muir, who made those wonderful crumpets; crisp on the edges and so light they were like to fly away. Jane had begged the recipe for both the crumpets and the cinnamon rolls, but she doubted that any cook she could afford to hire would do them justice. Perhaps she would have to learn the secret herself.

She paused just before she went down the back staircase. It was cold here in the upper hallway; far from any fires. There was a window which looked out on the stables. It was encrusted with frost, but still she leaned in to peer out of the window.

Thrice this week she had seen Lord Keegain ride out

early on his great black stallion. He was not so close that he might see her. He was quite a distance from the house, taking the lane at a swift trot. Jane recognized his form and movement against the frost on the trees. The fact that he too rose early, brought a smile to her lips. Where did he go? she wondered.

"Morning, Miss," said Nan, on her way to light the upstairs fires. "I shall have a fire in your room directly."

"Do not hurry, Nan," Jane said. "I am on my way to have tea with Mrs. Muir."

The girl laughed. "As if she were some fine lady," Nan said.

Jane laughed as she turned from the window and continued down the stairs.

⁓◦◦◦⁓

JANE SETTLED INTO THE HOUSEHOLD, choosing decorations with the other girls and their mother. She felt almost part of the family. She was going to miss the camaraderie when she had to return home. Jane missed Julia most ardently and wished her sister were here with her to share the season, but the joyous bustle of the house made her feel in a holiday mood.

The winter weather had fully taken hold, and the family retired to the parlor most evenings, with a roaring fire in the hearth to ward off the chill. On the nights where the earl would join them, Jane found herself most distracted. His very presence was a weight within the room.

She kept her eyes on the embroidery in her lap, just

as Lord Keegain's eyes were on his paper. At least he was holding the paper, like she was holding her sewing. Jane had knotted the thread twice, and it sat tangled once again in her lap. She could keep from looking at Lord Keegain, but she could not help but feel his eyes upon her. It was unnerving. She wished she knew what he was thinking.

When she glanced up at him, looking carefully through her lashes, a spark of passion like lightning struck between them. She looked down again.

She was falling in love with him, Jane thought suddenly.

Love? What a silly notion. She was a practical girl. It was better to marry for comfort and security than to moon over things that would not, and could not occur. Lord Keegain would never be hers. The denial brought a sharp pain to her heart. She felt a lump in her throat and tears prick her eyes. Jane hurriedly made her excuses to retire for the night although sleep was long in coming.

❧

THE BREAKFAST TABLE, as usual, was set with great piles of food, sausages, and eggs, as well as scones and crumpets. Jane had to smile at the ever-present cinnamon rolls.

"Today, we begin decorating in earnest," Lady Alice announced excitedly. "Ruddy promised to bring in the pine boughs today."

"Oh, no," Lady Charlotte said, disappointed. "I wanted to go with him to collect them."

"Charlotte, it is past time you gave up these

unladylike ways," her mother said. "Riding off into the wood to chop down trees and drag in branches! It is up to the gentlemen to do these tasks. Leave it to them and the footmen."

"It is only riding," Lady Charlotte groused.

"Are Mr. Fitzwilliam and Mr. Reynolds going to help Lord Keegain with the boughs?" Jane inquired, bringing the conversation back to the decorating.

"I am sure they will," the dowager said. "Both of them have been friends with my son since boyhood. You will meet their families at the Christmas ball."

Lady Charlotte peeked over her needlepoint at Jane. "I think Mr. Reynolds is quite handsome; do you not, Jane?"

Jane was surprised by the question. She had not given Mr. Reynolds a second thought, and now she stuttered with an answer.

"He's so tall, and Mr. Fitz too," Charlotte continued, "but Mr. Fitzwilliam is enamored of Miss Mary Wadsworth." Charlotte looked at Jane with a light in her eyes. "Mr. Reynolds would be perfect for you."

"Reynolds is as poor as a church mouse," Lady Helen countered.

"Not really. His brother is a baron. It is only that he doesn't have a title himself, and anyway, Jane doesn't care about such things," Charlotte told her sister, waving a hand.

"Oh, Charlotte," Helen said. "Everyone cares about money."

"Mostly when they have too little of it," the dowager added.

"Do you not want a better match for your friend?" Lady Helen chided. "There will be plenty of others at the ball, and Mr. Reynolds is so serious."

"I do not find him so," Lady Charlotte said, "Besides if Jane married him, she would be almost like family."

"He does visit an awful lot," Lady Alice put in.

"He's a second son," Helen noted. "He will never be a baron. It's doubtful he will even live at the barony. No doubt his work with the Crown will land him a modest flat in London."

"But you do find him attractive, do you not, Jane?" Charlotte urged.

"He is a handsome man," Jane agreed at last. "But I do not think he would do for marriage, at least not for me."

"You see," Lady Helen said knowingly.

"Why ever not?" Lady Charlotte persisted.

Jane felt a blush fill her face. She could not tell them she longed for their brother. She was reaching far above her station. She looked down at the sewing in her lap and tried to formulate a reply, but the dowager saw her distress.

"Leave off, girls," the older lady said, interrupting their interrogation. "It is clear Miss Bellevue's heart is engaged elsewhere."

"It is?" Lady Charlotte asked. "Oh Jane, pray tell, who?"

"I think I shall keep my own council, just now," Jane said softly. She concentrated heartily on her sewing.

"A secret then," Lady Alice scoffed, and Jane looked up, smiling at the young girl. She reminded her so of her own sister, Julia. She felt almost motherly towards the girl.

"I am sure you will have secrets of your own soon enough," Jane said.

The conversation gradually wound its way back to the hidden Christmas presents.

10

------

*L*ord Keegain had to hurry to get the pine boughs home. The family was going to add decorations to the great hall today. He looked forward to it, not just because he loved the Christmas season, but he also looked forward to seeing Miss Bellevue, and spending time with her. When he was with her, he could be himself.

His heart felt lighter than it had in a long while. He wanted to spend time with her, and with his family and friends. He felt relieved that Lady Margret would not be there. One should not feel so about one's own betrothed. He was sure of it, if his friend Fitz waxing poetic about his own lady was any indication.

Tonight, Keegain could decorate to his heart's content, and he would not have to stand back and allow the servants to attend to it. He knew Lady Margret would be appalled at his taking the decorations in hand. What would she say about his other activities in the village?

He would rather not tell her just yet. He shook his

head. Why should he worry? He was an earl. He was the master of his own house, and had been for nigh on eight years. He could decorate his own house if he wanted to do so.

Keegain's father had loved Christmas, and so did he. He would do what he willed, within reason of course. His thoughts went back to Miss Bellevue, and the joy in her eyes when his sisters spoke of decorating. It was a Keening tradition to trim the house with pine and holly boughs. He considered where to hang the mistletoe, and Miss Bellevue's lush figure came to his mind.

Keegain nearly groaned aloud. He had wished for passion this holiday season, and he had found it, only not where he should have done.

His mind should be occupied with Lady Margret, but his thoughts continually wandered to the petite brunette instead. He thought of her head bent, sharing secrets and giggling with his sisters. He thought of her heated blush upon their first meeting, and he wondered what it would be like to kiss her beneath the mistletoe. He attempted to push those thoughts away, but how could he, when she was under his roof? His eyes followed her, and he was sure she had noticed.

He should be like a brother to her. It was clear that she had affection for his sisters. He remembered watching her the past few evenings in animated conversation with his family. Her eyes sparkled and her smile was bright. She was enjoying herself, and her joy brought him happiness.

Even his mother had smiled upon her, and gave Jane her approval, which was no small feat, but that approval was as a friend of his family, not as his wife. Whatever was he thinking? He already had a bride-to-be, a woman that everyone approved of.

Well, almost everyone, he thought.

What was wrong with him? Lady Margret was perfect for him. Ted was constantly telling him what a lucky man he was to have Lady Margret. She was an incomparable beauty. She had status and poise and wealth. She was of his social standing, but he was not in love with her. Was he in love with Miss Bellevue?

He shook his head and handed off his coat to Hughes, the butler. What was he coming to? Love, what a daft thought. He had no need of love.

His friends, Reynolds and Fitzwilliam, re-entered the house just behind him.

"I say, Keegain," Fitz said with a shiver. "It's deuced cold. How about some eggnog to take off the chill?" He pulled off his gloves finger by finger.

"Or brandy," Ted added.

"Or eggnog with brandy," Fitz teased, "if I must make do with meager spirits for warmth instead of my Mary."

Fitz had been decrying the lack of Miss Wadsworth all day, and even Ted chided him. "Get a hold of yourself, man!"

Laughing with Christmas cheer, Lord Keegain waved over a servant to find something to warm them before they started the decorating in earnest.

The house came alive with Christmas cheer. Pine boughs were hung from every possible surface. Bows and ribbons adorned the staircase, and candles were lit in extravagant abundance. Charlotte suggested that they might enjoy the decorations with a Christmas story this evening, and there was agreement all around.

Mother was just finishing attaching the final boughs to a wreath that Helen was holding for her. Miss Bellevue held her fingers aloft for Charlotte to tie a bow for it, and she took the bow from Jane's fingers.

Keegain was amazed that Miss Bellevue fit so well with his family. Would it be so, he wondered, when he was married to Lady Margret? Or would she simply have the servants ordered to do all the decorating?

Mulled wine was flowing freely, and Fitz and Reynolds toasted the ladies before helping to hang the wreath above the fireplace. This was how it should be, the earl thought.

Even though the servants were rushing here and there as he directed them, he also put his hands to the task. Hernon, a footman, brought in a silver tray of the earl's favorite biscuits. Miss Bellevue's bright laugh brought his attention back to her, and he realized that she had said something to make the very proper Mr. White smile. Ted and Fitz set upon the biscuits, but he knew there was plenty.

Lord Keegain turned back to his decorating. He had hung several holly boughs himself and now held the mistletoe with thoughts of where to place it. He decided on several places, hoping to catch Miss Bellevue under it. He hung one mistletoe bough in the sitting room, and two in the corridor.

He had just placed one above his head in the arch between the library and the corridor, and he remembered that he might have left the Lord Beresford's letter on his desk. He went in to check. It would not do to leave such things lying about when there would be guests in the house. He picked up the letter and reread it, concern creasing his brow.

Keegain sat for a moment in his chair, his Christmas cheer dampened by the news contained in the letter, but after a moment, he pushed it aside. He would not let his concern touch his family. He put the letter in a drawer, locked it, and stood. He thought he would head back to the sitting room where he could hear laughter and singing, when he saw Miss Bellevue pause at the door to the library.

"Oh," she said, as she realized he was in the room.

"If you see anything that strikes your fancy, you are more than welcome to enjoy it while you are with us, Miss Bellevue." He gestured about the expansive library.

"Thank you." She blushed a little, though for the life of him, Keegain could not think of what he had said to elicit that response. It was rather charming, though. She seemed to have developed a shyness in the past few days. He did not want her to be shy with him. The singing continued in the other room as she came into the library, stepping under the mistletoe.

"That is very kind and very generous of you, Lord Keegain," she said, her voice and stance very formal. He wondered if he had done something to upset her. They were not truly alone, he thought. His sisters and mother were only a room away and the library door was open.

"Not at all. You are my guest, despite my deplorable lack of manners in closeting myself in the study. Please forgive me for acting like a hermit. I assure you I have taken no vows of poverty." He gestured around the opulent room to prove his point.

Jane looked around the room, her face expressing approval and perhaps just a bit of awe. He realized he was boasting. He wanted to impress her. Had he done so? He wanted to pull her out of her shell. He wanted to see her smile again, just for him, but she only nodded.

"Lady Charlotte suggested that I find something to read tonight," she said sweetly, concentrating on the books by the door. It was odd, the way her eyes slid off of him as they spoke, as if she did not want to look directly at him. "A Christmas story," she added.

"I know just the one," he said pulling the book from the shelf, and taking Miss Bellevue's hand and tucking it into the crook of his elbow. She felt right there, he thought, at his side. Lord Keegain glanced towards the mistletoe. Would she acquiesce or would she refuse him? It was only a bit of harmless fun, he thought, only he knew it wasn't. He wanted most ardently to kiss her.

"Lady Charlotte took me on a tour of the house," Miss Bellevue said. "I am sure that much effort goes into the running of an estate such as this. It must be very taxing,"

"It can be," the earl conceded. He paused in the doorway, mistletoe overhead. "Less so at the moment. I am glad you have come," he said seriously.

"And I."

The din from the sitting room drifted down the corridor. The laughter and singing had been raised to epic proportions. Keegain wondered suddenly if Charlotte had mentioned Miss Bellevue in passing. Could he have met her in Bath nearly half a year ago? *I really must pay closer attention to my sisters.* The thought made him grin.

"Is there something amusing, my lord?" Jane looked at him, wide-eyed. Innocent. Beautiful. Absolutely beguiling. He glanced up drawing her attention to the mistletoe.

"Oh," she said in surprise, but she did not move from under the bough.

"Happy Christmas," she said in a hushed tone.

"Happy Christmas," he replied as he tipped her face up, fully intending to kiss her mouth.

"There you are!" Charlotte's voice chastised him. "You are being a dreadful host, disappearing like that." She stopped suddenly, as if just noticing Jane at his side, and gave him a curious expression. He handed Miss Bellevue the book, as if that had been his intent all along.

"Yes, I suppose I am," Lord Keegain said, moving away from Miss Bellevue. "Will you have it out with me?"

"I shall be vexed," Charlotte promised, although there was a smile in her voice.

"I suppose that is a common quality of sisters," he said, but the truth was he rarely argued with his sisters. They got along swimmingly.

"It may be." Jane smiled, and her eyes once again ran to the book in her hand as if that was the only safe harbor. "I find it to be so with my sister, certainly, but I have no male sibling to gauge how a brother would take the same impetus."

"Remarkably similar, I would suspect." Lord Keegain must look a fool the way he kept grinning, but could not seem to stop himself. The girl was articulate and quick.

"You must make yourself at home," he said, once again taking hold of her hand. "If you want to borrow a book for yourself, you may. Whatever you desire, ask and it shall be yours." He found that he meant the sentiment. He wanted her to be happy here.

"Come along, dear brother," Helen called from the doorway. "There are other rooms to decorate."

"The lady was about to select a book for her own company later." He smiled and stepped back, magnanimously indicating his collection.

Jane shook her head and stepped back, away from him. "I thank you for the offer, but I fear that my time here is too limited to delve into something I would be unable to finish. Again, I thank you."

"If you wish to finish the volume, take it home with you. I am sure it will find its way back to me." The thought gave him a jolt of happiness to think that he would have an excuse to see her again. "If you decide to change your mind, I am sure my sisters would be happy to help you find a good selection." He looked to Charlotte for confirmation, but it was Jane herself that brought him up short.

"Or perhaps I could prevail upon Lady Margret," she said in a very quiet voice. "I understand she will soon be mistress here."

Lady Margret. The two words struck Lord Keegain as a blow. He had quite forgotten Lady Margret. He and Lady Margret were contracted to be married, but until this moment, the agreement had seemed little more than names on a contract. The inevitable union was the logical outcome of years of family association, but Lady Margret was not the vibrant woman who stood before him. He suddenly felt quite cold.

With another polite word of thanks, Jane joined his sisters and walked quickly through the library door.

Keegain bowed and nodded, following the rest of them out, letting the servants tidy up the room behind him. The conversation had unnerved him. Whatever joy he had found in those few minutes flirting with Miss Jane Bellevue was lost now, rubbed out by reality.

The mention of his engagement set a bad taste in his mouth, especially coming from her, from Miss Bellevue. It made no sense. He tried to shrug it off, and put it down to nerves at the seriousness of the marriage commitment.

He would speak to Margret upon her return and put Miss Bellevue entirely out of his mind. That was all there was to be said on the matter.

❧

Part 2

Holly & Heartbreak

11

──────────

The day of the Christmas ball was fast approaching. The halls were properly hung with pine and holly. Mistletoe graced several doorways, and Jane was careful to avoid them, especially when the earl was present. She had been quite sure that Lord Keegain was going to kiss her under the mistletoe when Lady Charlotte had interrupted them. It was only a bit of harmless fun, she told herself. Only she was quite sure it wasn't harmless, at least not for her.

Jane spent much of the night tossing and turning in her oversized bed, and when she finally fell asleep, it was quite late. Consequently, she awoke later than usual and she did not see the earl ride out in the morning. She felt quite vexed with herself, as if the day did not begin properly without seeing him.

When she opened the door to her chamber, she realized that the household was quite awake and in full swing. She thought since it was probably past nine, the ladies would be awake soon, if not already. She might see Lady Charlotte at breakfast rather than having tea with Mrs. Muir. She went down the front stairs and paused in the corridor. She could hear someone singing Christmas carols.

It was him. The earl. She recognized the sound of his voice. It sent tremors through her. She turned to go the other way, but she was not quick enough. There he was before her.

"Oh!" she said, startled.

He stopped singing. "I do apologize if I have frightened you," he said.

"No, of course not. I only…" She consciously stopped herself from babbling. It was the first time they had been alone, ever since he had almost kissed her under the mistletoe. Her heart was beating so fast it hurt.

She looked at him under the cover of her lashes. His hazel eyes sparkled with joy. He was so handsome, and his voice was surprisingly deep and melodious. She floundered for something witty to say.

"I had not thought you would have such a fine singing voice," she told him truthfully.

"My father taught me that one when I was small," the earl said, pulling off his gloves finger by finger and handing his coat to a footman.

"Your father? Did he sing too?"

"Yes. Now, he was the one with a wonderful voice. The gallery choir still misses him," Keegain said as he unwrapped the scarf from around his neck. "Although I do my best, I shall never replace him, I fear."

"You sing in the church?"

"I do, as did my father before me. There was much singing in our house when my father was alive. He was a jolly man."

"So is his son, I believe," she said, and blushed as he raised an eyebrow. He would know his secret was out. "I mean, I had not realized."

"Oh, I am full of surprises," he said.

Jane believed that. At least, so far, the earl had been very surprising; intriguing was perhaps a better word.

"As we become better acquainted, you will see," he said.

"Oh?" Jane said again.

He held her gaze.

Was the earl suggesting that they should become better acquainted? She knew she shouldn't. She was here to visit with his sisters, not with him. She was treading on dangerous ground. He had nearly kissed her last night, and she had almost allowed it.

"Shall we see if Mrs. Muir has tea?" he asked. "And sweet rolls hot from the oven?"

She stared at him.

"Or have you already broken your fast?" Lord Keegain asked. "Of course, you haven't. Come." He held out a hand to her.

Jane froze. "To have breakfast with you?" she asked, considering. Other than the servants, the household seemed to be still asleep. They would be unchaperoned; just the two of them across the breakfast table, like...why, like a married couple. Dangerous ground indeed.

"You are hungry, are you not?" he said, and Jane wondered if he noted that she did not always keep herself to ladylike portions. It was difficult with Mrs. Muir's wonderful cooking.

"Have breakfast with me," he said, his voice soft, coaxing, alluring.

"I think I shall," she said as she put her hand in his, "but I had called for tea."

Keegain turned to the footman that awaited upon his pleasure.

"Mr. Hernon, Miss Bellevue will have her tea in the dining room, and tell Mr. White we are ready for breakfast."

The man gave a short bow and hurried away.

Lord Keegain was a perfect gentleman as he seated Jane at the table, and it seemed that a member of the staff was always present. It wasn't exactly a formal chaperone, but it was more acceptable than being entirely alone with him.

As a huge plate of sausages was served, Lord Keegain spoke. "We all are very pleased to have your company here for the holiday, Miss Bellevue. I know Charlotte was near over the moon when I allowed the visit."

"Yes, thank you for agreeing," Jane said demurely, as she pulled off her gloves and laid them in her lap. She covered them with her napkin. Her heart seemed to be beating as fast as a hummingbird's wings. "I thank you for allowing me to share your holiday, Lord Keegain. It was very kind of you."

"My pleasure," he said, and the words somehow

seemed to bring back the memory of his touch in the library. She forgot to breathe with the very thought of it.

"I am afraid I spoil my sisters," he said, nodding to the footmen serving the sausages. "When Charlotte asked to invite you, how could I refuse, when I knew it would bring her joy to share the holiday season with her newest friend? I only wish your Father and sister could have joined us. If I had thought of it, I would have extended the invitation. It was remiss of me. Christmas is a time for those closest to our hearts."

Was she close to his heart?

"A time for family," he continued.

Jane shook her head, trying to concentrate on the conversation at hand rather than mooning over the man. "My father prefers to stay closer to home in the winter," she said. "He still gets relapses of the pneumonia that plagued him last winter, but he sends his best regards." She spoke between bites of breakfast sausage, wondering if Mrs. Muir made the sausages as well. One more recipe for her to collect.

"Only he and your sister for the holidays? Will he not travel to some relative?" Keegain asked.

"He is planning to spend the season with the Poppy family," she said. "They are good friends."

"Ah, the lady who accompanied you?"

"Yes. That was Mrs. Poppy. The family lives near Bath."

"I hope that you find joy in our company, as Charlotte has found in yours."

"I have. Thank you," she said softly.

And you, Jane thought. *Has my being here brought* you *joy this season?*

As if he could read her mind, the earl said, "I, too, am glad to share your smile." He laid his hand on hers and, with the shock of skin to skin, she felt her heart leap. She was reminded of the aborted kiss in the library. She realized she very much wanted him to kiss her.

Now Jane truly blushed. The sentiment made heat suffuse her body, and she knew her face was sporting colors. She looked down at her sausages and instead saw his hand still atop hers.

"Randolph, you know this is most improper," said a voice from the doorway. Jane recognized Lady Helen. "What would Lady Margret think?"

"I am sure she would think that we were hungry," Keegain said, rising at his sister's entrance and moving his hand from Jane's. "Anyway, Mr. Hernon has barely left the room, and the sentiment is silly. There is no one here to spread scandal."

"It is still improper," Lady Helen insisted, and Jane knew she should have refused breakfast.

"Oh Lud, Helen, do not be ridiculous," Lord Keegain grumbled as he seated his sister. "I do not intend to ravish Miss Bellevue on the breakfast table."

Jane had thought her blush could not get any deeper, but now she felt like her face was on fire.

"Randolph!" Helen said sharply, just as the dowager and Charlotte joined them in the dining room. Helen bit her lip.

"Are you arguing, children?" the dowager asked wryly.

"Of course not, Mother," Lord Keegain said as he kissed his mother's cheek. "Good morning. I hope you slept well."

"As well as I can at my age," the dowager said. "This cold seeps into my bones."

"I am sure you will get on once the sun is higher, Mother," Lady Helen said.

"And we still have the dining room to decorate," Lady Charlotte added. "The day of the ball will be here in no time. That shall cheer you."

The dowager's eyes lit with excitement, and everyone chuckled. Jane was glad the attention was off of her. It was no secret that the Dowager Keegain loved hosting social events and would easily become enthralled with all the details. Charlotte had said it was what her mother did to fill her time, and the lady loved to bring people together. Jane was beginning to get the impression that the Keening family didn't carry a large concern over social status, but instead simply enjoyed the good company of close friends and family.

The dowager called for the tea to be heated as Lord Keegain buttoned his tail coat. "Do find some more of those sausages for the ladies," Keegain said to the footman, and Jane realized, with no little embarrassment, that she and the earl had polished off the entire plate of them.

"I say, Jane. The Beatrams should be here today," Lady Charlotte said as she laid a napkin on her lap.

"I am excited to see Lady Patience," Jane replied. "I haven't seen her since Bath, or Lady Amelia for that matter."

Lady Charlotte launched into a story about the plans the trio had made for their season, adding the names of several ladies Jane did not know. Jane listened politely, but she knew she would not be a part of those London plans.

12

*L*ady Charlotte peered out of the drawing room window in a most unbecoming way.

"Honestly," Lady Helen said as she remained seated. "They will not arrive any sooner for your impatience."

"Is Reginald coming?" Lady Alice asked.

"Lord Barton," The dowager corrected in a patient voice. "And we shall soon see."

When a carriage finally pulled up the lane, Lady Charlotte squealed with excitement and announced Lady Amelia and Lady Patience had just arrived in time for tea. Charlotte rushed for the door. Jane was excited to renew her acquaintance with the ladies and hurried after Lady Charlotte to greet them, while the dowager urged them not to run.

Jane remembered her manners and curbed her excitement, but Lady Charlotte bounced on the balls of her feet and hugged her friends the minute the ladies shed their cloaks.

Lady Patience did the same, while Lady Amelia stood

a bit to one side. Ever the duke's daughter, she was poised and beautiful. Jane was nervous about meeting a duke, but she noted that Amelia's father, the Duke of Ely, was not with their party.

The two ladies were accompanied by Lady Patience's family: her parents, the Lord and Lady of Battonsbury, and her elder brother, Lord Barton, none of which Jane had met. The butler, Mr. Hughes, ushered the group into the house and the dowager did the introductions. The Dowager Keegain flatly refused Charlotte's request to accompany the group to their chambers.

"Give them a moment to freshen themselves," she insisted, and Lady Charlotte reluctantly agreed allowing their guests to get settled. "And Alice, you need not tag along."

Alice stuck out her lip in a pout, but acquiesced.

The Lord and Lady of Battonsbury were as different as could be. Lord Battonsbury was tall and nearly bald. Lady Battonsbury was a stout friendly woman with frizzy brown hair. She looked a bit like a sparrow, Jane thought, which was not unusual given the bird-like presence of her daughter Patience.

Lady Patience was tall as an egret, with a swan-like neck and graceful features. Unfortunately, she had bright red hair which was quite curly and escaped from her bonnet in all directions, making her look a bit like a waif no matter how she tried to tame the locks.

Lady Patience's brother Reginald's hair could also be called ginger, but it was a dark coppery color rather than so vivid a shade as his sister's. It fell in gentle waves rather than curls. He was also spared Patience's freckles, which did not seem quite fair. A gentleman who was one day going to be an earl could get by with freckles; for a lady, they were quite gauche. Both brother and sister had their father's height.

Lady Amelia Atherton on the other hand was diminutive, and yet, Jane thought for all her lack of stature, there could be no doubt that she was a lady of prominence. She was as short as Jane, but in contrast, her figure was perfect. In fact, Jane thought, Lady Amelia was quite flawless. Even after a day spent crushed in a carriage, her complexion was not flushed, her golden ringlets had not a hair out of place and her eyes were as bright and clear as a blue sea.

She looked like a lovely china doll, or a bauble, but Jane knew from her brief acquaintance in Bath that the lady was anything but. She had a sharp mind and a biting wit. When Lady Amelia entered a room, heads turned. Jane wondered how she, as a simple miss, could shine in the shadow of such a fine lady.

A little later, once they were reacquainted, the young ladies settled themselves at tea with their mothers while the gentlemen took brandy in the drawing room.

Jane wondered aloud where Lady Charity Abernathy might be and listened for the answer. Lady Charity was often found in the company of Lady Amelia and Lady Patience. Jane knew Lady Charity from her friendships in Bath, and had hoped that she might accompany the others.

Lady Charity Abernathy reminded Jane of her younger sister, Julia. The two young women could not be more different in appearance, but their forthright manner was the same. The two girls had become fast friends last summer. Lady Charity did not look down upon those of lesser birth, for although Charity's mother had married the Earl of Shalace, she also had humble beginnings.

"Lady Charity was sorry to decline the invitation," Lady Amelia said. "Her father was not well and the family did not wish to travel."

There were nods all around.

"That is understandable in this cold," Lady Charlotte said. "Travel is difficult. Did you stop at the Dovetail Inn?"

"No," Lady Amelia said with an exasperated sigh. "It burned down."

"Oh," Charlotte said sadly. "I did love their pumpkin pastries when we went to London."

"The effrontery of the place. It was done to spite you, I'm sure," Lady Helen said dryly, and her mother shot her a look. "Sorry," she said blushing, although young Lady Alice laughed and nearly spit out her tea.

The dowager gave them both a look and they settled into silence.

"We stayed at another inn in the next town called The White Mouse," Lady Battonsbury explained. "It looked quite nice."

"But, considering the name, we should have been forewarned," Lady Patience added, as she took a sip of tea.

"Whatever do you mean?" Jane asked.

"It was not one mouse," Lady Amelia said. "There must have been dozens."

"Hundreds," Lady Battonsbury corrected. "The things

were gnawing half the night. If I hadn't been so road-worn, I doubt I would have gotten a wink of sleep."

"How awful!" Lady Helen exclaimed sympathetically.

"Let's just say I shall never stop there again," Lady Battonsbury said, shaking her head.

"Not unless they change the name to The Copious Cats," Lady Amelia suggested, and they all laughed.

"I am sorry the trip from London was so unbearable," the dowager said, "but I am glad you are here now, safe and sound."

"Yes," Lady Charlotte agreed. "We are glad you are here."

"Oh, it was not so terrible," Lady Patience said. "It was only one night. We stayed the first night at the Amesford Arms not far outside of London. You know of it?"

Lady Charlotte nodded along with her sisters and mother. "Their service is superb," Lady Battonsbury added.

"And we had fine weather most of the way," Lady Amelia agreed. "It only rained a bit just outside of London, and there was no sign of snow until the last few miles, so we did make good time."

"Yes," they all agreed.

"Still, it was rather cold," Lady Battonsbury said. "I'd forgotten how brisk it might be this time of year."

"We did stop for warm drinks many times," Lady Patience said. "So much so, Father said we must press on if we hoped to make it here while the daylight held."

"And after The *Gnawing* Mouse, the thought of another unknown inn did make us consider our stops," Lady Battonsbury said, and the ladies laughed.

Lady Patience leaned in with a whisper. "I was fair to bursting by the time we arrived."

"Too many hot drinks," Lady Helen surmised, and the ladies giggled.

The conversation fell to speculation over whether or not they might have a dusting of snow for Christmas.

The Dowager Keegain directed the conversation to Lady Amelia. "Your father sent word of acceptance of our invitation," she said. "I expected the duke to accompany you."

"Father will be here later today," Lady Amelia assured all. "He had some business to take care of before he followed. He was not far behind us, although with all of our stops, I wondered if he might arrive before us." She laughed.

"Gentlemen should expect a lady's journey to be broken by stops," the Dowager Keegain added. "Men would ride straight on until morning without need to refresh themselves, on horseback no doubt."

"Indeed," said Lady Battonsbury. The ladies laughed at her expression, and she stirred her tea. "I must say the journey was longer than I remember, Agatha," she said to the Dowager Keegain. "I am at least grateful that I had good company." She smiled at Lady Amelia and her daughter. "We passed the time with a long discussion about our plans for your masquerade, did we not?" She nodded to her daughter and Lady Amelia. The ladies both smiled and told of their dresses.

"I cannot wait to see them," Jane professed, and Lady Charlotte and her sisters agreed.

"As soon as you are unpacked, we can compare them

all," Lady Charlotte said, and Lady Alice agreed, but her mother belayed the idea.

"Charlotte, I am sure the ladies are tired after their trip and would enjoy a lie down before dinner."

Charlotte looked disappointed, but nodded. "Of course, if you are tired, I would not want to disturb you." Jane thought her friend would entirely disturb them if her mother had not forbidden it.

After tea, when Lady Battonsbury went to rest, Lady Patience took Jane's arm and Lady Charlotte's. The redhead was grinning broadly. "This is going to be so gay," she said. "I cannot wait for the masquerade."

"Nor I," Lady Amelia agreed. "I have never been to a masquerade." She twirled around and the heavy fabric of her green wool traveling dress flowed like water around her. "It shall be an adventure to be someone we are not."

"Who shall you be?" Lady Charlotte teased.

"Someone mysterious," Lady Amelia said with a spark of mischief in her eyes. "Someone interesting."

13
————

*T*he ladies spent most of the day catching up on London gossip, and Jane felt a bit out of place because she did not know all the acquaintances. However, Lady Charlotte worked to include her and soon they were all talking like old friends. The ladies' excitement and acceptance lifted Jane's spirits and gave her courage, but the reprieve was not to last.

Before full dark, Lady Margret returned with her own entourage of friends. All of them were taller than Jane, and more comely. A cold supper augmented with hot soup and mulled wine was served for the latecomers, which allowed for a mingling of guests after supper. The gentlemen retired to the drawing room while the ladies remained in the dining room, talking in small groups.

Jane did not immediately renew her acquaintance with Lady Margret, but she noted the woman spoke briefly to Lady Patience. The redheaded girl returned to their group visibly upset; her freckles were standing out like spots on her pale face. Lady Patience seemed as distressed by the new arrivals as Jane, or perhaps more so.

"Patience, whatever is the matter?" Lady Amelia said, laying a hand on her friend's arm. Lady Patience only shook her head.

"It is nothing," she said.

Lady Amelia looked from Lady Patience to Lady Margret, who stood across the room with her friends. The new group of aloof ladies stood whispering. The word "tatterdemalion" was voiced a bit louder than the rest of the conversation, along with pointed looks in Jane's direction.

Lady Patience blushed hotly, and Lady Amelia's face darkened like a storm cloud.

Jane was not truly certain whether Lady Margret's companions were talking about her less than fashionable gown, or Lady Patience's waif-like hair. Lady Amelia assumed the latter.

Lady Amelia's eyes flashed fire at the affront to her friend. "I will speak to them," Lady Amelia decided.

"No!" Lady Patience said, catching Amelia's arm. "Let it go."

"I could speak to my sister," Lady Charlotte said hesitantly. "Mother would not condone such behavior."

"No," Lady Patience said again. "Leave it be. Let us talk of other things and be merry. I should not wish to allow harsh words to spoil the season."

Lady Amelia huffed indignantly, but agreed. She turned her back to the other women most deliberately and ignored Lady Margret entirely, as if she and her companions were not worth her attention. Lady Margret did the same. Lady Patience and Lady Charlotte became caught up with each other after a while, and the slight was forgotten, but Jane noticed that Lady Amelia's eyes kept straying to Lady Margret.

Perhaps Lady Amelia could not disregard the hurt of her friend, or perhaps she just did not take well to being ignored. In any case, they found themselves gravitating towards Lady Margret and her group, but not so close they might be overheard.

Lady Amelia turned abruptly to Charlotte and said in a low voice, "Charlotte, has your brother set a date?"

Lady Charlotte shook her head to the negative.

Lady Amelia made a short nod and with decisiveness began to move towards the other group of ladies.

Jane, Charlotte and Patience followed inexorably in Lady Amelia's wake as she approached Lady Margret and her minions.

"Lady Margret," Lady Amelia said sweetly. "I am sorry. I did not greet you sooner. I must have missed you when we arrived. I thought you would be hostess by now." Amelia caught both of Margret's hands within her own, which might have been a friendly gesture, but Jane wondered if it was to keep the lady from escaping.

"Not quite yet," Lady Margret said in a tight voice.

"Then you have finally set a date?" Lady Amelia said brightly, her oh-so-white teeth flashing.

"Not quite yet," Lady Margret repeated tightly.

Lady Margret's companions shuffled nervously, but Margret did not bother to introduce them.

Lady Patience, ill at ease with the animosity in the room, tried to smooth the way despite the previous insult.

"That is a lovely dress you are wearing, Lady Margret," she said.

Indeed the dress was exquisite and she wore it well.

Lady Margret turned her attention to Patience for a moment, as if perhaps searching for a compliment to return, but Lady Amelia did not let go of her. Instead, she eyed Lady Margret's dress critically.

"Yes, Margret," she said. "That is a most attractive dress."

Lady Margret began to preen at the duke's daughter's compliment, but Lady Amelia continued and Margret's face fell. "It fits you so much better now than it did in Town for the coming of the Masters," she said sweetly.

Lady Helen gasped and one of the other ladies in Margret's company sniggered, proving they were not as good of friends as Margret may have assumed. Lady Margret glared daggers at her companion, and the lady attempted to turn her snigger into a cough.

Lady Amelia went right on speaking. "Have you a new seamstress? You must give me the lady's name."

Jane was dumbfounded. Lady Amelia had managed to compliment and insult Lady Margret, all within the same breath. Jane was unsure if she meant to say her seamstress was of poor quality, or to imply that the lady had gained weight. Either way, Lady Margret was furious.

Her eyes narrowed, but she said nothing of the slight. "It is indeed a pleasure to see you again, Lady Amelia," she said tightly as she pulled away from Amelia's grasp.

"And you," Lady Amelia said with a full dimpled smile. She turned then, catching Patience's hand and pulling the lady to her side. She tucked Lady Patience's hand in the crook of her arm. "You of course, know my dear friends, Lady Patience and Miss Jane Bellevue." She gestured to Jane.

Lady Margret stiffened, but she was unable to fail to acknowledge Jane now that Lady Amelia brought her forward. One did not offend a duke, or even a duke's daughter.

"Of course," Lady Margret said through gritted teeth. She introduced her own friends, Lady Ursula and Lady Guinevere, but she turned back to Amelia as soon as was barely polite, changing the subject to one in which Jane could not participate. "The Masters was quite the event, was it not?"

Her companions twittered in agreement.

It was impolite to continue to exclude Lady Patience and Jane, but Jane was unsure what to say as the ladies spoke of music.

"Have you managed the Bach concerto yet?" Lady Amelia asked.

"Of course, but I strive for perfection. There has been hardly a single day where I have not had the chance to play the pianoforte," Lady Margret said.

She listed several teachers that Jane did not know, but Lady Amelia inclined her head, the picture of grace. Jane felt that there was some purpose to her speech, but she did not know what it was.

"I do remember your being partial to the instrument as well, Lady Amelia," Lady Margret continued. "I am sure you have not had the time to practice that I have, moldering away here in the country. There is positively nothing else to do."

"Miss Bellevue and I were just this morning discussing horseback riding," Lady Charlotte said, in an attempt to change the subject.

"I do love riding," Jane added.

"But we were speaking of music," Lady Margret said decisively, and Lady Amelia's eyes flashed fire at the affront.

"Oh no, Lady Margret," Lady Amelia said heatedly, and all attempts to change the topic ceased. "We were speaking of ladylike pursuits, riding, needlepoint, and of course, music. I must say, I do take the time to practice daily regardless of what other activities I may enjoy, including riding." She nodded to Jane and then continued. "I think if something is to be done, it should be done well. Do you not agree? That is a lady's prerogative."

"Of course," Margret said a little warily.

"Besides, Father bought me a new instrument," Lady Amelia said with a negligent wave of her hand. "I could not let it lie in waste. The very latest design shipped from Germany. The sound quality is quite amazing."

"I have heard that sound quality is dependent upon the skill of the musician," Lady Margret said tartly.

"Indeed, it is."

Jane heard a lace of steel in Lady Amelia's voice.

"I do hope you will grace us with a number during your stay," Lady Amelia offered. The words were spoken as a challenge, and Lady Patience nudged Jane's arm in camaraderie.

"Certainly, Lady Amelia. It would bring me great pleasure to play for you," Margret replied.

"Now seems to be as fitting an occasion as ever," Lady Amelia said, a smirk crossing her face as she looked across the crowded room. "The gentlemen will return soon." Jane was not exactly sure what was happening, but Lady Charlotte seemed to be excited. "Perhaps a duet? Since you have been practicing the Bach, we should not let such effort go to waste."

Lady Margret stilled for a moment. She kept a smile on her face as she considered the idea, but instead she finally turned to address Jane. "Do you play, Miss Bellevue?"

Jane was surprised that she was spoken to directly; in fact she had thought that Lady Margret would completely forget her name as soon as possible. The way Lady Margret emphasized *Miss* made Jane's stomach clench. Still, she answered politely.

"I play, although I have no great love for the instrument. Not like Lady Amelia. I prefer riding or when confined indoors, reading to any form of music," Jane replied, trying to keep her tone even. "I am all thumbs," she said self-deprecatingly. "I would not play for company."

"A pity, for sure," Lady Margret offered in return just as the gentlemen reentered the room. "Well, then, I should be returning to my Lord Keegain. I'm sure he misses me already."

"I look forward to our playing together," Lady Amelia insisted. "In fact, it is a shame that Miss Bellevue does not play, but I am sure Lady Patience can be coaxed into a trio."

"You play? Bach?" Lady Margret asked Lady Patience, the surprise evident in her voice.

"I do," Lady Patience said simply.

With that Lady Margret dipped her head and walked off, crossing the room without so much as a by-your-leave. Her friends followed at a respectable distance. Lady Helen seemed unable to decide which way to go, but eventually, with an apologetic smile towards her sister, she followed Lady Margret.

"Yes, run away," Lady Amelia said under her breath, and then to Lady Patience, "Do you feel better?"

"I did not ask you to do that," she said.

"Oh, I quite enjoyed it," Lady Amelia admitted. "A lady should always be cordial, even when patience is tried."

Lady Patience giggled at the pun on her name, and Jane noticed that Lady Helen had gone to her mother, while Lady Margret moved to occupy the chair next to Lord Keegain. However, he did not glance at Margret when she took the seat. He seemed to be far away and pensive. Jane wondered what was on his mind, but Lady Margret noticed her stare and fixed her gaze on Jane, forcing Jane to look away.

"Lady Margret used to be such fun. We were all friends, once upon a time," Lady Charlotte said thoughtfully. "I do not know what happened to damage our friendship. I do apologize. She was quite rude."

"I cannot abide rudeness," Lady Amelia whispered, frustration laced in her words.

"Pay no attention to her," Lady Patience offered. "It is

certain Lord Keegain does not. Though I thought they were supposed to be a love match."

"Obviously not," Lady Amelia observed. "Do not let that woman upset you," she soothed Lady Patience. Her eyes came up to meet Jane's. "Either of you," she added. "A true lady is proud, but never cruel."

Jane tried to offer her friends a grateful smile, but she felt that she could not. Her attention to the earl had been noticed by Lady Margret, if not by others, and she did not feel as brave as she had earlier.

She was no lady. She did not belong in these circles. Perhaps her mother's advice had been wrong, and Jane would have benefitted better from guarding her heart instead of following it. Lady Charlotte linked arms with her and smiled.

"We shall go riding before the week is out," she insisted. "I am glad you ride, Lady Amelia. I hope you and Lady Patience will accompany us."

"Of course," Lady Patience said and launched into a tale of riding in Hyde Park last spring. "Although I do try to stay out of the sun," she explained.

As the night wore on, Jane schooled herself not to look towards the earl. She had no desire to watch his reactions to Lady Margret. Instead, she spoke pleasantly with her friends. Even when joyful laughter would erupt from the other side of the room, Jane did not dare look to see if Lord Keegain was joining in the laughter with Lady Margret or not.

By the time Jane was able to return to her bedchamber, finally alone with her thoughts, she was relieved to be free of the company. How did the pleasant holiday feeling that had been with her all week, suddenly vanish?

She knew why. All week she had settled into the rhythm of the household. All week she had felt like a member of the family, and now that Lady Margret had returned, it was clear Jane was most definitely not family.

She allowed Jacqueline to help her dress for bed.

"You are: how you say? *Mélancolie*?" Jacqueline observed.

"Only pensive," Jane corrected, but that was not quite true. Jacqueline had seen the truth. Once Jane was completely alone, she let down her guard.

She crawled into bed pulling the blankets up to her chin. The maids had left the bed warmer and the soft feather bed was comfort itself. She blew out the candle and as darkness completely enveloped her, Jane pulled the pillow to her chest and fought the tears that tightened her throat. She would not cry. She would not allow Lady Margret's cruel dismissal to upset her.

Lord Keegain was never hers, and he never would be hers. She had to let go of this silly fantasy. He was an earl. He was engaged. Jane was a practical girl, and she knew when reality could not be changed. Hadn't the death of her mother taught her that? Some things would not, and could not change. They just had to be borne. Finally, she could hold back the tears no longer, and she muffled the sobs against her pillow as her heart broke in two.

14

———

Randolph Keening, the Earl of Keegain, gently swirled the brandy snifter in his hand, warming it as he stood by the window. The Duke of Ely stood with his own glass.

"I say, it is likely a bad storm brewing, Keegain," the duke said from behind him. Keegain nodded silently, wondering whether the duke was referring to the gathering gray clouds on the horizon, or their earlier conversation: the gathered armies of France amassed under a mad little dictator, who seemed bent on taking over the world.

Keegain hoped that the more literal storm would hold out until his guests were all safely ensconced in the house. He knew that where the lane drew close to the river, it became icy in inclement weather. He had ordered a fence around that section of the lane to keep conveyances from sliding over the bank and into the water. Several carriages were still due to arrive. At least most had made it safely.

His intended, Lady Margret, had returned to residence. Many of the ladies had already arrived; including his sisters' friends, and most especially, Jane.

Miss Jane Bellevue. He remembered her face, sweet and serene as she had looked sitting across the parlor from him; sitting across the breakfast table from him. It was a most domestic moment, and yet it was a moment he treasured.

Jane. The name suited her; simple, yet elegant. He remembered how her hand trembled under his at the breakfast table, and how her face turned up to him under the mistletoe, so expectant. He should not have considered kissing her; now, he could not forget it.

As his eyes studied the horizon, Keegain took a sip of his brandy. He considered the Duke of Ely's words, and wondered if there was any safety left at all. He swallowed hard. All that he had to lose made the duke's warning that much more dire. The responsibility for so many lives lay upon him, his guests' and his sisters'. How would he bear it if anything happened to any of them while they were under his roof?

The Duke of Ely's voice echoed in his thoughts. The duke was no alarmist, although there were many lords who were unnerved by Napoleon's bluster.

Keegain and the duke were Englishmen and stood proudly for their country. Yet, the war in the colonies had been taxing, especially trying to fight the colonies and France at the same time. The King had gone mad, yes, but the Regent was fully in control now, and the Crown was stable. Well, as stable as any monarch's seat on a throne could be while Napoleon raged. That did not vouchsafe security for anyone.

But this? This madness was surely beyond the pale. The fact that the duke had sworn to the veracity of it; and that, in fact, there was a history of such horrifying events, made Keegain pause. His estate was days from London, and even if he had been active in the *Ton*, the very nature of secrecy and the deuced paranoia of anything that even hinted of scandal would doubtless have kept them all in the dark anyway.

"Can I count on you then?" the duke pressed gently.

Keegain dropped his gaze from the horizon and brought himself back to his guest and the troubling conversation. He nodded. "Of course." He strode to the crackling fireplace, as if to warm himself, but all he felt was the cold draft around the flames. He dipped his fingers into the pocket of his waistcoat. The sharp crackle of the letter stored there made him pause in mute apology. He had chosen to not believe the contents of the letter, doubted even the authenticity of Lord Beresford's hand, but to hear it again from the Duke of Ely sent a chill through his frame that could not be blamed on the occasional draft.

"How is this possible, Your Grace? In my own home! Are you completely sure?" Maybe it was not well to question the veracity of a man in the duke's position, but the words came in a strangled cry of unexpressed anguish, a plea that the older man might tell him that the world could be a safe place; that his home could be a safe place.

The duke took no offense. "Yes, Keegain, I am sure."

"Then perhaps your informants erred?" Lord Keegain waved that off. "I am sorry – I'm just..." He pulled himself to heel and straightened his spine. "Please, Your Grace, just so I do not misunderstand, would you tell me again?"

"If you cannot credit it, Keegain," the duke said kindly, "then you have not misunderstood." He set down his glass and took a breath, meeting the earl's eyes. His expression was soft, but his voice was hard and rough.

"There is a traitor among us." He spoke patiently, his tone somber. "He moves in circles only open to the peerage. For this reason, several King's men will be at the ball tomorrow, mingling with your guests. I believe you have already met Mr. Reynolds."

"Ted Reynolds is friend. I understood him to be in His Majesty's service, yes, but as to the others..." Lord Keegain trailed off.

The duke clapped Keegain's shoulder. "I shall introduce them all to you straight way. That way you'll have a good idea what they look like behind their masks." The duke's expression fell then, and the grasp on the earl's shoulder tightened with the weight of importance. "Keegain, whatever you may do, keep your sisters close." The duke gave a little shake on the last word, the elder generation imparting wisdom on the younger, and Keegain nodded.

"Damn this ball." Keegain set his glass on the mantle. "Would it not be better to send the ladies away, someplace safe?"

The duke shook his head sadly and headed back to the padded chair he had so recently occupied. "No, Keegain. I sympathize, I very much do. My daughter,

Amelia, is at risk as well. She is the very light of my life. I desire to protect her as much as you would your sisters, but if they were sent away, the traitor would be warned and would crawl back into the woodwork, only to arise again and cause more trouble. No, the only way to catch the traitors is if they believe they have the upper hand, though I very much doubt the villains will be caught in their cups. Too much is at stake." The duke sat down heavily in one of the winged leather armchairs in Lord Keegain's private study. "Now, you must keep your own counsel on this, Keegain. Not even your own sisters should suspect anything amiss."

The earl nodded, but reached for the glass again.

"I will need your oath." The duke's face was iron now as he leaned forward in his chair.

Lord Keegain's head whipped up and he returned the duke's look with one of fire. "My word is my bond."

"Do not bristle your feathers at me, lad," Ely warned him. "If I had a moment's doubt about your word or your loyalty to the Crown, I would not have brought this to you in the first place."

Keegain took a sip of brandy to cover the effort it took to get his emotions under control. "Of course, you can count on me." He managed a small smile and a shrug. "I am English, am I not? I am sworn to the Crown, to protect King and Country. It is only...." He turned pleading eyes to the older man. "I simply cannot credit so heinous a plot is afoot. There was no sign, no..." He searched Ely for some reprieve. "Is it not possible you are mistaken?"

The grandfatherly expression returned to the old

man's face. "No matter how hard you may wish it, I am not mistaken."

"But... why here? I'm not exactly on the route to London, we are days from there."

"You say you are remote, but others may say you are far from prying eyes. Additionally, you are holding a masquerade ball which is, by its very nature, an invitation to deception and intrigue."

It felt like an accusation, though Lord Keegain knew it was not. He cleared his throat. "I never meant it to be so."

"I know, but perhaps it is for the best, eh?" The duke smiled and winked. "We can catch the traitorous bastards." His fist clenched in the air, as if already grasping the villains.

Keegain smiled politely and returned to the window, finding himself too keyed up to sit again. The clouds looked as if they held the promise of snow. Ely sat quietly next to Keegain. Apparently Keegain's doubt was forgiven. The Duke of Ely was not a man to be questioned. Keegain had known the man for years.

Ely had argued in the House of Lords for caution, had used his own wealth to bolster that of the Regent's when the costs of fighting two wars at once began to bleed the coffers. Now, to suggest that the little dictator was getting money funneled to him from Britain, worse, from a member of the Peerage...Keegain did not want to credit it. Highwaymen, he understood; a man might steal to feed his family or for greed. But to become a traitor to one's own country left a sour taste in Keegain's mouth.

He shuddered. No, not from the cold, from the raw deception of such a plot. From the fact that those he loved would have to be placed in danger, before he and the duke and the King's men could put a stop to it.

Napoleon had turned his eyes to England. They had expected as much. What was beyond the belief of any rational Englishman was that there were those who waited to welcome him with open arms, and that they did not wait idly. They sent gold bullion to aid in the madman's butchery. And how they got that gold...that was the thought that made his bones ache from a cold deeper than any storm cloud.

"Do not fret, my young friend." The duke spoke lightly, but his voice was strong and sure in its confidence. "We'll catch the brutes!"

Keegain nodded and finished his brandy, but it left a bitter taste behind.

15

*J*ane had a fitful night. Although she awoke early, she remembered that Lady Margret was returned, and she did not want to accidentally encounter the lady. Jane moaned, fluffed her pillow, and buried her face in it. She did not even wish to rise to go down for tea in the kitchen. No matter how she had felt like a member of the family, the truth was that she was not.

She closed her eyes and willed herself to go back to sleep. It must have worked, because some time later, she heard a faint knocking in the distance and dismissed it. She remained in dreamland until the sun was streaming through her window. She had not drawn the draperies last night. She was surprised that Lady Charlotte had not come for her. Surely it was after ten. Once she had lain in bed for as long as she could, Jane rang for tea.

While she was dressing for the day, Jacqueline informed her that the ladies were awaiting her in the sitting room. Jane steeled herself for another encounter with Lady Margret. She could not avoid the woman. Margret was soon to be the lady of the house.

Jane braced herself and thanked Jacqueline for her help and direction as the maid opened the door to the sitting room. Jane peered into the room and breathed a sigh of relief. She saw just the ladies she wanted to see: the Lady Battonsbury, Lady Patience, and Lady Amelia, as well as the Dowager Lady Keegain and young Lady Alice.

"Welcome to my solar," the dowager said, and Jane smiled.

"Thank you for inviting me." She hovered uncertainly in the doorway.

"Come, come," the Dowager Keegain urged, and Jane came further into the room. Jacqueline curtseyed politely and closed the door behind her as she left.

"Where is Lady Charlotte?" Jane asked. "Surely she is not still abed?"

"No," the Dowager Lady Keegain said. "Her brother roused her sometime this morning to go for a ride with him. Helen, Margret, and the others have had their gowns planned and did not need our input."

Jane felt a bit sad to be left out of the riding this morning, but perhaps Lady Charlotte wanted a bit of time with her brother, so Jane could not be cross. Besides, the knocking she remembered on her door may have actually been Charlotte. Jane thought it served her right to be left out when she was so dour this morning.

"Humph," Lady Amelia said with a bit of a huff. Jane was not sure if she too was upset about being left out of riding, or if she was thinking of Lady Helen and Lady Margret.

Lady Alice assumed the later. "Oh, Helen is ever antisocial," she said from where she had draped her long limbs over a chair.

"Alice, that is a terrible thing to say about your sister," the dowager scolded.

"It's true," Lady Alice said with a shrug. "Unless, of course, you wish to discuss novels."

"No matter. We shall enjoy ourselves in their absence," Lady Patience said, smoothing the situation. "We have decided to trade gowns."

Jane looked around her. The room smelled of pine and was filled with Christmas cheer, but it had been nearly redesigned into a fitting room, complete with dressing screen, and ball gowns rested over the settee and chairs. Jane smiled with ease as she took in the view.

"Has Lady Charlotte chosen?" Jane asked.

"Indeed she has," Patience said, showing Jane a pink confection of lace and bows. "She has chosen mine."

Jane wondered what mask the lady would wear with the elaborate gown.

"We were starting to grow worried that you were not well," the dowager commented. "Charlotte has said that you are usually an early riser."

"I was simply overly exhausted from yesterday's festivities," Jane lied.

Lady Amelia and Lady Patience shared a look, and Jane pleaded silence from the two of them with a glance. She did not want to make a fuss.

"Why, of course, my dear. This is quite a lot of

excitement for you, I am sure," the Dowager Keegain commented, turning back to the other girls and the dresses they were perusing.

Jane's smile faltered then, but she was glad no one was watching her. It gave her a moment to regain her composure as she neared the spectacle of gowns, lace, ribbons and masquerade masks.

The dowager introduced the seamstress, who had gone unnoticed until now, as Mrs. Greenly. She was a slight woman of uncertain age, but surely as old as the dowager or older. Her nose was rather long, like a beak, and her arms were long and thin. She looked rather like a stork in the white smock that covered her dress. She had pins stuck in a line along the pocket, and from that pocket she took out a measuring tape and went to work.

The dowager spoke in a hushed voice as she picked up a mask and handed it to Jane. "Now, I must share a secret with you, Miss Bellevue, and ask that you keep it between us."

"Of course, my lady," Jane said as she took the mask the dowager had handed her. Whatever did the lady mean?

Jane looked at the exquisite mask in her hands. It was white with swan's feathers adorning it and cut glass, or perhaps they were truly diamonds, around the edges. The thing glittered. Another mask that graced the table was blue and purple with enormous gems placed around the eyes. Surely they must be glass, Jane thought. A mass of peacock feathers framed the top of the mask. Both masks had ribbons fixed to the sides to allow the wearer to tie it around their head and hair.

"I have a fascination with masquerade masks and have designed these especially for you three," the Dowager Lady Keegain said, beaming with satisfaction as she picked up a third mask of raven feathers and dark stones which may have been onyx. "You must keep my secret, and of course, you may have your own, dear, and that is quite all right if you do not want to use one of these."

"I have nothing quite so grand as this," Jane said examining the mask in her hand. She had planned to wear a simple black mask across her eyes. This was lovely, and she told the lady so.

Jane admired the expert craftsmanship. The care made her suddenly miss her sister. "You are an artist, Lady Keegain," she said. "But why would you not want to tell people of your talent?" She carefully handed the mask back to the Dowager Lady Keegain, who lifted a shoulder in a delicate shrug.

"Because, Miss Bellevue, I enjoy making them, and I do not want to be revealed as a countess who enjoys a tradesman's art. So, I share this secret only with those whom I trust." The dowager put the mask carefully aside.

"I am honored," Jane said seriously.

The dowager raised a finger and wagged it before Jane's nose. "Remember now, if you ever are questioned about the maker of your mask, you must tell them a secret friend from Town fashioned it for you," the dowager explained with a wink, "and I shall be your secret friend."

Jane felt quite overwhelmed to be included in the lady's surreptitious activities. "It will be our secret, Lady

Keegain, and I shall give you all the praise when we shall talk alone together, so that you might be appreciated for your wonderful talent," Jane said, hoping to please the dowager. By the way the lady smiled, Jane knew that her words had truly warmed her heart.

"Do you still make Christmas decorations, Agatha?" Lady Battonsbury asked the dowager.

"I do," she said, and the two older women began discussing decorations.

"You are an angel, Miss Bellevue," Lady Patience said, picking up the swan feathered mask, "and so, we thought the white mask for you. Lady Charlotte said that your gown was white."

"It is," Jane agreed.

"We've been fussing all morning on which gowns would be best for the ball," Lady Patience said. "I've changed my mind at least a dozen times, but I am leaning towards the black and blue with the black mask, although Lady Amelia did want to be the mysterious one and the gown is hers, so she should choose first." Lady Patience peered at her friend, a question in her eyes.

"The purple one is mine as well," said Lady Amelia in a teasing tone. It seemed the duke's daughter had brought an entire trunkful of ballgowns.

"So it is. Choose then, Amelia."

"Perhaps the peacock," Lady Amelia said. "The blue and purple will go well with my sapphires."

"And which would suit you, Miss Bellevue?" the dowager asked, as she gestured to the dresses laid out on the bed.

"Oh, I couldn't," Jane began, but Lady Amelia interrupted.

"We want to share," she said, "unless you wish to wear your own gown."

Jane did have a gown, but not nearly as lovely as the dresses laid out for her perusal. She suddenly felt as if this was a plan to dress her, so that Lady Margret would not make crass remarks about her clothing as she had done. Jane hesitated.

"I do have a dress," she said, "but these are beyond beautiful." She was torn between her pride and the lovely dresses before her, dresses her father could never afford. All were silk with imported lace and stones, or glass beading and embroidery. The labor alone would cost more than a common man made in a year. This was part of the reason she would not have a London season, but she could have a taste of it. For one night, she could be a lady, or at least dress like one. The thought was tempting, but such extravagance was not her. She made her decision.

"My dress is white," she said at last, "and I have my mother's pearls, but the swan mask is beautiful, if I may."

"You may," the dowager said magnanimously.

Lady Patience picked up the blue and black gown and danced around the room with it. "Do you think I could possibly meet my future husband tomorrow night, Mama?" she asked dreamily.

"Anything is possible, my dear," Lady Battonsbury said.

"You must remember tomorrow is a masquerade, and the unveiling isn't until midnight," the dowager added. "It will be hard to judge one's character without knowing what they truly look like."

"For all we know, a gentleman could be covering a rather large wart on his face," Lady Amelia added, and they all laughed. Jane thought of Mr. Reynolds' comment about his brother, who was called Wort, but was most warm and chivalrous.

"I do not think I should mind, as long as he is kind," Jane said, and the ladies laughed again at her unintended rhyme.

The ladies were in high spirits, and Jane felt a part of the happiness. It was as if the ladies were family, and the Dowager Keegain and Lady Battonsbury fussed as mothers should. As Jane thought her mother might have done. Jane felt the warmth of Christmas cheer, and when Lady Charlotte joined them, Jane's joy was complete.

"What have I missed?" Lady Charlotte said breathlessly, clomping into the room still wearing her soiled riding habit.

"Everything," Lady Amelia said dryly, but Patience laughed. "We shall have to tell you everything, and bring you up to scratch."

"Darling," her mother said. "Do remove those boots before you soil the carpet."

"Sorry, Mother," Lady Charlotte said, sitting and attempting to pull off the boots. "It is only that the pasture was uncommonly muddy with all the rain."

Lady Patience moved to help Charlotte, but the dowager rang a bell, calling back a maid so quickly that Jane wondered if she were waiting outside the door.

"You missed a wonderful ride, Jane. You should have

come with us," Charlotte said, proving that she had indeed tried to invite Jane this morning.

"You could change in your room," the dowager said as the maid moved to help Lady Charlotte with her boots.

"Why, if we are trying on dresses here?" Charlotte said as the boot came loose and she fell back on the chair with a plop.

The girls burst into laughter, and the dowager just shook her head. "I am never going to marry you off, am I?" she said.

"Probably not," Lady Charlotte agreed. "I shall stay here and care for you in your old age, Mother."

"Here?" the dowager said. "Oh, are you sure that Lady Margret will accommodate us both?"

A frown of worry crossed Lady Charlotte's features before she waved it away. "Lady Margret prefers her time spent in London. She shan't bother us here at all."

"Indeed," the dowager replied dryly, and Jane wondered what the elder lady thought of her soon-to-be daughter-in-law.

16

Lord Keegain realized he had been neglecting his guests whilst speaking with the Duke of Ely. The ladies were engaged with dresses, and he found the gentlemen in the drawing room.

"You've been quite ensconced with the duke," Edgar Fitzwilliam began without preamble.

The earl grimaced. "Not entirely by choice, Fitz. Have you seen Ted Reynolds?"

"I have." Fitz nodded toward the grinning man by the door. "In fact, we were catching up while we waited for our betters to finish their conclave."

Keegain gestured toward the tall blond man, and he moved to join them, moving back to the study.

"Then you are aware that Reynolds is in His Majesty's service?" Keegain asked Fitz.

"Aren't we all, old boy?" Fitzwilliam grinned. When neither man reacted to his jibe, he frowned a little, looking from one to the other uncertainly. "I say... what am I missing here? The tension could be cut with a knife."

"Ted is here in an official capacity, I fear." Lord Keegain poured each of them a drink, but refrained from taking one himself. The brandy he had finished earlier with the Duke of Ely was still working on him, and he wanted to keep sharp. Reynolds also politely declined, though Fitz took his eagerly.

"Official capacity?" Fitzwilliam echoed, his expression curious as he lifted his glass to drink.

"It seems there is a group of Englishmen calling themselves the…" Keegain turned to Reynolds. "What was their name again? Some fool society, I know."

"The Society of Second Sons," Reynolds supplied.

"Quite. At any rate, these men are unscrupulous types who are supplying funds to Napoleon."

"Englishmen financing that… despot?" Fitzwilliam's eyebrows raised considerably.

"I'm afraid so." Reynolds' expression was serious. At a nod from Keegain, he continued. "The funds are drawn from a spate of kidnappings that have been vexing the gentry of late. Ladies of quality taken by force and held for ransom. Mostly the daughters, but there have been wives taken as well. The ransom is always in gold and is sent south to France."

"Good God in heaven," Fitzwilliam exclaimed. He seemed to forget about the drink he held, an indication of his upset, as he gestured wildly. "But what are Reynolds and the King's men…" His head swiveled to Keegain. "Here? You think there will be an attempt here?"

"The duke certainly is convinced," Lord Keegain said, crossing to the fireplace.

"It is most likely," Reynolds agreed with a nod. "I wish I could say otherwise, but a masquerade ball out of sight of London? It is tempting indeed."

"Why have I heard nothing of this before?" Fitzwilliam slammed his drink down on the desk, sending brandy out in a wide arc and staining the wood dark.

"Because of good old-fashioned *sensibility*." Keegain nearly spat the response.

He too had been enraged when he heard. He still was, but had gained control of his features before leaving his study. He waited now, letting Fitz take in the shock. Truth be told, his own control was shakier than he let on.

Lord Keegain could not think of the danger to the ladies' person. Thus far, the women had been returned, but at what cost? His voice was terse as he continued.

"Imagine what a scandal it would be for one of our own to be made a victim: a wife or a daughter. What would be said of a gentlewoman left in the hands of ones so unscrupulous? Even returned, she would be ruined, and through no fault of her own. We must be vigilant. I cannot allow for my sisters, nor the wives or daughters of any of my guests, to bear that burden."

"Or your betrothed." Reynolds heaved a heavy sigh.

"Of course," the earl agreed hastily, but Reynolds continued.

"Unfortunately, I am afraid you are right. The scoundrels are well-versed in the ways of the *Ton*. None would breathe a word for fear of scandal."

A knock on the door interrupted whatever he was going to say, immediately followed by a frontal assault of merriment with gay dresses and smiling women. Keegain's sisters took the forefront, with a small group behind them.

"Here is the most common fixture of the house, our brother," Lady Charlotte said breezily, dismissing his scowl. "Oh, cheer up, Randolph, you have been hiding in here all afternoon with your brandy. It is time to join the world as it were."

"Yes," Lady Helen announced. "You must share the benefit of your company with the rest of our guests. Do join us in the parlor for tea. All of you," She called over Charlotte's shoulder.

"Especially you," Charlotte added, seizing Mr. Reynold's arm that she might draw him toward the door, while Helen took Fitzwilliam.

The youngest of the trio, Alice, nearly doubled over giggling behind them as they turned to exit, the gentleman in tow.

Reynold's gave him a pleading look, but was swallowed up in the group before a rescue could be affected, a man drowning in the quicksand of femininity. "Stay strong, old chap!" Keegain called with a sharp glance at Fitz, who was laughing at the ladies' antics with his customary good humor, though Keegain knew him well enough to know the sound was forced.

They would have to let the matter go for now. Their somber discussion had no part in this time of frivolity. If the ladies knew of the danger, it would only create a panic. No, it was best to stay alert. In the meantime, this was meant to be a house party celebrating the birth of the Christ Child and peace on earth. *Humph*, he thought of Napoleon. *May the man rot.* Still, it was a party. He was meant to be jovial.

There came with that thought the realization that a certain young lady was likely part of the flock invading his library. Jane. The earl looked around for her now, spotting her near the back of the group. He shouted good-naturedly at the throng as he moved to join them.

"Forgive us, ladies, we have been negligent in our duties to you all," he said, taking the long way around the group, that he might be nearer to Jane as he spoke. She did not, however, look at him. He wanted her to look at him.

"Indeed," Fitzwilliam lifted his snifter from the desk as he was herded out, that he might toast them, even if the glass was nearly empty. "When it comes to entertaining the fairer sex that is the single profession at which I would not fail."

The women gathered Fitzwilliam and Reynolds in their wake and began to edge out of the room. Keegain spotted Jane eyeing him from beneath her lashes a moment before Lady Margret took his arm. Jane looked hastily away. Miss Bellevue, he reminded himself sternly. He could not be so familiar now that guests had arrived, Lady Margret most especially. It was for the best, he thought.

He smiled at Margret and followed the others from the room.

By the time the earl returned to the library, all of his guests were abed. The day had been eventful, but all were accounted for and safe. He poured himself a brandy. Now that he no longer needed to be alert for danger, he could take his ease here in front of the fire, but his mind kept going over scenarios in his head, each one worse than the last. The Christmas ball was still to come. He could not yet relax. Was the villain already in his house? The notion brought fear and rage in equal measure to his mind. He clenched his fist around his glass and tried to consciously settle his apprehension.

The thought of any guest hurt while under his roof was giving him a nervous upset. Who might be in danger? Margret? His sisters? His guests? Jane? He did not think he would sleep a wink until all of this business was concluded. He sipped his brandy and looked at the papers the duke had left in his care willing them to say something different, but the words remained the same while the fire crackled and burned down to embers.

17

Jacqueline brushed Jane's hair with lavender oil and braided it. Jane closed her eyes with the sensation, trying to relax with the sweet scent and let the day go, but her stomach still felt jittery.

"Goodnight, *Mademoiselle*. Sleep well," Jacqueline said, and Jane thanked her.

After the maid had left the room, Jane read for a while by the light of her candle. She had already finished the book, so it was not very satisfying to re-read it. Eventually, she laid it aside. The thought of Keegain's library tempted her, but if she wanted a book, she should have chosen it earlier in the evening. Truth be told, the thought of Lord Keegain himself tempted her, but she knew that such thoughts led nowhere. Still, she knew she was not going to fall asleep any time soon.

Her thoughts kept going back to the incident with Lady Margret yesterday, and then the conversation over the dresses today. Was the whole day simply a way to give

her a gown that would not seem out of place in the finery
of the upper circle of society?

Perhaps she should not have eschewed their charity.
Lady Amelia seemed excited to dress her, and Lady
Patience too for that matter. Lady Patience had wealth
enough for her own dresses. Jane reconsidered; perhaps
it was not charity at all, but friendship. The ladies were
trying to help her. The thoughts ran round and round her
head. Obviously, sleep eluded her just as it had the
previous night.

Jane sighed and slid out of bed. She donned her
wrapper, tying it tightly around her. No one else was
awake. She was fairly certain of that fact, and she was
also fairly certain she could find the library again. She
would just pop out; retrieve another book and pop right
back to her room. A good book would take her away from
her troubles. She would relax into the words and after
reading for a bit, she would fall right asleep. She would
not spend another night tossing and turning worrying
about Lady Margret Fairfax.

Jane picked up the candle with determination and
began working her way toward the darkened library.

LORD KEEGAIN AWOKE WITH A START. He had fallen asleep
in his desk chair with papers spread before him and a
half glass of brandy by his elbow. The fire had burned
down and the room was nearly dark.

He had a sudden awareness that someone was in the
room with him. His immediate thought was for the

villain who dared invade the sanctity of his home. He wished for his pistol, but the fireplace poker was within reach. Surreptitiously, he reached for it as the candle the intruder carried bobbed along his shelves, coming closer. A moment, he thought. The man must be within reach and then he would have the villain.

He leapt to his feet, brandishing the fireplace poker.

"Oh!" cried a very feminine voice, and she very nearly dropped the candle. Miss Bellevue.

Lord Keegain, all in one motion, dropped the poker and jumped to her side to save the flame from falling. Hot candle wax spattered across the lady's hand and his own, and she cried out again, this time in pain.

"Miss Bellevue," the earl said. All of the air had quite gone out of his lungs, and he stood, one hand on her candle and the other steadying her, holding her, candle wax burning them both.

"What are you doing here?" he asked, but even as he said the words, he knew why she was here. She could not sleep, and was taking him up on his offer of a book. He had been quite the fool attacking her with a poker.

"I thought...I only..." she stuttered, looking up at him with the widest doe eyes he had ever seen. She was less than a step away from him, and she smelled like lavender. Her chest heaved under her scanty night robe, and it was all he could do not to pull her sweet softness into his embrace. Sweet heavens, she was lovely. He raised the candle a bit to see her better.

She grimaced at the wax stuck to her hand.

"You are hurt," he said.

"It's nothing. Just a bit of wax," she said as she pulled

the globule from her hand. He winced sympathetically and stepped to the liquor cabinet where he kept a decanter of water to mix with the spirits. He sat the candle on his desk, wet his handkerchief and applied the cool compress to her reddened skin.

"It's nothing. Really," she said, but she did not move away from his touch. They stood for a long moment, with her hand in his and the lavender scent of her invading his senses. His body was intimately aware of her soft femininity. He wanted to pull that softness close, but he could not. Instead, he breathed her in. Neither moved as if aware that to move would break the spell.

"I am terribly sorry," she whispered.

"No. It is I who should apologize. I offered you a book, and then I nearly attacked you."

"You were startled. Were you asleep?"

"Yes."

The implied vulnerability of it stretched before them. The rest of the house was sleeping. That they were the only two stirring in the dark created a strange intimacy. The white muslin of her night dress teased him where her dressing gown had fallen open. There was only a ribbon at her neck, begging to be pulled. And then what? Nothing but cool white muslin over warm skin. He still held her hand in his.

She blinked at him, and he thought he could kiss her now. She was so lovely, so soft, so trusting. He could pull that softness into his arms and kiss her. Just a kiss. And even that would betray her trust.

He could not.

He pulled in a slow deep breath, ignoring the lavender scent of her.

"What sort of books do you like?" he asked. He transferred her injured hand to his opposite, and with the damp cloth still held on her burn, he led her toward the shelves, the flickering light of the candle sending their shadows dancing along the wall of books.

"Novels mostly," she said. "Or history."

"History?" he repeated. "Truly?"

"Well, the purpose of the book was to put me to sleep," Jane said, pulling her hand from his but keeping his dampened handkerchief wrapped around her injury.

Lord Keegain chuckled lightly. "Oh I see. May I choose one for you?" he asked.

"Please do," Jane said, and he pulled two of his favorites from the shelf. He paused, still holding the books, unwilling to give them to her. Unwilling to see her go. "I also enjoy history," he said.

The shared topic seemed to be more than it should have been. In the quiet night, it was a secret thing.

She reached for the books, but he shook his head. "Let me escort you back to your room," he said, and she nodded.

"Thank you."

They walked through the darkened hallways in silence, as if they were two ghosts who could not quite touch one another, as if they had just realized the danger of touching.

When he reached the door of her bed chamber, he paused, giving her the candle in her left hand and taking her right hand again in his. He was not sure why he did it, but he tucked the books under his arm and unwrapped the moist cloth slowly and gently from her hand.

"Oh yes. Your handkerchief," she said almost breathlessly, but instead of taking the cloth, he lowered his lips to the burn on her hand, kissing her in the only way he was able. His lips found her soft flesh, and a jolt of desire rushed through him. The chaste kiss was not nearly enough. He ached to feel her hot skin beneath his lips. She quivered beneath his touch and he was nearly undone.

All the while, his conscience was screaming at him. He ignored it, just as he ignored the fact that her bed was only steps away. At last, he wrapped the damp handkerchief around her hand again.

"Keep it," he said and handed her the books. He gave her a short bow. "Good night, Miss Bellevue. Pleasant dreams."

He turned and walked away from her, while everything in him wished to stay.

❧⌘❧

18

*J*ane came down too early for breakfast. She knew it the moment she stepped into the dining room, surprising a bevy of servants who were laying out the spread. She sighed and considered retreat. After her encounter with Keegain in the library, Jane had lain awake thinking of him. When she at last fell into a fitful slumber, she woke at her normal hour, just after dawn. Now, she was too early.

Lady Margret would think her entirely the country bumpkin if she caught Jane having tea in the kitchens, but she had foolishly come down the front stairs entirely too early, and unfortunately, she had no idea how to get to the kitchens from this part of the house.

She could backtrack, she thought. Return upstairs and come down the servant's stair instead. She would not upset the balance of the household. She would not see Lady Margret, but she would also not see the earl. Her heart leaped at the prospect of seeing him again this morning, and that was just the trouble. She should not wish to see him.

Jane turned, intent upon retracing her steps. She would return to her room now, and come down later, she told herself. She turned, only to bump right into Lord Keegain, who had just entered the dining room behind her.

"My lord!" she gasped, stepping back hastily to bob a quick curtsey. The closeness was too like the closeness of last night when he had surprised her and caught her. When for just a moment, he had held her close, even if he had not meant to do so. His eyes went to the red mark on her hand where the wax had splattered, and she knew he was remembering the moment too. She felt the heat of a blush fill her face, or perhaps it was just the heat associated with his nearness.

"We are the first, it seems. Come. I expect the others will be along soon enough. Although," he leaned in to whisper conspiratorially as he passed, "I shall not wait for them. I prefer my eggs hot."

She should not follow. Jane knew she should return to her room.

Still, her feet seemed to have a mind of their own. She fell into step beside him, trying to ignore the way his warm breath in her ear had sent delicate shivers throughout her body.

"You are one who rises early as a habit then?" she asked, even though she knew it was so. Still, she could not say she had watched him ride out in the mornings from her window. She settled in the chair that he pulled out for her.

"I have been known to. Though I think the storm kept me awake."

Was that what kept him awake, Jane wondered? She glanced at the tall windows. Heavy velvet draperies blocked out the chill, leaving only a thin line of glass between them where the fabric did not meet exactly. She could see the wild tossing of branches on the trees outside, and the thick gray snow clouds releasing a deceptively fine snow, but as yet it had not accumulated.

She attempted to make polite conversation. "Are you worried for the ball then?" she asked, smiling her thanks at a footman who came forward to assist her with her plate.

"I expect the snow will likely not be heavy, but I hope the rest of our guests arrive safely in this weather."

So they were speaking of the weather then. It seemed a safe subject, after their closeness last night. Surely he had felt the pull too. Was it only her feelings that had so nearly overwhelmed her? She had to know.

"Was that what kept you awake?" she asked primly. "Worry for your guests?"

"I must concern myself for the safety of my guests," he said, his voice deep and low.

"And such things keep you up at night?" Jane felt her face warm at the unintended innuendo. They were treading too close to forbidden desires, but she could not seem to help herself. The sensual moments of last night were one thing, but now, in the light of day, shouldn't her passion have cooled? Their moment in the library seemed a dream. She would almost think she had imagined it if she did not still have his handkerchief.

Lord Keegain put down his fork and gazed at her. His warm brown eyes seemed to see right through her.

"Certainly that was the case last night," he said seriously, and when she seemed flustered, he reached across the table, catching her hand and rubbing a soft thumb against the red mark on her wrist. A shiver ran through her.

"Are you cold?" Lord Keegain asked.

"Quite the contrary," she whispered.

"I should not like my guests to be uncomfortable," he said. His fingers on hers were hypnotic, tracing a path that brought tremors to the very core of her.

A servant came in carrying a platter, and she pulled her hand away, self-conscious. "I expect it was the noise of the wind," she said. "That...that kept you awake."

"Was that what kept you awake, Miss Bellevue?" he asked.

"Yes. I was uneasy all night through."

"I would not wish it so," Lord Keegain said.

"I mean, I am afraid of winter storms," she admitted. Jane rarely admitted her fears, and had surprised herself by being so candid. She shuddered and picked up her fork. The idea of being out on ice-encrusted roads in that gale terrified her. It seemed a recipe for sure disaster.

She shot a look at the earl, seeing his expression thoughtful as he stared at the window. He was troubled by something, and it was not just the weather, she was sure.

For a moment, Jane entertained the idea that he had been left wakeful for the same reason that she had been. He had been thinking of their encounter. Their encounter last night had left her with a yearning that even now tugged at her. She had spent much of the night staring at the fire in her room, trying to sort out her reaction to the earl.

Never before had she understood the attraction that occurred between a man and a woman. She had read about such things in romance novels, and heard it talked about in whispers between young ladies. The idea of romance was something she had considered a fantasy until now. Something that would remain forever locked within the pages of a book. Until last night. The reality of it had near taken her breath away and left her heartbroken. The earl was not hers to covet in this way, nor could he ever be.

He is the brother of a friend of mine, Jane reminded herself. *For Charlotte's sake as well as my own, I must remember that fact.* Jane vowed to be polite to the earl, but to keep a distance. At dawn, it had seemed the easiest solution. Now, in light of day, with the object of her desires before her, Jane's resolve wavered.

"You are not eating," Lord Keegain said, concerned. "Is the sausage not to your liking?"

She took a bite of the sausage on her fork, not really tasting it, even though it was her favorite breakfast food. When she swallowed, she forced herself to speak.

"Tell me about your other guests. Will there be many attending beyond what was at dinner last night?" she asked suddenly, desperate to break the awful silence that had fallen between them.

Perhaps if she talked as one would to a casual acquaintance, she could convince herself that he was just that. And only that. If only she could still her galloping heart.

"A few," the earl said, turning towards her with a smile as he lay down his fork. He started listing names and family connections that she could not follow. In truth, Jane heard nearly none of it, for her attention was on his strong fingers as he gestured, the way his half-smile seemed to light his eyes and the sooty fringe of his lashes when he looked down in thought.

Jane was caught by Lord Keegain's handsome profile, and she remembered anew the way he had bent over her hand when they'd met; the way he had bent over her hand at her bedchamber door last night. The feel of his lips on her skin. The very thought sent shivers of delight through her.

"Do you not agree?"

Jane blinked. She realized she had not heard the rest of the question and had no idea what he was asking. She must have held a panicked look in her eyes.

The earl laughed then, and she blushed, for it was clear that he had seen Jane had not been attending his words.

"I do beg your pardon, my lord. I think my mind was on other things. The library last night…"

She broke off. She had not intended to say the last. Her traitorous lips had betrayed her in the worst way. She felt her face burn with the flush of embarrassment.

"Yes," he said, and there was a long silence between them as the footman poured her tea and the earl's coffee. When they finally withdrew, Lord Keegain asked, "Did you enjoy the books I recommended?"

Jane had not yet read them. She did not know what to say.

Lord Keegain pressed on. "You mentioned you enjoyed history and novels. Which are your favorites?"

Although Jane loved many novels, at the moment she could not think of a single title. She only stared at him while she attempted to get her brain to function.

"I too have thought of little else," Lord Keegain said, his voice soft and resonant. It went right to the heart of her.

For a moment, their eyes met. She could drown in those eyes, hazel with flecks of green and gold. They were suddenly so dark. She must have leaned into him; just a bit. Then, hastily, they both looked away, him to his toast and her back to her sausages, which had grown cold on her plate. Still, looking down, she began, "I should not have..."

"I wish we could..."

They had both started talking at once, and the pair laughed now, some of the tension easing.

"Do go on," Lord Keegain urged, and Jane shook her head, for the words seemed silly now, too trite to explain this oddness that came over her when she was with him. How did one explain that her heart could not stay within her breast properly when he was near? She felt it now, giving strange staggering beats that seemed too fast by far when he looked at her in that knowing way. As if he could see straight through her. Her hand touched the space just above her heart, as though to still the organ. *Slow down*, she wanted to say. *He cannot be yours*.

"It is no matter, my lord. What say you?"

"Only that I wish we could have met...sooner."

Jane gasped, color flooding her cheeks for a second time. It was as much a declaration as any she had ever heard. Such talk should be confined to his betrothed. *He is betrothed*, her heart screamed, but she spoke. "You should not..."

"No. I should not," he agreed quietly. "I beg your pardon, Miss Bellevue." He dropped his gaze to his plate, and pushed his fork around, chasing potatoes, but eating nothing.

A noise in the hallway told them their moment of solitude was over. The other guests were awake. They burst in together, a large noisy bunch who settled themselves around the table in a jolly group, greeting one another and taking muffins and sausages from the copious platters passed before them.

It was clear that the family did not stand on ceremony. A year ago, Jane would have loved the chaos and thrown herself into it with abandon. Was this not the event she had come for? She had left Bath thinking to enjoy her time spent amongst the lords and ladies. Only days ago, she would have enjoyed the happy bustle. Now she could not bear it. The precious peace of her time alone with Lord Keegain had been shattered, and now everything was only so much noise.

A tightness filled her throat. Jane knew now she was no longer in danger of falling in love with the earl. She had already fallen, and she saw no way to reverse the descent.

She could not have him. She had known that from

the moment she met him, but she could not stop her heart wanting him.

"If you could but excuse me. I had…I had promised a letter to my sister. I should have written it long ago. I must write it now if it is to go out in the morning post," Jane stammered, and rose to leave.

All the gentlemen around the table stood with her rising, but only Lady Charlotte looked at her, her face full of questions. Still, Charlotte did not ask, a fact for which Jane blessed her silently. Charlotte sat between her sisters, Helen and Alice. Jane smiled politely and turned quickly, only wanting to escape.

She felt more than saw the earl watching her as she left. Surely it was his eyes which she felt heavy upon her, those beautiful hazel eyes. She knew it was him, though there were other young men present: Lord Barton and Mr. Fitzwilliam, and some of Keegain's other gentlemen friends. Mr. Reynolds was near the door making droll comments to all and sundry.

Jane had to step a little sideways to get clear of the group, and so nearly walked into Lady Margret, who was only just coming through the door, the last to arrive. Margret paused, like a queen assessing her court and wondering how a plebeian managed to block her path.

It truly was the last straw. To be so clumsy as to walk straightaway into Lord Keegain's intended seemed too much like fate laughing at her. Jane froze. She could not make her feet move, and yet she must. She must escape him, from these feelings, herself.

Jane did the only thing she could think to do. She fled.

"Pardon me," she said pushing past Margret and heading for the door.

As she reached the corridor she heard Margret say, "Well, I do believe my maid owned a dress quite similar to that one a few years ago, but she discarded it after I gave her a raise."

Margret's friends all tittered with laughter at Jane's retreating back.

19

$\mathcal{K}$eegain fumed at the slight. He noted that none of his sisters smiled. They were stone-faced at Margret's comment, as were Lady Patience and Lady Amelia. *At least they are not all sheep*, he thought as the servants cleared away the used dishes and laid a new place for Lady Margret.

Lady Margret turned with a bright smile to the risen guests to accept their accolades as they laughed.

Keegain had never felt such disgust.

Charlotte started to stand and then hesitated. Keegain knew he could not follow Jane himself, but he hoped, as her friend, his sister would. He gave Charlotte the most imperceptible nod.

"Are you well, Charlotte?" he asked and there was a moment of communication that they had not had since they were children.

"No," she said succinctly. "Something has disagreed with me. Please excuse me." She pushed in her chair and headed for the door.

There was a moment of shared decision that passed over the other girls' faces. Lady Amelia stood, and then Lady Patience. "We will help you," Patience said, and just like that, the threesome was gone.

Margret stood smiling, waiting at his side, for him to pull out her chair for her. Mechanically he performed the duty and she sat at the place next to him.

Once the ladies had departed and Margret was seated, the gentlemen all retook their seats, Keegain included. Lady Guinevere leaned over to say something to Helen, and even if his other sister wished to, she was no longer able to smoothly leave the table.

Lord Keegain tried to calm his ire.

He could not chastise Margret without causing a scene, but she would hear of his displeasure. He smiled at his other visitors and said all right things for a polite and affable host, but inside he seethed. Margret's rudeness to a guest in his home disappointed him greatly. This was not acceptable. This was not how a lady acted towards her guests.

He had the ungracious thought that if someone were to be kidnapped, perhaps Lady Margret would be an ideal candidate. It was an unworthy notion; borne of anger, not rational logic. Keegain regretted the thought immediately.

The Christmas season was a time of goodwill. He could wish no harm befall Lady Margret, but neither would he allow a guest within his house to be treated poorly. *Any guest, or only Miss Bellevue?* a small voice in his mind chided him, as the scent of lavender and the feel of crisp muslin invaded his thoughts.

Why was he so distracted? He felt near besotted. He
should have kissed her, he decided, and not just her
hand. He should have kissed Miss Bellevue thoroughly in
the library, where she stood looking up at him so dewy-
eyed and soft. Just the mere thought of her made his
body react. He told himself he should have found out
then and there whether his attraction was real. As it was,
she haunted him.

Jane was petite, but buxom, with dark hair and dark
eyes that seemed to hold mystery. He wanted to discover
that mystery. He could not deny that he had developed a
fondness for the woman, and he knew that was wrong.
He was engaged. Still, he could not seem to quell the
emotion. He should have kissed her, he thought. But
would a kiss have been enough? He very much
doubted it.

Lord Keegain sighed. There were more important
matters to think upon than his own muddled sentiment.
His mind turned back to the duke's warning. A dark
cloud loomed on the horizon, and there were villains
within his house. He could not be so distracted.

By the time the men were ready to retire to the parlor,
Lord Keegain had his body and mind under control. He
had nearly convinced himself that it was only the
thought of dire criminality and intrigue that had put him
in such a foul humor. Lady Margret was his intended.
The woman was his to protect, just as his sisters were his
to protect, and he would shield them. Who, then, would
shield Miss Bellevue? The thought left him bitter and he
lingered over his coffee, nursing it as if the drink were
something stronger.

⁓⁓⁓

JANE FELT ENTIRELY EMPTY. She could not sit calmly at the table and watch Keegain with Lady Margret. She could not bear it, and so she had run and she had cried. She had poured her emotion out upon her pillow. Now she felt numb. Perhaps she was wrung out; wrung dry of tears. After the tears came lethargy. She felt as if she could not move. She lay on the bed, defeated. Perhaps she fell back asleep. Perhaps she just felt as if the world moved on past her, without her.

She wondered what she should do. She did not want to see him again, or worse, see Lady Margret, but how could she not?

Sometime later, she thought a cup of tea would be heaven, and she was a bit hungry. Understandable, since she had missed breakfast. Yes, she had gone to breakfast early, but she had not eaten. Jane considered ringing the bell, but she did not want company. She wanted to feel sorry for herself. She rolled over and buried her face in the pillow. She closed her eyes as if to shut out the world.

At first Jane ignored the knocking on her bedchamber door, hoping to pretend she was still sleeping so she could just breathe for a few more minutes and once again recapture control over her emotions. When the knocking came a second time, Jane knew she could not hide any longer, so she called out to the person, bidding them enter.

"Miss Bellevue, are you quite alright?" Jacqueline said as she opened the door and stepped inside the room, her voice full of concern.

Jane opened her eyes and blinked. "I'm quite alright, Jacqueline. Simply tired is all." It was true, after a fashion. Jane did not feel any more rested than she had at dawn, though she must have fallen back asleep. It was strange that the more she slept, the more exhausted she seemed. Jane finally sat up and moved towards the edge of the bed.

Jacqueline met her there and pulled back the curtains; the sunlight glinting off snow caused Jane to squint for a moment. *Snow*, she thought. It had snowed and there was every indication that there might be a white Christmas. Still, it was England, and the snow might melt before midday, she thought. Then she realized it was midday.

Once she stood, Jacqueline took one good look at Jane and released a heavy sigh. "The other ladies are worried about you," the maid said.

"They are?"

"They came to check on you, but you were asleep," Jacqueline said. "Lady Charlotte thought it best not to wake you."

"Oh." Jane looked in the glass. Her face was red and puffy. Her dress was wrinkled. "I look a fright," she said.

"Oh, my dear. Come, let's get you washed up. I know just what to do to brighten that pretty face of yours," Jacqueline said, and Jane nodded.

She always was an ugly crier. Her face turned red and puffy and stayed blotchy for hours even after she had gained control of herself. It was one of the reasons she usually kept a tight rein on her emotions. Crying solved nothing.

"Thank you." Jane offered the Frenchwoman a soft smile as she followed the maid to the other side of the room, where a water basin was positioned. The maid poured a pitcher of water into the basin and soaked a flannel before handing it to Jane. Jane looked at the cloth in her hand and thought of Keegain's handkerchief. She had tucked it into her valise around her mother's pearls. Oh she was a wretch!

"The water might be cold, but it will help diminish the redness," Jacqueline explained. "Just hold the cloth to your eyes."

Jane obeyed.

It was colder than Jane had imagined as she placed the wet cloth over her face, pressing it against her cheeks and around her eyes. It was shocking at first, but then relaxing, almost numbing the soreness she felt. Jacqueline had Jane repeat the process several times before she helped Jane slip out of her wrinkled gown and apply the cloth to the rest of her body. Though it was cold, it felt soothing, and by the time Jane was dressed in a clean gown, she was feeling quite refreshed. No doubt Lady Margret would think this dress ugly as well. Jane tried to convince herself that she did not care what Margret thought of her.

"There now, Miss Bellevue. *Magnifique!*" Jacqueline said with a smile as she finished pinning up Jane's long brown hair. "I shall take you to madam's sitting room and bring a fresh pot of tea. The other young ladies have joined there. The musicians have come early, so there will be music and perhaps singing."

Jane's heart sank at the idea. She couldn't do it. There

was, of course, no easy way she could bow out, but she wasn't particularly interested in allowing Lady Margret to make fun of her dress, nor did she relish watching Lord Keegain and Lady Margret spend another evening together. It would just hurt all over again. Jane tried to put the thought out of her mind. She did not want to spoil the other ladies' holiday fun with her morose mood. She only hoped that Lady Margret had found another occupation, but Jane doubted her luck.

"I need a moment," she told Jacqueline.

"As you wish," the maid said taking her wrinkled dress to press, and closing the door softly behind her as she left the room.

Jane thought she could not appear so melancholy when arriving to the sitting room. It was Christmas. One must be jolly. With effort, she turned the corners of her mouth up into a smile, but she did not feel an excess of Christmas cheer. She was grumpy and hungry. She realized she had completely missed breakfast, and there would not be another meal for hours. Mrs. Muir would have something good to eat, she thought, and Mrs. Muir would cheer her.

20

*J*ane had begged Mrs. Muir for the recipe for her crumpets, but she doubted that any cook she would be able to hire would do them justice. They were so light; they were like to float away. Perhaps she should have Mrs. Muir show her how to make them. It would be a wonderful way to spend the afternoon. Oh, that would cause quite a stir, she was sure. She nearly giggled at the thought.

A fire was already blazing in the kitchen and the morning meal for the upper house servants was prepared. The room was pleasantly bustling and smelled of Mrs. Muir's wonderful baked goods.

Today, the cook greeted her with more than her marvelous delectables. She had a small hand-written book with a ribbon round it, and handed it unceremoniously to Jane. "It's a Christmas gift of sorts," Mrs. Muir said. "It's from the whole staff, because they helped me by doing some of my work while I got it all written out. It was a shared effort. Most of these are just in my head, you see."

Jane opened the book to find a plethora of recipes for many of the delectable dishes she had been served in the past weeks at Kennett Park.

"Oh, how wonderful," Jane said. "Thank you, but now, I am embarrassed. I have nothing for you, Mrs. Muir."

"Oh, never you mind," Mrs. Muir said.

Jane busied herself looking through the recipes printed in Mrs. Muir's neat hand, and only looked up in surprise when Mrs. Muir said, "It's enough you make his Lordship happy."

"What?" The comment startled Jane, but Mrs. Muir went right on talking while she rolled her dough.

"His Lordship already does so much for us. Why, he has been out every day this week delivering gifts. Just yesterday the master delivered a haunch of venison to my nephew and his wife." Mrs. Muir smiled. "We will eat like kings this Christmas. Then he went about the town with rabbits and birds for the other's dinners and sweetmeats for the children. Playing Father Christmas, he was, just like his own father used to do. God rest his soul."

So that was where the earl disappeared to, Jane thought, and the warm feelings that she had already entertained for the lord of the manor flared in her heart. Was there ever such a man? How could she not love him?

Mrs. Muir was still speaking while Jane was woolgathering. "And you make his Lordship happy," she said.

The words tugged Jane sharply back to reality.

"I'm sure I don't know what you mean."

Mrs. Muir fixed Jane with a stare. "The master has a generous heart. He deserves someone who will match him."

"Oh, no. Mrs. Muir, no," Jane said shaking her head. "He has a betrothed."

"He'll never marry the ice queen. You'll see," said Jack, the kitchen boy, as he brought in more firewood for the stove. He dumped it with a crash on the hearth.

Some of the kitchen maids nodded, but Gilly, Mrs. Muir's assistant, hushed them. "Lady Margret will be our mistress," she said, "You shouldn't speak ill of her, Jack." Her voice dropped to a whisper. "You will find yourself wanting a job and no references about it. She would sack you in an instant, and your dreams of becoming a footman will be gone. Just like that." She snapped her fingers under his nose.

"He won't marry her," Jack muttered. "He doesn't love her."

"Love rarely enters into society marriages," Jane said sadly.

"But his Lordship is a romantic," Mr. White said.

Jane was surprised that the kitchen clerk joined in the conversation. He usually held himself apart, as he was one of the upper servants, along with the housekeeper and the butler. She had not heard him speak more than a "yes, my lord" or "no, my lord," to the earl. Now, he sat at the table with Jane, and Mrs. Muir put his breakfast in front of him as some of the other upstairs servants took their places around the table. Jane recognized the warmed sausages from earlier.

"That is true," Mrs. Muir agreed. "His Lordship

allowed Lady Sophia to marry Mr. Gibbon when the Viscount Cornish wanted to wed her. Even his lady mother was furious that he allowed it, but of course, he is the earl."

The staff was silent for a few minutes, and Jane had a moment of feeling guilty for listening so unabashedly to gossip, and servant's gossip at that. And yet, she was learning more about the earl than Lady Charlotte had ever told her.

"And yet," Jane began. She stumbled to a halt. She could not outright ask, could she?

"What is it, Miss?" Mrs. Muir asked.

Jane hesitated, the very words causing her pain.

"Speak, Miss Bellevue," Mr. White said softly. "Nothing you say shall leave this table. You have my word."

Jane spoke barely above a whisper. "It's only that, if Lord Keegain is a romantic, he must love his intended. He asked for her hand."

"Oh no. It was not like that," Mrs. Muir said. The staff stood all around, shaking their heads, but it was Mr. White who spoke.

"I am sure it is not my place to say, but I think someone must. When the late earl fell ill, God rest his soul, he was concerned about the young master. He wanted him settled, and so, on his deathbed, he made his son promise to marry."

"He did not have to choose Lady Margret," Jane said hesitantly.

Mr. White's voice turned hard. "No, but then Lady

Margret was a friend of the family and companion to his sisters. She was an obvious choice."

"So she swooped in and took the spot," Mrs. Muir spat. "And his Lordship is too kind to disavow her."

Jane had never heard the friendly cook speak so. The others were nodding all around. Jane realized that none of the staff liked Lady Margret, or relished the idea of her being the countess.

"If he had actually wanted to marry her, he would have done it already," Jack added. "The earl is not indecisive. After all, there is no impediment, except that he does not want to set the banns."

Jane shook her head. She doubted it was as simple as all that. Surely there was some feeling between them. One had only to look at Lady Margret and see that she was stunning, tall and willowy with golden hair and an air of a queen.

She was everything Jane was not. Her father might call her Lady Jane, but the truth was she was just plain Miss Bellevue. Lord Keegain could never be hers, could he? No. She could not allow herself to hope. It was too painful. It was best she put him out of her mind. As she had said, society marriages were rarely based upon love. For a woman, marriage meant comfort and security. It was time she sought those things with more fervor.

The others went back to their work and suddenly Jane felt uncomfortable. "I think I shall have my tea in my room," she said. "If it is not too much trouble."

"No trouble at all, Miss," said Mrs. Muir, and at a gesture from her, one of the maids poured boiling water into a pot with leaves to steep.

"I will be up directly with your tray," the maid said, and Jane smiled.

"Thank you." She turned to leave the kitchen with her recipe book in hand, but her heart was confused.

Part 3

Friends & Finery

21

*L*ord Keegain thought he should be happy. Margret's behavior aside, his house was full of guests and Christmas cheer. Everyone who was going to arrive was here safe and sound in spite of the storm, and for that he was thankful. The snow was quite beautiful as long as one could admire it from the warmth of the parlor. The day had mellowed into evening, and he was with his friends.

He loved this time of year more than any other, but his heart was heavy. He knew at the center of that was one Miss Jane Bellevue. He tried to put the thought of her from his mind. He had other things to worry about, namely the villain that had invaded his home, but there was nothing he could do about that at the moment. He should enjoy his guests and the holiday season.

Fitz was waxing poetic about his lady, telling anyone who would listen of her virtues while gesturing wildly and sloshing his drink. Was that his third or fourth?

Keegain had no idea. The drink had been flowing freely for some time now.

Fitzwilliam, an energetic sort of man at the best of times, became positively animated as he spoke of his love. Despite his outrageously flirtatious nature, it was plain to see that no one else would hold the keys to Fitzwilliam's heart as did his Miss Mary Wadsworth.

He was even now spilling more of his drink than he was actually drinking. He was animated and restless, unable to settle in one place, and he had only just gotten from the hair on her head to his new fiancée's eyes.

"I tell you, old boy, they are the brightest, deepest eyes I have ever seen. Like cut jewels."

The earl's mind went invariably to Jane's eyes. They were brown, but so dark it was like looking into a mysterious night.

"Rubies," Reynolds said dryly. Keegain nearly choked on his drink at the jest.

Fitzwilliam went on expounding on Miss Mary's beauty. "Emeralds, by God. They sparkle at the best of times, but I swear they glow when she is up to mischief."

"And have you been?" Reynolds shot a wink at Fitz. "Up to mischief, I mean."

Fitzwilliam laid his index finger astride his nose, still holding his drink. "I do not kiss and tell!" He announced with mock affront. "Such would dishonor the lady."

He should have kissed Miss Bellevue in the library, Keegain thought. He should have pulled Jane into his arms and kissed her, well and thoroughly. Then perhaps he would not feel so restless now. The very thought of her moved him.

Fitz seemed to take sudden notice of the glass in his hand as it lay directly under his nose. He grinned and took a healthy sip before continuing. "I tell you gentlemen, I never knew there could exist one so beautiful in this world. She is an angel. With skin like alabaster and the dulcet tones of a nightingale."

"I have to admit, old friend, I would never have pegged you for falling for the charms of Miss Wadsworth." Reynolds said.

"She is quite the quiet one," Keegain added, pouring himself another and holding the decanter aloft. Reynolds looked at it askance for a moment and nodded, taking it from him.

The other gentlemen, either unfamiliar with the object of discussion or familiar enough to have heard this many times already, clustered in the corner among a game of cards or searched through the library for some distraction. Fitz, Reynolds, and Keegain were left to their own devices around the fire.

The discussion of the kidnapping and Napoleon was still fresh in their minds; however, they did not mention the plot. It was a secret shared between the three of them, and whichever gentlemen were King's Men.

Keegain glanced at the card players. Were any the villain? He did not know. Somewhere in that grouping were likely others like Reynolds, and the earl wondered which ones they were. Reynolds had a partner among them.

Keegain shook his head. This was not something he had wanted to think about just now. The greatest danger would come during the ball. Now, they were just passing time, waiting for something to happen. In order to distract his friend, he had started the conversation regarding Miss Wadsworth, and now had begun to regret it as Fitz waxed poetic.

Fitzwilliam snagged the bottle from Reynolds and began refilling his glass, but in his animation began gesturing with both glass and bottle. Reynolds leapt from his seat to rescue either the scotch or the carpet. Either way, it was appreciated. Keegain thought of his own dash to save the candle that Miss Bellevue held.

"At first, yes, she was quite shy," Fitzwilliam continued. "In fact, at the ball in Northwick, she was so quiet I had to lean close just to hear her. I think now that it was an affectation designed, so that I would whisper in her ear."

"Affectation?" Lord Keegain asked. "And yet you call her sweet?"

"Oh yes," Fitzwilliam waved that off with a slosh of scotch, which rose in a magnificent wave before landing directly back in the glass without losing a drop. "I knew her as a child, and she was ever the adventurous thing, but as a woman, she was uncommonly shy. It was as if we had only first met, once again. Twice met, and yet both times new. As we became better acquainted, she became more warm and comely."

"Warm, was she?" Keegain teased his old friend.

"And comely," Reynolds repeated.

"Oh, get on with the both of you." Fitzwilliam snorted. "I refer to the warmth of friendship; something I find lacking in the present circumstance." He took another drink and shook his head slowly.

"She soon became more welcoming," Fitzwilliam said, as if from a great distance. "We spoke about everything. We danced. Oh, how we danced. To hold her in my arms is heaven, but to speak my heart, that is a pleasure that defies even heaven's place of grandeur. You cannot know, old boy."

"I see." Keegain had no clever retort for his friend. Fitz was right. He did not know and likely never would if he married Lady Margret, as he must. He had given his word.

Lord Keegain thought for a moment of speaking his heart to Margret. Was such frank discussion too much to ask of a woman? Perhaps it was the fact that she was a lady. Fitzwilliam seemed content with his bride, although she was a simple miss. Perhaps it was just Margret herself. He could not imagine sharing the inner workings of his mind with her. Could he speak his mind to Miss Bellevue? Keegain wondered suddenly.

"The more visits I paid to her..." Fitz added quickly, "to her family, that is...I knew her family from way back." He sloshed his drink again. "We were almost like brothers."

"Brothers?" Reynolds scoffed aloud.

"I mean her brother is like my brother. Oh, you know what I mean."

Reynolds laughed. Fitz was well and truly within his cups now.

"Oh, gentlemen, she may be without a title in her family, but I have never met one with more poise or graciousness than my Mary. Not among the *Ton*, nor among the finest diamonds of the first water; not within all of England." Fitzwilliam took a slow drink staring at the fire, his eyes focused on his love who even now was miles away.

And Miss Bellevue, Lord Keegain thought. Was she not as poised as any trueborn lady? Had he ever met her like? He could not say that he had. She was as singular a woman as Fitz's lady love.

"Your Mary sounds lovely, Fitz," Keegain said into his drink. "It is a shame she could not be here. I cannot wait to meet the lady who has so charmed you, my old friend."

"Charmed is right enough." Fitz sighed. "Bespelled more like. I know that a storm approaches, but I tell you true, I would brave any storm to see her, to hold her again. I would ride to her house, now, this very minute to feel her in my arms, and muss her hair."

Lord Keegain's mind conjured an image of Jane as she had been last night. Her night clothes were rumpled, as if she had only just tumbled from her bed. Her deep eyes shone in the soft light of the candle. Her curls had escaped her braid; he imagined freeing them entirely and burying his hands in her sweet-smelling locks.

Fitz blushed suddenly, and glanced over at his oldest friend with a wry smile. "I believe she perfumes it," he explained, "or perhaps the heavenly scent is the lady herself."

Keegain's thoughts were inundated with the scent of lavender, and heat suffused him.

"I want to hide her in a tower as in one of those fairy stories, and keep her all to myself. But, listen to me, going on!" Fitzwilliam chided himself. "Of course you know how I feel!" He clapped Keegain upon the back. "You are engaged to Lady Margret! You have been for nearly as long as I have known you. I do not understand why you've waited so long to take the plunge, old boy."

Why indeed? Keegain thought. He found he did understand his friend's longing. Thoughts of Jane would not leave his mind. He longed to touch her. Every moment he was apart from her felt like a unique form of torture. He knew if it were Miss Bellevue he was to marry, he would not have waited so. But it was not Miss Bellevue. The thought chilled him.

Lord Keegain took a long pull of the scotch and let it burn his mouth and throat. "I am simply in no hurry to marry," he said flatly, standing to poke at the fire which had gone to embers. He was reminded of the soft glow of the fire in the library when Jane had woken him. He threw another log on the fire, and the sparks danced and caught, warming the room, although Keegain thought his blood already thoroughly heated.

Lord Keegain was truly happy for his friend, but he couldn't fight off a wave of jealousy. Margret had some good features. Certainly she was beautiful; her breeding and vast fortunes were considerable assets, but the woman herself was cold perfection.

One did not muss perfection. Or hold it in one's arms expecting warmth.

"Time enough, Fitz," Keegain said with a forced laugh. "Enjoy these dwindling few days of freedom, before you are leg-shackled."

22

---

*J*ane walked back to her room, feeling somewhat cheered by her conversation with the servants, but the truth was, she had nothing to compare with Lady Margret's beautiful wardrobe. Her gowns were fashionable and pretty, but not of the quality of the other young ladies in the house. Still, she thought, she did not need such things. She would be herself, and she would not let Lady Margret's comments upset her.

When Jane returned to her room, she found her friends waiting for her.

"Where have you been?" Lady Charlotte scolded. "We have been looking all over for you."

"I went to the kitchens," Jane said.

"The kitchens? Whatever for?" Lady Amelia asked.

Lady Charlotte and Jane exchanged glances. "Biscuits and scones," they said together, laughing.

"We have come to cheer you," Lady Patience said. "It is good to hear you laugh."

"I cannot believe how rude Lady Margret was to you," Amelia said. "No true lady would act so."

Lady Patience was nodding her head in agreement. "Now come," she said taking Jane's arm. "We have a surprise, and we shall not be denied." Lady Charlotte fairly bounced and Jane could not bear to stifle her excitement.

"What is it?" Jane asked curiously.

"Come along, Jane," Lady Amelia ordered.

The girls led Jane to Lady Amelia's room, which was down the hall and around the corner from her own.

While they were walking, they met Molly in the corridor with Jane's tea.

"Bring the tea along to Lady Amelia's room," Lady Charlotte said. "In fact, bring a few more cups and sandwiches. None of us ate much at breakfast."

They reached Lady Amelia's room, and on the bed and dresser were an abundance of gowns.

"Oh," Jane said in surprise.

Her friends were all grinning ear to ear.

A lady's maid that Jane did not know was waiting for them. She curtseyed to Lady Amelia who said, "Thank you, Gabby."

"We have decided to outfit you," Lady Charlotte said to Jane.

Jane bristled. This was about Lady Margret's comment. "I do not want to be someone I am not," she said.

"But my dear, a masquerade is exactly the time to be someone you are not," Lady Amelia said.

That brought Jane up short. "I don't know."

"If you want to wear the swan, you can wear my white gown," Lady Patience said, laying a hand on a crème and white gown, which had a layer of golden lace descending down from a bodice of intricate design. One look told her that the golden threads were actually made of that precious metal. The sleeves were short, and the neckline low.

Lady Patience held it up to Jane, but she shook her head. She was quite a bit curvier than the thin redhead. "It is lovely, but I am afraid I would be exposing too much of my décolletage," Jane said.

"Oh pooh," Lady Charlotte said. "I am sure we can find some ribbon or lace for it."

"Perhaps Lady Keegain still has some of the swan feathers she used for the mask," Lady Patience suggested.

"That would work," Lady Amelia said.

Jane looked at the other dresses laid out on the bed. They were all so beautiful. Avarice got the better of her. Perhaps Lady Amelia was right. For one night she could be someone new. The purple gown called to her. It was exquisite. She had to at least touch it. She realized as soon as her fingers brushed the cloth that it was silk velvet. It felt like a cloud.

"This is beautiful," she sighed. "I do not think I have ever seen anything like it."

"I doubt you would have, Miss Bellevue," Lady Amelia spoke up as she extended her hand and rubbed the fabric between her fingers, much like Jane had done. "It is a recent present from my father who brought it from Town. He says it is of the latest design from Madam

Sullivan, a very premier dressmaker, silk velvet with Venetian lace."

"But surely you would want to wear this gown then," Jane said as she pulled her fingers away from it. Aside from expense, it was a dear present from her father, the duke.

"Not at all, Miss Bellevue. I shall be very pleased to see you wear it." Lady Amelia's eyes sparkled with an ulterior motive.

"Why ever would you?" Jane inquired.

"I enjoy dressing my friends," Lady Amelia said, and Jane felt a warm glow that she was included in Lady Amelia's friendship. "Ask Patience. Was it not my suggestion to give that hideous pink gown to your maid?"

"On the other hand, if you prefer the pink," Lady Charlotte offered, picking up the equally pink gown that she had chosen, and the others laughed.

"Only you can wear something so shocking, Charlotte," Lady Patience said. "The rest of us would look like some candy confection."

"Shouldn't you be someone you are not?" Jane teased Lady Charlotte. She thought it was funny that Charlotte was a study of contrasts. She was most comfortable in a stark riding outfit or an overabundance of bows and lace, the more elaborate the better. The thought made Jane laugh.

"Very well, I shall have to part with it," Lady Charlotte said with a hand over her heart. "You may have it, Jane."

"No, thank you." Jane shuddered at the thought, although she certainly would not seem herself in the pink gown.

"It is settled then," Lady Amelia said. "You shall have the violet and the peacock feather mask."

"I do not know what to say," Jane replied.

"I believe the common response is thank you," Lady Amelia said, blue eyes sparkling with excitement. "Now, the jewels."

"Oh no," Jane protested. "I could not possibly."

"Don't be silly," Lady Amelia said. "If you are going to be a great lady, you must have your jewels." She waved a hand at Jane and the violet gown, while she dug in her jewelry box. "Go on, try it on," she said. "We are about the same height." Amelia's lady's maid came forward to help her, but Jane still hesitated.

"You are taller," Jane said, but Amelia eyed her critically.

"I am sure your curves will fill it enough that it will not be too long. Go on, try it on."

Still Jane hesitated, but Lady Charlotte spun her around. "Turn around," she said. "And I will get your buttons." Jane turned, and without further ado, the gown was pulled over her head.

"Oh," Lady Amelia said as she viewed the dress on Jane. "It looks perfect on you. That is the one. You may have it."

"Oh, no," Jane said. "Only to borrow."

Lady Amelia lifted a delicate shoulder. "I have gowns I have never tried on. Patience knows." She nodded to the other girl. "She says Father spoils me."

"Oh, I am certain you are not spoiled at all," Jane said, brushing her hands over the lovely gown. It was exceedingly soft. She had never worn such a garment. It made her feel like a queen.

"Consider it yours," Lady Amelia said looking at Jane with a critical eye. "I think diamonds would look best, or perhaps the sapphires."

"Definitely the sapphires," Lady Patience said, adding her opinion.

Lady Charlotte nodded. "Sapphires," she agreed.

"I have pearls," Jane said. "They were my mother's."

"But today, you are not Miss Jane Bellevue," Lady Amelia insisted.

"You shall be Lady Jane," Lady Charlotte said, remembering that Jane's father called her that.

Jane felt tears spring to her eyes. "You are too kind," she said as Amelia hung the expensive jewels around her neck. They were a glittering mass of sapphires and diamonds.

"There are earrings here somewhere," Lady Amelia said.

Lady Patience held up the glass so that Jane could take a look at herself. She touched the jewels. They were possibly worth more than her father's house.

Lady Charlotte brought up the peacock mask, and Jane thought she did not even recognize herself.

"Excellent," Lady Amelia said, nodding her approval.

"Thank you. All of you." Jane said sincerely.

Lady Amelia only grinned at Jane as she turned this way and that, observing the whole effect in the glass.

"Oh, that's lovely," Lady Patience said.

"It is a bit long," Amelia noted, and Jane felt

disappointment fill her. For just this one night, she had wanted to be a true lady.

"It is nothing," said the maid as she knelt to take the measurement of the gown. "It is only a hem, and the ball is not until tomorrow night."

"Will it be done in time?" Jane wondered.

"Of course it will," Lady Amelia said. "Gabby is quite quick with her needle."

"Thank you, my lady," Jane said to Lady Amelia. "I shall feel like royalty in this gown." She traced her fingers over the fine fabric.

"As you should, my dear," Lady Patience said, a knowing smile on her face. Jane simply smiled as she continued to examine the dress, deep in thought.

"You shall surely catch a husband in that dress," Lady Charlotte said, and the thought brought Jane up short.

Yes, she thought. She should be looking for another beau, one who was completely eligible. Still, none could capture her heart like Lord Keegain.

"Perhaps even the one you are thinking of," Lady Charlotte whispered. "You know, my brother's favorite color is purple."

Jane opened her mouth to speak, but found there was nothing she could say. She only squeezed Charlotte's hand in silent thanks. Jane found she could hardly contain her excitement.

Perhaps she would impress the gentleman that she wanted to impress. Perhaps it was possible. A flutter of delight filled her at the thought. With Lady Charlotte and Lady Amelia on her side, she felt bold.

23

The earl looked around the dining room. Jane was not at breakfast.

Considering Lady Margret's treatment of her yesterday morning, Lord Keegain did not blame her for eating in her room, but the thought filled him with sadness. He wanted to see her. Still, on this of all days, she was probably safer in her room. He was in a high state of awareness, and he had spoken with Ted so many times already today that the man snapped at him.

"I do know how to do my job, Keegain."

"Of course you do," the earl apologized. Still, he was wound tight as a top. He forced himself to eat slowly and chew, lest he find himself with indigestion.

Margret was holding court at her end of the table.

"Ladies, I simply must insist on it," Margret said, as she leaned over the table as if in silent conspiracy with everyone in the room. She had gathered them all so close that Keegain wondered who was left to hide from. He found that ever since her castigation of Jane yesterday, he found a dozen little things about Margret which annoyed him.

He made an effort to relax and pay attention to the conversation, but he had been woolgathering too long and he had lost its direction. What mischief was Margret planning?

"But Margret," his sister Helen protested, a look of horror on her face. "It is cold and about to storm." She indicated the threatening clouds.

"Nonsense." Margret said gaily, "Those clouds have been building for hours and we are not walking to London, just a simple stroll through the gardens."

"The gardens?" Keegain regarded her quizzically. "In the middle of winter? Whatever for?"

"Ah, but that is the duty of it. I am given to understand that the Queen herself takes a walk in the garden every day, regardless of the weather. She attests it is, in fact, the secret to her good health."

"To the Queen," Reynolds raised his glass. The table joined in.

"Besides," Margret continued, "it does get beastly stuffy inside all day, do you not agree?"

"Well," Charlotte looked from one woman to the next with a devilish grin on her face. "Well, and why not then?"

"I think it should be bracing indeed!" Margaret continued.

Lady Patience nodded. "I do love walking," she said. "I believe I would like a walk after breakfast." One by one the other women agreed, much to the consternation of the men.

Keegain stole a look at Reynolds, but the man did not so much as frown. Keegain shook his head at his own foolishness. Of course, there would be little enough risk to walk on an overcast morning in the company of others. The garden was walled, and private. It was when everyone wore masks and there were shadows behind drapes and curtains that would be the danger, not now in the daylight.

It was quickly agreed that the ladies were to stroll the grounds, despite the muddiness of the pathways and the mounting breezes, though why precisely, Keegain could not guess. Sometimes women were unfathomable. There were certainly no flowers to enjoy at this time of year, nor would the trees be in leaf. There would be little enough there to look upon, but their excitement grew and the ladies began excusing themselves to go and prepare for their outing.

The gentlemen stood to see them off, but they too wandered from the table in search of distraction. Reynolds promised to escort the ladies, as if they were going to a ball. Keegain did not understand. They had no need of an escort. They had no need to go outside at all, but he supposed that Reynolds would keep them safe. He had admonished the man to do so.

❦❦❦

JANE DECIDED to stay in her room, rather than risk breakfast. It was the day of the Christmas ball, and she was sure that the staff would be busy, so she ordered tea in her room. She spent the morning reading one of the books that Lord Keegain had given her while sparing glances at the beautiful gown that hung ready to wear in her room. Lady Amelia kept the jewels in a locked box, but promised she would bring them to Jane before the ball.

Jacqueline had come and gone. Molly had brought her breakfast tray and returned to take away the leavings.

Jane laid her book aside and picked up her mother's pearls. She would not wear them tonight, but she would still have her mother's spirit with her.

The more she thought about it, the more she decided it was cowardly to hide in her room. What could Margret do, that she had not already done? So, she might ridicule her dress. Jane had expected that.

What was much harder to bear was the knowledge that once she left Kennett Park, it was doubtful she would ever see Lord Keegain again. Even if she did, it would not be in the same manner as now. Was she really hiding from Lady Margret, or was it her own tempestuous feelings that frightened her?

Her mother had said, *trust your heart and you shall never be unhappy*, but Jane had been afraid to trust her heart.

She pulled together her determination and opened her bedroom door. She would not hide from the likes of Lady Margret Fairfax, or from her own feelings.

As Jane descended the stair, the ladies returned from their walk, flushed and excited. Even within the walls of the small formal garden behind the house, the wind had been incredible. The ladies laughed and chatted amicably.

"You should have come!" Lady Charlotte scolded Jane as she removed her cloak. "I would not have thought of walking outside in this weather, but Margret was right, it was an invigorating experience!"

Jane saw what the others did not. Cheeks flushed, hair askew, skirts muddied. Lady Margret stood among them, serene and perfect, her pale cheeks, and the alabaster of her skin without a mark from the wind. She had stepped out with them, to be sure, but no doubt the lady stood out of the wind. How many of the ladies had noticed that Margret had stayed within the shelter of the door, and entered with them as though she had been one of their number all along? Jane reached for Lady Charlotte's hand, drawing her aside with a nod toward the others.

"Is it time for tea yet? I am absolutely famished!" Lady Alice exclaimed, and the others called their assent. Lady Margret laughed and urged them to come and sit. They followed, laughing at their appearances, still not seeing how askew all were, even as they passed the door to the study where the gentlemen lounged at cards.

When Lady Charlotte saw the difficulty to which Jane was trying to draw her attention, her face went pale. "Oh no. I see."

Lady Margret in sleek perfection trailed behind the rest of the ladies, and it was supremely obvious to Jane and Lady Charlotte both as the men's eyebrows rose at the disheveled appearance of the rest. Their eyes came to rest in appreciation of Lady Margret, who strode past with not so much as a hair out of place.

Jane noted that even the unflappable Lady Amelia

looked a bit out of order, though her color was high and her eyes were bright. Lady Patience's hair had turned into a frizzy orange ball in the misty snow. Her freckles stood out sharply on her pinked skin. Most of the ladies' hair was in some disarray.

"She has made us all to look …" Lady Charlotte murmured.

"No," Jane interrupted her, feeling her chin come up at the injustice of it all. "She has made herself to look better than everyone else."

The others had not noticed. If they had, there might have been a revolt. Instead, the group made its way to the parlor for tea. Lady Charlotte looked from them to Jane and back, and called after them, "Ladies, let us not be overly hasty. Our tea will keep. Is it not our duty to look our best? Dear Margret was correct in thinking the crisp air would freshen our attitudes and restore vigor to our limbs, but let us next freshen ourselves, lest the gentlemen see us in such a windblown state."

The ladies looked at one another and laughed. "That is so!" Lady Helen called out, though Alice looked longingly at the cakes through the open doorway.

As the ladies filed past, Lady Patience touched Jane's shoulder and bent near. "That was wise; to draw Charlotte's attention to what was happening, but you might expect trouble for it." She nodded toward Lady Margret, who had stayed behind, her lips pursed.

Mr. Reynolds said something to her that brightened her attitude, and Jane could only hope that her ire stayed at bay.

Lady Amelia, who had joined them, nodded to Jane.

"Maybe you had best come with us." She winked a startling blue eye. "There is safety in numbers."

Jane was heartened by Lady Amelia's grace and friendship, but she shook her head. She was no coward.

Indeed, Jane wanted a moment alone with Lady Margret. In truth, she wanted to speak to Lady Margret, perhaps to propose a ceasefire, she thought. "I shall be fine." With that Jane smiled and stepped into the parlor where Lady Margret awaited her. Perhaps Jane could discover what made the lady's tongue so acid. Regardless, she must say something.

It was just the two of them, save a single servant who hovered near the tea cart ready to pour.

"I suppose you think you are clever," Lady Margret said as Jane approached.

Jane only smiled. "Shall I serve us both while we wait for the others?"

"I daresay you should be more at home serving, would you not, *Miss* Bellevue?"

It was a nasty dig. Jane had been acutely aware that she was the only lady present whose family did not bear a title of some sort, but that Lady Margret would make an assumption that not being of the nobility put her on the level of a servant was highly insulting. Jane took a calming breath and nodded to the maid to pour out two cups of tea. She wanted to upend her cup into Lady Margret's lap. Instead, she smiled blithely.

She was a lady in bearing, if not in name. Her mother had always said so. Her father had ever called her Lady Jane, even though she had no claim to the title. She would not lose her manners now.

"There is nothing demeaning in being able to be of service. Thank you, Miss Marple," Jane said as she took the cups from Molly, who looked at her in surprise, then smiled as she curtseyed. "I would say it even shows a great deal about a person's character, would you not agree? Many writers have espoused service and humility, from St. Augustine to Shakespeare himself." Jane smiled. "How would you like your tea, Lady Margret?"

It was hard to be kind, but Jane couldn't help but wonder if Lady Margret had known somehow of the tension between herself and the earl. If so, could she blame Margret for being out of sorts?

Jane wondered how she would feel if their places were reversed. She flushed as she added cream and sugar to Lady Margret's tea, before settling opposite her with her own cup. Jane thought she would want to tear the lady's hair out. She smiled benignly.

Lady Margret looked at her, face flushed and angry. By all rights, as one who was soon to be lady of this house, Lady Margret should have been the one to pour the tea. Such actions were usually left to the one who was considered the hostess. As the home was Lord Keegain's, and would soon be hers, the duty fell to Margret, or at least, it would soon.

In fact, upon consideration, Jane thought, Lady Margret might even consider that Jane was stealing the right of hostess, which would be the case were she trying to steal Lord Keegain from her. Was she? For a moment, Jane wondered. She had acted without thinking, doing what felt natural.

"I did not mean..."

"Then what did you mean, Miss Bellevue?" Lady Margret asked, looking significantly at the cup in her hand.

The other ladies chose that moment to return, hair tidied, several having changed their dresses. They came in chattering, Lady Amelia and Lady Patience coming first through the door. Never had Jane been more pleased to see her friends.

"Oh, do come in," Lady Margret called as the group entered. "Miss Bellevue has been regaling me with stories of what it is to be common. It is quite entertaining to speak to someone who is so much lower than one's own station, is it not? One gains such a unique viewpoint."

Jane seethed. A teacup in her lap was too good for her. Lady Margret deserved the entire pot over her head. Indeed, Jane had expected something scathing. This was far beyond that. She looked up at the staring faces. Lady Helen and Lady Alice appeared uncertain. Lady Charlotte glanced her way with what could only be sympathy.

Several of the other ladies seemed to have difficulty in meeting her eyes. In that instant, Jane knew it had been a mistake to come here. She had thought that she would be welcome on the strength of her association with Lady Charlotte, but in truth, she was an oddity who never quite fit in.

Lady Margret's voice cut through her thoughts. "I am sorry, dear, but I wonder if perhaps it might be best if you lie down before it is time to prepare for the ball. You look rather pale. We would hate to have you miss the festivities." It was clear that what Lady Margret wanted most of all was for Jane to miss the festivities.

The message was clear. She could either leave now, or leave later. Either way, Lady Margret would have her way.

Jane surprised herself by wanting to stay. *I am not missing that ball. I have come here with a clear purpose. Tonight, with a mask on, I can become anyone at all. I can win the heart of a stranger, a man of means and title both. I can do whatever I wish, but I cannot do anything unless I yield here, now.* She would yield, but she would not let Margret take this night from her.

Jane set her cup and saucer carefully on the table next to her. "It is, as you say, Lady Margret. It would be best if I perhaps spent some time resting before tonight. I would not miss the ball for anything. Ladies," she paused to curtsey to the gathering. "I hope you enjoy your tea."

Jane walked to the door with what she hoped was stately poise. She would not let them see how bothered she was by Margret's acid. She would not be ruffled; only inside, she was upset.

She brushed past the gentlemen who were just coming to join the others in their tea. The earl was with them. She would find him in any crowd, she supposed, given the way her senses came alert whenever he was near. Perhaps she drew a measure of strength from him as she passed, for somehow she managed to make it all the way to her room without bursting into tears.

24

———

*L*ord Keegain and the gentlemen came to attend the ladies after their walk and tea. For their part, the ladies seemed to have pulled the miracle for which their sex was known, and presented themselves once again clean and coiffed as they filed into the room. Lord Keegain smiled at their flexibility, and waited to cross the hall until they were all safely ensconced. As he walked past the open door, he heard Lady Margret speaking.

"Miss Bellevue has been regaling me with stories of what it is to be common. It is quite entertaining to speak to someone who is set so far lower than one's station, is it not? One gains such a unique viewpoint."

Keegain felt suddenly ill, though it was difficult to discern between nausea and rage.

I will not break my word, Keegain thought. It seemed such a hollow sentiment.

He let his anger simmer while the ladies finished

their tea, his ire growing all the more for being contained. When he saw that the ladies were finished, he suggested they retire to the sitting room together where a fire had been built up against the chill.

Twittering, the ladies filed out, but he signaled Margret to him catching her before she could follow. "A word," he said simply.

She looked up at him with her blandly beautiful face as if she could not imagine what would be wrong. He gave Reynolds a pointed look and the man stepped away from them.

Lord Keegain felt out of sorts with the trouble afoot. He did not need further upset. He waited until the room emptied before confronting her.

He lowered his voice so that it did not carry. "I do not appreciate my guests humiliated or humbled. Guests in *my* house are exactly that: guests. And not the target of your malevolent gossiping."

Margret looked stunned. "I am sure I do not know what you mean."

"I think you do. I refer to the comment you made about a guest who was clearly upset and did not deserve being treated unconscionably by your sharp tongue."

"You mean the common girl?" Margret could not have been more surprised at Keegain's ire than if he had suddenly burst into flame. "Oh, darling, why would you care? No one else does."

"No matter what you think of her," Keegain said through gritted teeth. "She is *my* guest."

"*Your* guest, is she?" Margret hissed. "I thought she

was Charlotte's guest." Margret looked unaccountably flushed and Keegain calmed himself.

"Regardless, such behavior is unacceptable to guests in my house."

Margret smiled at him. The smile did not reach her eyes. "Perhaps I might remind you, my dear, that very soon this house will be mine as well."

Her words lit a fire of anger in him. This was *his* house. Margret was getting above herself. She was not his wife. Not yet. He thought to remind her of that fact, but he held his temper. The marriage was to honor his father and her mother who had been enamored of a bond between the families. He could not break the engagement. He had given his father a deathbed promise, and he kept his word. He sucked his breath through gritted teeth and bit his lip against the harsh words that sprang to it.

How was it that she raised such an ire in him, when they had been childhood friends? He approached the problem from that manner. "We were friends once, but when I see you behave in such a manner, I find myself wondering when you gained such venom."

"Now, Keegain," she said putting her hands on his chest and blinking up at him. "Certainly you don't mean that." She pulled at his cravat, straightening a stray wrinkle and letting her hands wander.

He was fully unaffected. He grabbed her wrists and firmly set her away from his person. "Curb your tongue around my guests, or I shall find another way to silence you," he said.

Margret's face went as pale as milk.

He wondered what on earth she had thought he would do; cut off her allowance, most likely, once they were married. He knew he was out of his depth, but since their engagement, this new grating personality had taken root in Margret, and it vexed him greatly. He found that his own tongue was as sharp as hers and more focused. Further, he seemed to have little enough control over it. He did not know how to retract his words or if he truly wanted to do so. Let her think what she will.

"I see," Margret hissed, but kept her expression carefully neutral. "Will that be all then, *Lord* Keegain?" She spoke in a voice colder than ice, and just as implacable.

"That is all." Keegain tried to match her icy tone, but the woman had a talent for acid.

"Very well, my lord." She curtsied with a smirk dripping sarcasm, and spun on one heel, her back straight and unyielding her head high. She left the room in a leisurely pace, unhurried and seemingly unshaken. It was as if she wanted him to know that the world played on her timeline, not his. *We shall see*, he thought. With this business with the brigands looming, the last thing he needed was dissension in his house.

"Tell me, old boy," Fitzwilliam said from the serving table. Keegain started. He had thought the room empty, but his dear friend was placidly eating late-bloom blackberries from their hothouse. He popped one into his mouth, and chewed before continuing. "Do you find it wise to put needles in your bed at night?"

"You heard her," Keegain snapped. "I will not accept such cheek. Guests are to be treated with respect."

"Oh I agree." Fitzwilliam said, eating another of the fruit. "One should always be polite to ladies with deep dark eyes." He grinned knowingly and clasped his friend's arm. "Come, I am sure the men have decided to use this lovely hour given to us by the ladies by smoking your cigars and drinking your brandy. You should join us."

Keegain grinned in spite of himself, but with the possibility of villains in his home tonight, he did not want to start in on the brandy, and said as much.

"Indeed," Fitzwilliam said and considered the matter very seriously. "In that case, we'll drink your Scotch. I like it better anyway." He winked outrageously and headed toward the parlor.

Keegain shook his head, and wondered what kettle of worms he had opened this morning. He wanted to crawl back into bed and begin the day again. His imagination conjured Miss Jane Bellevue, there amongst the sheets, gazing at him with her dark and mysterious eyes. How had she so captured his thoughts? Miss Bellevue was an enigma he could not unravel.

He looked around the room. "Where is Reynolds?" He asked.

"Oh, he went in search of Lady Margret," Fitzwilliam replied.

"Good. Good," Keegain said distractedly. He could not have the woman wondering around unescorted when there were villains about. "Reynolds will protect her."

"Oh, is that right?" Fitz said, raising an eyebrow with his sarcastic tone.

"What?" Keegain questioned.

"Never mind," Fitz said. "I am sure Reynolds will protect your intended as if she were his own." Fitz shook his head. "You cannot see what is right in front of your nose."

Keegain frowned. Whatever did Fitz mean by that?

Fitzwilliam just shook his head. "Do you love her, Keegain?" He asked seriously.

Keegain blinked.

"Lady Margret," Fitz clarified with a small smile at the earl's hesitation. That Fitzwilliam asked him outright was something of a surprise, although in retrospect it should not have been.

"I am avowed," Keegain said sternly. "Both to Lady Margret and to my father's dying wishes. I shall not break my word, not to either of them."

"Lud, Keegain, how old were you when you made that vow? Thirteen?"

"What does that matter? A vow is a vow, and a man's word is his bond," Lord Keegain said turning away.

"You were but a child," Fitzwilliam spat.

"I was not," Keegain said. "I was fifteen, and within the year I was the earl. I have not been a child for a very long time."

"I know, my friend," Fitz muttered as Keegain turned away. "You always were too honorable for your own good."

Keegain did not know what Fitz was on about, but he did not want to argue with his friends. It was bad enough he and Margret were out of sorts. With a brigand lurking, they should have solidarity.

Keegain excused himself from the room. He needed air, and just now, the idea of walking in the garden in a freezing gale did not sound so bad, even if he came in disheveled and mud-stained as the ladies had been.

---

25

*I*n the end, Jane did curl up on the massive bed with one of the books Keegain had given her. The first was a history tome. The other was a light-hearted romp that made her laugh, and she needed to laugh.

She read for a while, but her eyelids were feeling heavy. She had not slept much the night before, and with the ball commencing in a matter of hours, it seemed the wisest recourse. She honestly thought she wouldn't sleep now, not with the way the wind rattled at the windows. In the end she must have dozed, or surely she would have noticed the knocking on her door that much sooner. As it was, she lay there for the duration of several such sharp raps, trying to puzzle out the sound.

After the day she had, Jane was somewhat unsure if she wanted visitors. It was likely Lady Amelia and Lady Patience come to console her, or perhaps Lady Charlotte. Was she ready for company and their sweet pity?

I would not be here if it were not for them. I should not be avoiding them, she reasoned as she swung her legs over the side of the bed, and lifted one hand to her hair to smooth it. It was a rumpled mess and would need Jacqueline's careful hand, but it did not matter.

Jane threw open the door with a smile. "As you can see, I am fine..." she started only to find that she had been mistaken in the identity of her visitor. Jane found herself looking into the very pair of eyes she had been trying so hard to forget.

"Lord Keegain, this is most unexpected!" she murmured, lifting a hand to her heart in silent protest.

"I am here only for a moment. The others are downstairs, and I have asked Fitzwilliam to let me know if anyone comes."

Jane's eyes opened wide.

"I did not mean to alarm you."

She peered past him down the hall, seeing the second gentleman stationed at the head of the stairs. He seemed to be taking the role seriously, standing with all the attention of a soldier on guard duty. "I am duly impressed, but you are still taking quite a chance in coming to my room in such a manner. Was there something that you required?" she asked, hating this conversation, hating that not only did she have to dispel him from her mind, but from her very threshold as well.

"I only wished to apologize for the behavior of Lady Margret. As she is my betrothed, I feel responsible for her actions."

"You are not," Jane said. "Her actions and her words are her own."

"I...overheard what she said to you earlier and as your host, I am most regretful of the entire affair."

Jane drew back into the room, feeling suddenly chilled. "I am sure it does not matter," she said softly, "and I would thank you to leave."

"Of course it matters," the earl argued. "And you are trying to handle the matter so tactfully that I cannot help but be grateful. But you are a guest in my home, and I would not have you form a poor opinion of us here."

As Jane looked into his eyes, she became positive that there could be no such thing as a poor opinion of him personally. That he cared enough to come apologize was endearing and sweet, but that he stood in her bedchamber door was terribly dangerous. To be seen so would be considered compromising, aside from the fact that Lady Margret was like to scratch her eyes out, and she could not blame the woman.

Besides, Jane really did not wish to discuss this with him. He would ask, he would have to, what the entire incident had been about, and it all seemed petty now and ridiculous. She had imagined Lady Margret's reaction to her pouring the tea. She was being too sensitive.

"You have spoken your piece, and I thank you," she said again, starting to close the door. "As I said, I have no wish to discuss it."

Lord Keegain stopped the door, only inches from closing, one hand shooting out to hold the edge of the door. His hand was so near her own that she could have touched it had she wanted to. His hands were rather large for his stature. Large and powerful. His signet ring shone in the light of the hall sconces. Jane swallowed hard, trying to ignore the temptation, the flutter of danger that moved deep within her belly.

Having this conversation in the doorway of her bedroom could ruin her if any should see. She could invite him into her room, a reasonable voice in her mind urged. Then no one would see him hovering upon her threshold. That of course, if discovered, would be infinitely worse.

"I would have your forgiveness."

"There is none needed," Jane said, and indeed that was true. Margret's actions had not been his. The idea that a man must take the blame for his wife's action did seem silly, although it was not the first time Jane had heard it. It was not even the first time she had heard it in conjunction with an engagement, but Lady Margret was not his wife, only his intended. Lord Keegain was not yet married.

Jane could only see a piece of his face between door and jamb. The earl's eyes probed hers, filled with an agonizing sadness. "Why do you work so hard to push me away?" he asked in a hoarse whisper.

For a moment, Jane found herself wanting to push the door open enough to draw him into the room, and into her arms, so that she might comfort him. Oh, such thoughts were dangerous. Lord Keegain could never marry her. He was an earl, and she was no one. It was ludicrous and could not be.

He was promised to another, a proper lady, and yet he stood at *her* bedchamber door.

Jane licked at lips that had suddenly gone dry and gathered her mettle. "I have noted the difficulty before, and wonder that you have not. It is simple. You are engaged, my lord. And not to me."

With that she shut the door with infinite care that it would not slam.

She had half-expected him to push his way in after all. It was something of a disappointment that he did not. Her heart was beating as if she had run a race, and she put a hand to it to gain some perspective. When she leaned against the door, she could hear him in the hallway, just on the other side. Moving. Breathing. He stood there a long moment. She wondered if he stared at the wood and thought of her there, leaning on the other side. Waiting. By the time she worked up the courage to reopen the door, he was gone.

She felt tears well up in her eyes and she tried to blink them back. If she cried now, her face would be a splotchy mess. Still, she could not stop the tears from coming. The pieces of her broken heart seemed to clog her chest. How could she let him go? Because he was never hers, she reminded herself.

❧❧❧

26

*J*ane used the water in the basin to cool her eyes and wipe away the redness, when she heard a tap on the door. She paused, holding the cloth aloft, thinking for a moment perhaps it was the earl returning, but it was not.

"It's us, Jane," said Lady Charlotte from outside the door, and Jane moved to open it. The girls trooped in with their dresses and their ladies' maids.

"Oh," Jane said surprised at the veritable parade.

"Alice is moping in her room, and Helen is dressing with Lady Guinevere," Lady Charlotte said as she turned to her maid who carried her dress, directing her to hang it in the armoire for the moment.

"We have brought everything," Lady Patience said, as Lady Amelia placed her jewelry box on the writing desk.

"I thought it may be too crowded," Lady Amelia added looking around, "but I do believe that your dressing room is as large as mine. Apparently, Lord Keegain thinks highly of you."

The words brought a blush to Jane's cheeks. Could she have been so transparent?

Jacqueline curtseyed and brought Jane from her musings. "May I start *ta coiffure, mademoiselle*? Yes?" She held the hairbrush in her hand.

"Yes," Jane said, rather overwhelmed by it all. She steeled her resolve as Jacqueline fixed her hair.

Tonight was the event for which she had originally come to Kennett Park. She had greatly anticipated the Christmas ball when she left Bath, and she would not allow it to be spoiled. Jane was no lady, but tonight she would look like one. She would have this one night, to remember forever. She would laugh and dance and be merry. Tonight, she would be Lady Jane.

Once she and the other girls were dressed, they tied on their masks, and Lady Amelia put a veritable fortune in jewels around her neck.

"I shall be apprehensive all night," she said, touching the glittering necklace at her throat. "What if I were to lose them?" Although, that was not the only reason Jane was nervous.

"Do not be silly," Lady Amelia said, as her maid fastened a similar cascade of emeralds around her own neck. "Tonight, you are an heiress. You shall find a wonderful gentleman, and dance the night away."

Jane nodded. Lady Amelia was right. She would worry about the earl and Lady Margret tomorrow.

Lady Patience grinned and hugged Jane, her smiling eyes glittering behind her mask.

"Oh, I could just die with excitement," Lady Charlotte said, still moving this way and that, much to her maid's consternation. Lady Charlotte was dressed in her pink confection complete with diamonds. Jane was not sure what Charlotte was supposed to be: perhaps a bouquet of pink flowers, for surely she could not be only one flower in that dress.

"Lady Charlotte," her maid said, as she tried to fasten the jewels around Lady Charlotte's ever moving body. Charlotte stilled, and in the next moment, the group was ready to go down to the ball.

"I am a lady," Jane said to herself as several gentlemen came forward to escort them. Jane recognized Mr. Fitzwilliam and Mr. Reynolds, but did not see the earl with them. The third man, she realized, was Lady Patience's brother, Lord Barton. Patience waved her fan at him when he would have taken her arm. "No, Reginald, you escort Lady Charlotte," she said.

Before Jane could blink, Lady Amelia had found a partner, and was already halfway across the floor.

Mr. Fitzwilliam bowed over Jane's gloved hand. Jane smiled at him, and they joined Lady Charlotte and Lord Barton who were lining up for the set.

THE APOLOGY HAD NOT GONE AT ALL as Lord Keegain had planned. He realized that rushing to Jane's door and asking Fitz to be his guard at the stairs was presumptuous. In retrospect, it was also dangerous. A scandal could cause Margret to rethink their promise and call off the engagement. Maybe, deep down, he wished for that, but the damage it would bring to Jane's good name was something very different.

The shame would have been an insurmountable obstacle in her case, one not soon forgotten and possibly never forgiven, if he had been found in the doorway of her bedchamber. Her hair was mussed, and he wanted to raise a hand to smooth it, or perhaps muss further. He had glimpsed the rumpled bed beyond her shoulder, and for a moment, his imagination had taken flight. He had wanted her to invite him in, but of course, Jane would not. She was a lady; as much a lady as Margret, in his eyes. Miss Bellevue was noble in manner if not in name.

What Margret had against a perfect stranger other than the poor girl's lack of social standing was beyond him. Why would Margret care about a guest's background? To that point, if he wished to set up a chimney sweep in one of the guest rooms, it would be her incumbent duty as hostess to supply the man with clean sheets and hot water.

Maybe what had set Lord Keegain on edge was the fact that, aside from the men brought by the duke, he had invited each and every individual here today. Granted, Lady Margret had quite a bit of input, but he personally knew each man here tonight and most of the women. Many of them had spent considerable time under his roof in the past, and would likely do so again, for he loved to share his home. To think that one or more of those he called friends could be a criminal, a traitor, was enough to make him regret hosting the entire affair.

The duke had personally introduced Lord Keegain to the men under Reynold's command. Ted could have just as easily done so himself, but the Duke of Ely was not to be questioned, and if he introduced the host of the celebration, it meant that the duke and House of Lords guaranteed Keegain's innocence in any complicity. High praise, to be sure, considering the stakes involved.

The men of the Crown were young, brash, and eager. They had been raised around the gentry, and were able to ape the mannerisms and talk as well as any blue-blooded aristocrat, but Keegain could not dispel his worry.

There would likely be an attempt on a young woman's life tonight. That it would serve to see justice done was of little consolation when his mind put Jane in the young woman's place. Or one of his sisters. Why did his mind not picture his betrothed? Instead, he saw Miss Bellevue held prisoner for an exorbitant price her father could never afford.

That was of a strange comfort, though. If her family could ill-afford a ransom, did it not follow that she was in less danger of kidnapping? If they were to take someone, it would be someone of means. Like his sisters. The thought chilled his blood.

Lord Keegain knew it was best to do as he had been advised. Let the whole thing play out. Wait for the villains to make their move and catch them in the act. Kennett Park was a remote estate, which meant that the perpetrators would have no place to hide once the deed was done. There would be no better time or place to end this terrible business.

His father would have cautioned Keegain to steer clear of the King's Men. Let them do their jobs and not get in their way. The duke said much the same, but Lord

Keegain was made of sterner stuff, and protecting his sisters and Miss Bellevue was priority. He realized that when it came down to it, there was not a person here he would wish to see put in harm's way. Every life had value. Meaning. No one was expendable. Not even Lady Margret.

In the distance, he heard the musicians strike a lively tune, appropriate for the beginning of the ball.

The earl strode, mask in hand, to the ballroom, and stood outside of the doors to take a breath. The mask was singular, something Margret had picked out for him, or perhaps she had it made for him; he did not know, but it was gaudy. Mother would have made him something tasteful. Normally, he would have balked at wearing such a monstrosity, but tonight it was the least of his worries. The mask had great wings that were reminiscent of a dragon's wings, or perhaps it was the great horns of some angry god or devil. It was a powerful mask; one of strength that held a certain threat to wrongdoers. Or at least tonight, he hoped it did.

Two liveried servants stood, one on either side of the door and waited. He knew them both but did not speak. He only gave them a brief nod, donned the ridiculous mask and paused.

There was mistletoe overhead, and it reminded him of his aborted kiss in the library with Miss Bellevue. He sucked in a breath and his senses were filled with the sweet scent of pine. The lights of an extravagant amount of candles flickered across the room, and laughter came to his ears. The room was filled to bursting with holiday cheer, but for once in his life, he could not enjoy the

Christmas spirit. He was too agitated. He looked across the room. He knew all of these people. They were good Englishmen; only one, or more of them, was not.

The earl straightened his shoulders and proceeded into the room. No one was announced, not tonight, for that was the object of the masks, to let people be anyone they chose to be for the evening. Some had chosen to be traitors.

27

*W*ith the hideous mask covering his face, the earl surveyed his guests. The mask was more like whatever Margret wanted him to be. Strong, but arrogant and prideful. Was that how his fiancée saw him, or what she wanted him to become? It sounded much like her, when he thought on it.

He wore the ugliness she kept hidden. He pushed that thought away as hard as he could.

Perhaps not all marriages were meant to have attraction, or even more preposterous, love. Most marriages did not. Despite her vitriol, theirs was a business relationship, and as a respectable Englishman, his word was his bond. It was unbreakable.

Focus on the immediate issue, Keegain reminded himself. *There is a traitor in the room, most likely more than one.* There would have to be, to abduct a woman and keep her isolated, quiet and safe enough to return when the money was paid. It would require a team, would it not?

The earl searched the room as if he could spy the culprit. Apprehension clogged his senses.

The Duke of Ely passed by him with a curt nod under his own extravagant leather formed mask. It covered more of his features than most, but few people could mistake his tall figure and gruff exterior.

The duke had been a great help to Keegain after his own father's passing, but for those who were not familiar with the older man's deep emotions, he often seemed brusque and terribly serious, except for when he spoke of his daughter, Lady Amelia. The girl was the duke's heart and he would keep a careful eye on her tonight.

Reynolds pointed out that everyone who had been abducted was returned unharmed, although if word got out, the lady's reputation would certainly be in tatters. No one would believe that a woman taken and held in the company of a group of men, nay, scoundrels, would still be pure and marriageable upon her return.

Once more Lord Keegain ran the guest list in his head. He could not conceive of any of them being a traitor to the Crown, or such a cad as to endanger the life and reputation of one of the fairer sex. It was unthinkable.

The musicians shifted into a new tune, a lively little number. It lacked sophistication, but it was generally well-received, as it was a local favorite. He wondered if it would make Jane feel more at home, to hear music not quite so pretentious.

Strange, how his thoughts invariably returned to Miss Bellevue. Perhaps it was more that Jane consistently entered his head when he was distracted? It was a glorious thought, as though she could wander in and out of his mind at will. He smiled at the notion.

Miss Bellevue had been scandalized at his appearance at her door, and rightly so. Would he have done the same to someone of the nobility? Would he have barged into Lady Amelia's suite, for example, in such a manner?

Lud! The duke would have had his guts for garters.

Lord Keegain stopped in his tracks so abruptly that a server nearly crashed into him with a silver tray laden with sweetmeats. There was a precarious moment while the man righted the tray, but the earl's thoughts were elsewhere.

If his sister had been wronged as such while visiting a house far away, would he have wanted the gentleman of the house to confront her alone in her room while his friend stood watch?

The earl suddenly realized that he was every bit as uncouth as his betrothed. He had assumed Jane's sensibilities would be less acute than a member of the elite. In short, an untitled individual could be imposed upon, where a titled individual could not. *In short, old boy, you've been a perfect ass.*

Lord Keegain fought the urge to seek out Miss Bellevue, to track her down and offer his apology. That would only compound the problem, apologizing for apologizing. *Great, why not trap her again so you can say you are sorry for trapping her?*

He could not do that. His heart spoke to him. If he could see her again, speak to her, touch her, perhaps he could explain. He shook his head, feeling the fool, but gazed around the room, still hoping to spot her.

The men and women were dressed to the extent of fashion, the ladies in elaborate ball gowns and the gentlemen in tailcoats of superfine or velvet brocade. Masks covered every face. The masks were grotesque or humorous, elegant or flamboyant, and everything in between. Other than those of exceptional girths or the very short or very tall, it was most difficult to tell who was who.

Certainly, the culprits were men. Women would not have the physical strength for kidnapping, and no doubt had better sensibility. So it was the men upon whom the earl focused his attention. Yet, he found himself wondering what mask Jane wore this evening. Hadn't she mentioned her mother's pearls at one point? He looked for pearls, but could not spot her.

The earl began a new search, simply looking for her rather than jewelry. He knew her. He knew how she moved; poised but not haughty, with an air of delicate grace.

There. He saw her across the room in a lovely deep purple gown and a peacock mask. She took his breath away.

One of the men from Reynold's group passed between them, and he lost her to sight. He spied Reynolds pacing the ballroom, keeping to the edge of the crowd and the shadows, leaving Keegain to handle the part of the gregarious host. It was a position that Lady Margret had already assumed, flitting from one guest to the next, uncannily avoiding the King's men. It was as if she could sense who was and who was not gentry.

It occurred to the earl that he was taking up space on the floor as those not paired up headed toward the sidelines and cleared the room for the dancers. He retreated to where Reynolds stood. At least the man was easy to find; his mask was distinctive.

"I trust you are enjoying yourself, Lord Keegain," Reynolds greeted him quite formally.

"On the contrary," Keegain admitted. "I find myself a veritable mass of nerves, being concerned about the... other events this evening."

Reynolds leaned close and spoke. "The Crown has charged me to do that very thing, my lord. If you worry all night, there will be nothing left for me to do to occupy my time."

Keegain snorted his amusement. It felt strange that his friend should be working tonight when the room was filled with so much Christmas cheer. "You could try dancing," Keegain said.

Reynolds shook his head. He took his eyes off of the crowd and turned to the earl. "Tonight I have a more important task."

"You should dance with my intended," Keegain said.

Reynold's expression was unreadable behind the mask. The eyes that peered out from the holes spoke of a quiet intensity.

"Please, Keegain, do not worry for Lady Margret. I give you my word she will come to no harm. Leave the worry to me and my men. I know my job."

"Of course you do."

"It is, in fact, imperative that you relax. The host of the ball must not appear to be agitated, after all. We mustn't let the cat out of the bag until we spring the trap."

Lord Keegain nodded, sighing inwardly. It made sense, but he did not have to like it. He did not have the temperament for subterfuge. Reynolds could be unruffled in any situation. Keegain envied him his cool exterior.

Keegain was not so calm, not when people he cared about were involved.

"Very well. I shall enjoy the ball, as you say, but I shall not like enjoying it, I can assure you," he told Reynolds as he took a drink from a passing footman's tray. He raised the glass in toast to the man and set off in search of Margret. Or perhaps Miss Bellevue.

28

---

*J*ane soon lost her friends in the crush. She
had danced with several gentlemen, and like
Lady Patience and Lady Amelia, was
escorted back to the Lady Battonsbury and the Dowager
Lady Keegain several times, but she soon lost track of
them as well. With all the color and masks, it was difficult
to keep everyone in sight. Jane did see Lady Charlotte.
She was dancing; floating like a pink bubble across the
floor.

Jane paused, edging as far from the dance floor as
possible so she was not stepped upon by some whirling
dancer. She could feel a blessed breeze coming in from
the corridor. Perhaps someone had opened one of the
doors to the garden. Despite the winter chill, it was
terribly warm in the ballroom with all of the people.

"Milady, would you care to dance?"

She turned to see a tall man in the guise of a knight.
Even with the shallow visor of his Medieval helm, she
recognized him from dinner two days past. Though she

could not remember his name, the young man was easy to identify. Tall and gangly, made more so by the modified knight's helm that he used as a mask, he might have been Don Quixote himself, come to tilt at windmills.

"Thank you, but no. Pray excuse me, good Sir. I must rest a moment." Jane bobbed a curtsey and turned away.

"Then, may I fetch you a refreshment?" he persisted. Surely, he did not recognize her.

Jane nodded.

"I shall return in but a moment," he said.

She had turned him down, and perhaps she should not have. She knew that the knight met her various criteria for a potential suitor. His family was well titled, with the funds to match. That she knew him to be looking for a wife, made him that much more appealing. Why, then, had she refused him?

She sighed. That particular puzzle was easy to solve. He was not Lord Keegain.

And if you found the earl, what then? You and he both well know that he is not available to you. Have you forgotten your entire reason for being here? You are meant to enjoy yourself. Jane tried to remember the resolve she had when she left her own home.

Oh, but how could she flirt and dance now? She felt false looking for courtship and commitment in the space of a single evening upon a dance floor. The gentlemen here were looking for ladies, and she was an imposter at the ball.

Jane took a deep breath, trying to remember to hold her head high, telling herself that she did, in fact, have every right to be here. She had been invited, had she not?

Did that not lend a certain legitimacy? After all, her host had thought well enough to include her, or to at least allow her upon the guest list when asked. Lady Charlotte wanted her here, and Lady Patience was ever welcoming. Lady Amelia had lent her the dress and jewels. What difference did it make if one particular lady felt she had no place here?

Except that this particular lady would someday be lady of the estate and Lord Keegain's wife. His wife. Not to mention that selfsame lady had made it abundantly clear that Jane was not welcome in her august company. More so, she was not welcome near her imminent groom. Jane could not really blame Lady Margret.

It is only one night, she told herself. *Does it truly matter what Lady Margret thinks? You are here for the ball tonight and tomorrow it will be over. You are not likely to be invited again; especially not once Lady Margret is the hostess here, so why not enjoy the night? Let Lord and soon-to-be Lady Keegain enjoy their night far from your eye.* The ballroom was huge, and Jane certainly knew enough to stay clear of the both of them.

She had not spotted Lord Keegain at all.

The thought hurt more than she expected. Jane sighed. She had spent the better part of the afternoon sternly reminding herself that Keegain was not to be hers. She could no longer entertain the ridiculous fantasy that had taken hold while they shared the manor, when Lady Margret was not in residence. She was returned now. There was nothing for Jane with the earl.

Oh, she knew he was attracted to her, but unless she would deign to be his mistress, that attraction must come to naught. She should not even think of such things, but she did think upon it and the thought made her blush. Perhaps it was just the heat of the ballroom filling her face.

The earl had come to her bedroom door. She argued with herself; was it only to deliver an apology, or had he expected something more? She had turned him away, as was proper, but oh, she had been tempted. The fact that she longed to see him even now gave credence to her desire. She would give into temptation if she stayed, but she had come for a reason. If she did not find a husband in this dignified company, when would she do so? The time must be now.

Perhaps, she should have accepted the invitation to dance after all. Hiding in a corner was not the way to find a husband.

Don Quixote returned with her drink and she tried to be sociable, apologizing for not dancing and giving some excuse about the tightness of her slippers. She sipped her drink and tried to be gay, but in a moment, he realized that she was only half-paying attention to his witty banter, or perhaps he saw a lady more agreeable. He excused himself, and Jane promised herself she would dance the next dance no matter who asked her.

Jane stopped at a vantage point at the edge of the dance floor, where she might watch the couples that had already begun the set. Don Quixote was already in line, holding the hand of a bright sunflower, who smiled in such a way that even Jane could see the lady was clearly smitten, and the knight seemed most solicitous.

Another missed opportunity. Jane could not feel

badly about it though. Perhaps the knight and sunflower were meant for each other. Who was she to stand in the way of a love match? *As you stand between Lord Keegain and Lady Margret?* Were they once a love match? The thought gave Jane a sour feeling, and she tried not to feel so. She would not think of them. Still, she found herself looking for the pair on the dance floor. She did not see them.

Her eyes found Lady Charlotte again across the room. She and Lady Amelia were together for but a moment, and then they were both off dancing again. The sunflower and the knight danced an immediate second set together. Well, wasn't that scandalous, Jane thought, but with the crush, she wondered if anyone would notice. Why should anyone care if they did? she wondered.

Her toe tapped in time to the music as she watched the sunflower and the knight dance. The tune was a bright and lively country reel, one she had heard many times in the past, though it surprised her to hear it here in this fine company. The song seemed a touch common. Not that the dancers minded. She smiled at the thought. She did not imagine that Lady Margret chose it. Perhaps Keegain did, or perhaps it was a novelty to the dancers, something new that they had not enjoyed before.

Maybe Jane herself could likewise be considered something of a novelty. Something worth pursuing, she told herself, but still, she stood apart.

With the Dowager Lady Keegain's help, the ladies had completed Jane's costume with an elegant fan of the lovely plumy feathers left over from the mask. She had been surprised when the dowager suggested it. The earl's family was so welcoming. It was not just Lord Keegain she loved. She loved Charlotte, and young Alice, and even Helen, as if they were her own sisters. Jane wanted to be part of this family, but she was not.

You are being a wallflower, she castigated herself. *Your friends have outfitted you in a most spectacular dress complete with jewels and mask, and you are wasting their efforts.* The jewels that Lady Amelia had pressed upon Jane had truly complemented the outfit, and Jane did not look out of place, or a country bumpkin. She would not act it. She would be bright and gay, she told herself, even as she hung back in the alcove.

She would try. Mingle. Talk to others. Any gentleman here would be suitable for a dance, if not a match. *The next person that asks you to dance, accept. It is that simple*, she told herself. *You do not have to marry the first person who asks. It is only a dance.*

Applying an air of false cheer, Jane contented herself with glancing around the room at the fine masks and elaborate gowns worn by the ladies. The guests wore masks so incredibly detailed that it was obvious that many had hired special artists and costumers to provide for their wardrobe. They truly were exquisite. Jane glanced down at her own dress, a daring deep purple that matched the feathers of her mask. She did not feel much like a peacock. It was a bright and creative bird, but Lady Amelia had been so gracious, she could not squander this chance.

Jane raised her feathered fan now as she peered around the room, feeling safe in the sanctity of her disguise, knowing she looked every bit as fine as the others here, especially with the expensive ring of diamonds and sapphires around her neck and glittering at her ears. The jewels felt warm and heavy at her neck and the feathers bobbed, tickling her, as she shifted her head.

It was disconcerting, not recognizing more than a few individuals. This was not the general crowd that came to Bath. This was the *crème de la crème* of the *Beau Monde Ton.* Everyone who was not at parties in Town during the Christmas season was here. In fact, Jane knew, some had come from Town to enjoy this event in spite of the weather.

She tried to find her friends again. She looked for Lady Charlotte's outrageous pink dress. It took several minutes of hard searching. It was with relief when she spotted them and decided to make her way towards them. The group was just across the ballroom now, a bevy of fine ladies clad in a rainbow of silks and satins.

Lady Patience was easy enough to spot; her red head stood out no matter what costume she chose to wear. The gentleman talking to her then must be Lord Barton, for those bright shining heads certainly complemented one another, although Reginald's hair was considerably darker than his sister's.

Lady Amelia was there in her cat's mask with a collar of emeralds. Lord and Lady Battonsbury were with them. Lady Charlotte turned to dance with a gentleman in a fool's hat. The two of them were a riot of color. Keegain's other sister was more difficult to find, but Jane did not know Lady Helen as well as she knew the others, and she had not seen the mask that Helen had chosen.

She could not find Lord Keegain at all. Where was the earl? It was his party!

She should not be looking. Jane chastised herself, unable to believe that she had once again allowed herself to be distracted. What was it about the man that enthralled her? She was here to dance. Just that, to find someone for the next dance, or, more accurately, to allow herself to be found for the next dance. The last thing she wanted was to sit out the rest of the night, afraid that if she did, she would be forever bypassed and forgotten. Jane noted that as she was working her way towards her friends, all three of them had found partners to dance with.

Anyone. I will dance with anyone.

As if in answer to her thoughts, a gentleman approached. He was a burly man, with large fleshy hands that looked more accustomed to work than those of many a man here. His dark hair stuck out at odd angles under his hat, a rakish affair that went well with the simple black mask he wore beneath. He had gone all out in his outfit. He looked the very picture of a pirate, right down to the cutlass he wore at his hip.

"Never have I seen a more elegant fowl," he said, bending low over her hand. "Might I interest you in a turn around the dance floor, Lady...?" He held the question as if he expected her to answer with her name.

Jane laughed a little. "You are wicked, good sir, for I understand that we are not to be unmasked until midnight. Would you have me give away my true identity so early in the evening?"

"I am a pirate, after all," he said and gave a comic leer

that caused Jane to laugh as she took his hand, allowing herself to be led to the dance floor for the next set. Lady Charlotte was two pairs over from her. She would find her way to her friends after the dance she decided.

Once Jane set her mind to it, it was quite easy to lose herself in the dance. She let all her troubles and uncertainties fall away. Even realizing that it was Lady Margret who danced near to her did little to spoil her fun. Of course, Jane realized it was not Keegain with whom Lady Margret was dancing. It was another gentleman who apparently stepped on her toes.

Jane turned away with a smile. It was easy to laugh with the pirate, who, despite his foreboding expression, seemed to have a good sense of humor, and kept her laughing as he made witty, even if somewhat bawdy, remarks about those around them. Jane did not take offense. It was all in the fun of the masquerade. In fact, she had a few choice remarks of her own regarding Lady Margret, although she kept them to herself.

The pirate was intent upon finding out who was whom, but Jane was not much help to him even if she wanted to be.

"What of your family?" The pirate asked after he had pointed out one disastrous couple that was easy to identify by their bickering. Jane thought they should keep to the convention that one did not dance with his or her spouse at a ball. "Perhaps they are siblings," she considered.

"Perhaps," he agreed. "My brother and I fight constantly."

"That is a shame. Siblings should be one's best help in

this world," Jane countered.

"Do your parents get along well?"

Jane nodded a touch wistfully. "My mother is no longer with us. My father doted upon her though. It is hard for him to be alone, I think, although he is often occupied with business."

"As most gentlemen are," the pirate commented.

Jane nodded. "We still miss Mother a great deal."

"Your father has not remarried then?"

"No," Jane admitted.

"I am sure he feels blessed to have a daughter such as yourself, on which to spend his affection."

Jane could not help but laugh at that. "You speak as though you know me, when I know for a fact you do not. I am certain I would have remembered your voice, if not your face. Whether or not I am a blessing, I am sure I worry him enough."

"I can hardly imagine such a thing, although I suppose it is in the nature of all fathers to worry," the man answered with a smile, as they danced their piece and rejoined the line.

"Such fine plumage," he said, nodding at her bright feathers as they waited their turn to dance down the center line again. "Does your family enjoy many such birds?"

For a moment Jane did not know how to answer. Peacock was a meal fit for the wealthy. To answer honestly would reveal her true state. Did not Lady Amelia say this was the point of the masquerade then, to become anyone for a night? Well, if that were the case, why should she not be a fine lady? The pirate would find out the truth soon enough, but perhaps by then, he would be well on the way to being smitten. Not that she truly wanted this stranger to court her. She knew nothing of him, and he seemed rather coarse, but perhaps that was just his act to go with the pirate visage. Given time, she might like him.

Given space. Away from Keegain and the confusing feelings he raised within her, she would find another suitor. Why not this man? Her heart felt heavy at the thought, but she smiled brightly and allowed the pirate to dance her down through the center, a little further than necessary for they bumped into another gentleman. The man was dressed as a rakish war hero in full uniform, complete with saber. His eyes glittered at her from another black mask, plain and simple, much like the one of her pirate.

"I beg your pardon," the pirate said with a bow, and led her back to the other dancers, who seemed to notice nothing amiss.

Jane could not shake the feeling, however, of being watched from that point onward. Every time they danced to that end of the room, the soldier was there watching. Her own partner seemed to have little else to say after that, although he pressed her for a second dance as the first finished. She berated him for his forwardness and refused. When he persisted, she pleaded exhaustion and a desire to sit the next one out.

"I must find my companions," she said. Something about the pirate had disturbed her, and the flirtation suddenly did not seem such a good idea.

He seemed ready to protest her decision, and Jane

finally had to refuse him again in a rather firm tone.

"Very well, then. Allow me to return you to your chaperone," he offered.

He was just being solicitous, she thought, and then she spotted her friends across the room. "Oh, there is Lady Patience," she said. "And her brother, Lord Barton. One can always find her red hair." Jane gave a quick curtsey to the pirate and turned away, in an attempt to disappear into the crowd, but the press was so great that it was hard to make the exit she truly desired.

The pirate stepped forward, and for a moment she thought he might pursue her. Desperately, she pushed between the knots of ladies talking and escaped him, ending near a window and laughing at herself for being so foolish. This was the Earl of Keegain's ball. No blackguard would have been invited.

Outside, the wind beat at the windows whistling and drawing her attention. Branches rattled against the glass. Her gaze was drawn to the rising storm and she shivered. The room seemed suddenly a touch darker, more sinister. The exotic masks and the crush of strangers joined into a queer combination that seemed more suitable for a re-enactment of Dante's Inferno than a simple ball.

Thunder rattled the pane and she looked up in surprise as did those near her. Thunder in winter? It seemed an ill omen, and Jane found herself fleeing, away from the glass that showed only the black of the night and the strange distorted reflections of the masked dancers.

Jane's heart raced within her breast and Lady Amelia's jewels felt hot against her throat. There were too many people here. She could not catch her breath. For a moment she panicked, wanting nothing more than escape. Jane twisted around, looking for a familiar face, for the cat mask. Yes. Lady Amelia. Nothing unsettled the duke's daughter. Jane could not find her in the crush, or any of the other young ladies she had so recently befriended.

It had been a mistake to dance with the pirate. Something had seemed off, as though he were too interested, and now she was completely on the other side of the ballroom, and she had once again lost her friends to the whirling crowd.

You are unfair. The pirate is quite likely here for the same reason you are: to find a marriage match. The worst he would be was a fortune hunter. Of course he would try to find out about her family. Had she not been trying to do the same? Only she had lied, had she not? If any were the deceiver, it was she.

Someone bumped into Jane, and then another. The room was too crowded. For a moment she thought the pirate might have come back, wanting to claim the next dance after all. She felt a large hand close on her wrist and near panicked. Jane pulled frantically away, catching her breath upon a sob, because she had lied and been caught out in that lie. The pirate would have his revenge.

Jane opened her mouth to scream; only she recognized the calming voice in her ear, deep and endearing, "Miss Bellevue, will you dance with me?"

29

---

*L*ord Keegain again spied Miss Bellevue's lithe form across the dance floor, and made his way towards her. They were both in masks, he thought. Who would know if he danced with her? There was anonymity in the mask and freedom in the dance.

"Miss Bellevue, will you dance with me?" Lord Keegain said quietly, and led Jane toward the floor.

When he approached, the poor girl looked frightened half out of her wits. Perhaps she had seen something? Something to frighten her? He needed to know what it was. As the earl, the safety of his guests was of paramount importance.

If the villains were about to strike, he needed to know and quickly, so that he might alert Reynold's men. He glanced across the floor, his sisters were encircled with his mother and Lord and Lady Battonsbury. He spotted Reynolds and his brother, Lord Wortingham with Margret. They were safe. It was with that thought in mind that he was able to take a moment to calm Miss Bellevue.

"My... my Lord Keegain?" Jane looked at him for confirmation and he nodded. No doubt his monstrous mask had frightened her, but now she let out a breath and gripped his arm tightly. She was, at least pleased to see him, despite his botched apology, and that filled him with a sense of pride.

"Are you ill, madam?" he asked as they prepared to line up for the opening notes.

"No." The word came out a rushed breath. She gathered herself and tried again. "That is to say... I fear I do not know my own mind. I felt.... I felt as though something was amiss." She shook her head, causing an abundance of feathers to flap in every direction. "I am sorry, my lord, I really do not know what came over me. I expect I was overcome by the music and the proximity of so many people. It is quite the crush."

"I suppose that it is a bit stuffy in here, with all the windows closed." Lord Keegain conceded, looking over the sea of faces.

Miss Bellevue frowned. She was indeed out of sorts.

"Are you sure you are quite all right?"

"Yes," she said still a little breathless, as they took their places.

It was unaccountably warm, but he did not want to open windows, not only because of the biting cold outside, but due to the fact that the traitor might allow some of his compatriots into the room. Or perhaps escape.

The dance began. Keegain bowed and dipped and spun as the cadence required and reached out his hand to Jane. She took it and he felt her slender gloved fingers in his own. He grasped them gently, only too happy to be touching her again, even so innocently as this.

There was no explanation for it, but holding her hand made him want to smile. Too soon, it was time to separate as the strictures of the dance required, but soon enough they were reunited as the music played on.

"I think, my lord, I am unaccustomed to so many people so closely together. In truth, the dances I have attended are somewhat less..."

"Crowded?" Lord Keegain supplied helpfully.

"Less well-attended." Jane laughed lightly, but the laugh was enough to send a warmth down his spine. "Especially by so august a crowd," she added in a whisper.

Lord Keegain was sure he was not supposed to have heard that last part. It was said with such a heavy weight, it made him start. The dance pattern at that moment called for the couples to be looking aside, so Miss Bellevue did not see his reaction, and truthfully, she might have missed it anyway for the way the mask hid his features and his expressions.

The mask also helped in other ways. He was able to gaze at her without seeming to stare. The dress she wore was lovely, but the color was truly striking. The purple alone made her stand out like royalty, although the earl was sure he would notice her in anything. Miss Bellevue's strength and bearing overshadowed any other lady in the room.

The dance came to an end, and Lord Keegain was

suddenly and unaccountably sad to hear the final notes playing. He knew that he must leave her. He bowed to her curtsy, but they moved toward each other unwilling to part. In the silence that followed, the dancers applauded politely and the musicians smiled and nodded to their accolades, but Keegain had the unworthy thought that it was not the musicians the couples approved of, but each other.

Keegain was transported back to another time, a freer time when the world was his; when the earldom was still his father's, and when he was at liberty to choose his companions as he wished. Would that he could still do as he chose.

"The crowd of popinjays applaud the end of a set," he had once told Fitzwilliam in dogmatic manner worthy of Master Thomas, "because they are always startled that everyone else was successfully able to maneuver without crashing into each other like so many drunken draft horses."

"Do you often feed your draft horses an excess of spirts, then?" Fitzwilliam had inquired out of the corner of his mouth, while to all intents and purposes attending their professor.

Keegain was not so lucky. He broke out in a loud guffaw, nearly spitting on Master Thomas himself. This action caused him a detention, as Master Thomas did not approve of mockery. The story, told again, had Fitzwilliam in stitches. Yet, in all the years since, Lord Keegain had never seen a reason to alter his views on the fallaciousness of balls. Until now: until this dance, with Jane which had seemingly changed everything. Suddenly, the ball he hosted seemed less a duty of nobility and more like a gift: a wondrous and marvelous heavenly gift.

He had not felt so free since he was a boy. He could ask her to dance again, and no one would be the wiser. He could even waltz with her. Thank heavens for the masks. He could not stop smiling, until he saw her tense face. Even with the mask over her features, he could sense the tightness in her shoulders, the way she held herself apart.

Something had upset her. Or someone more like, he thought uncharitably. "Miss Bellevue," he said, approaching her cautiously. "If you forgive me for saying so, you seem uneasy. Might I suggest something cool to drink? It should help take away the residue of your discomfort. There is wassail punch or wine if you prefer?"

Jane seemed to think about it more intently than the question merited. Finally she nodded, the feathers bouncing and fighting one another as she moved. "Thank you, my lord." She nearly curtsied again. She was certainly distressed.

"Punch or wine?" Lord Keegain asked.

"Wine please," she answered after a brief hesitation. Was she fortifying herself, he wondered?

"Wait but a moment," he said, but he did not want to leave her alone, even for that brief instant.

"Have you seen my sisters?" he asked. "Charlotte?"

"I do not know," Jane answered, and so with a nod Lord Keegain stepped away to secure two glasses. A footman carrying a tray was only a few paces away. If Miss Bellevue had seen or heard something that had set off this mood, he needed to know. He returned to her side, only a few minor drops falling from the cups. "Here we are."

He handed her the glass and took out his handkerchief to assure no drops of wine fell on her dress. Again, he felt the thrill of her touch as she took the cup and beamed up at him.

With his handkerchief he gently wiped the droplets of wine from the edge before it might stain her gloves. He wanted to bring those fingers to his mouth and kiss them, to suck away the taste of wine from her skin. Her eyes darkened under her mask, and they were already impossibly deep. He knew she was remembering the same moment as he, when he had brought her bare hand to his lips outside of her bedchamber and stole a sweet taste of her.

The music started again, lively and quick and featuring a flute. While the group was highly skilled, the high-pitched instrument did hinder conversation.

Lord Keegain leaned in to speak to her, his lips nearly at her ear. He could kiss her behind the ear, he thought. They were masked. No one would know. He would know and he could not. He spoke.

"Could I prevail upon you to move to the far end of the ballroom?" He said into her ear. Miss Bellevue whirled on him and he could see the whiteness of her eyes behind her mask. "No need to panic," he assured her. "We will be quite visible." Had he so upset her by coming to her bedchamber door? He had not meant to do so.

"You are the host. It would not do to have you

disappear. I would not harm your reputation," the girl said under her breath.

Yes, he thought, he had come to her room and now she was nervous around him. He did not wish her to feel so. "Nor would I endanger yours. You have my word. Come," he said taking her lovely slim gloved hand within his own.

She nodded and let him hold her hand. The heat of it moved him in ways that Lady Margret's touch never did. Silently, they picked their way through the crowd until they were at the far end of the hall, further away from the music, but still able to be seen by many of the ballroom guests.

"Thank you." Keegain was relieved that they were more easily heard. "I simply wondered, Miss Bellevue, if there was something that had upset you?"

She blinked and looked away and seemed about to say something when she shook her head and smiled instead. "No, my lord, no I was just a little... flushed from the excitement, I fear. Please forgive me that weakness."

"I would forgive you anything," he said honestly.

Lord Keegain thought he should have been relieved that nothing was amiss, but all he could consider at that perfect moment was her person. Even from behind the mask, he was only too aware of how Jane looked up at him. Her eyes were truly so large and bright and liquid that they seemed to hold the secret to the mysteries of the world. He had not remembered them so bright; yet they seemed now to shine. Perhaps it was the rich purple of her dress and the peacock feathers that accented her dark features. Her breath raised her bosom, and the jewels resting there rose and fell, sparkling in the light.

For a moment, the sound of the dancers and the music and revelers all seemed to fade, and only Jane and her lips existed; reddened with the wine. Lord Keegain imagined how it would taste on her lips. Her scent was heightened with the heat of the room, and he wanted to breathe her in, to taste the skin of her bare neck and shoulders. He wished to see her dressed in only jewels, and to remove even that from her and muss her hair. He shifted nearer. It was as though he was drawn to her by some ancient and undeniable force. He brushed a thumb under her chin, tilting her face to his. She seemed so...

"My lord," she said quietly, and put her hand on the middle of his chest. Her hand was small and warm. She surely could feel his heart beating in her palm. She must, for the organ pounded within his chest. He wanted to kiss her, but she deserved better than stolen kisses.

Jane deserved everything. Still, he caught her other hand and shifted further into the alcove beyond. The hallway led to the gardens. It did not matter that the corridor was cool, in fact, it was preferable. Heat was coursing through him as he pulled her close, and she came; without protest. She came to his arms.

His lips brushed hers at first, a chaste touch, as if he could just touch her and be done, but a fire took hold of him and pulsed through him as he tasted her. She was so sweet and when she innocently parted her lips to allow him entrance, he was undone. He crushed her to him and plunged his tongue into the warmth of her. He wanted all of her.

His body sang with her touch. Her fingers reached past the mask to his hair. She touched him; clung to him. Sweet heavens, he had never felt such bliss. It took him a moment to realize that her hand had left his hair. It was back on his chest. There was a hesitation in her, a trembling motionlessness he did not want to feel.

She startled, as if she only just realized what they had done. Her hand was still on his chest and she snatched it back. It was colder over his heart now, colder and emptier.

Jane stepped back slowly.

The corridor was still as stone.

The music and the dancers and the noise of the ball flooded back, so loud for a moment, Keegain would have run mad from the overwhelming sound of it.

"I cannot... I think," she stammered. Her lower lip trembled, bruised by his kiss. She drew a shuddering breath. "I should return. I thank you for the dance." She curtseyed.

She curtseyed as if they had not just kissed, as if his world had not been upended.

"It was just what I needed to... to clear my head."

"And is it clear, then?" He spoke through a dry throat. His certainly was not. His head was filled with her. Only Jane, and he had never been more confused.

"It is, my lord."

So blasted formal, he thought.

"I cannot...and I would not..." Her voice broke and she cleared her throat again. "I would not keep you from Lady Margret. I would not wish to create any undo...." She faltered again, and then gained control of herself.

259

This time her voice was sure. "Thank you for the dance." She curtsied once again, and shot him a pleading glance. He did not know what it was for which she pleaded, only that he felt the same inexpressible need.

Lady Margret indeed. The name gave Keegain a moment's pause and cooled his desires. He took his own deep breath, wishing he had delivered Jane back to his mother or the Lady Battonsbury, but the girl had turned and fled so quickly, he was still held within a daze.

Feathers flying, he watched Jane's bright dress disappear into the milling crowd and vanish from sight. He should not have let her go. He fought the desire to chase after her, to pull her back into his arms and kiss her again in the very center of the ballroom for all to see, propriety be damned. He hoped she found her way back to his sisters or her other friends.

Keegain stood alone as the party continued around him, a solitary figure in a little pocket of stillness, as his guests laughed and danced around him.

"Yes." He said to the place where Jane once stood. "Lady Margret." He nodded again and snatched a drink from a passing footman. He downed it in one swallow. "Her."

He turned and scanned the crowd. Not for Margret nor Jane, although he struggled with the latter. He had once again overstepped the bounds of propriety. Overstepped hell. He had dived happily over the cliffside, found himself fallen and did not know what there was to do about it now. He only knew his lips still burned for want of her touch, and he would never taste wine again without also tasting her lips. Never had his vow to

Margret been so repugnant. Blast it all. He needed male company.

He sought out another solitary figure, Fitzwilliam. The gentleman was already well smitten to his own lady fair. Perhaps Fitz knew something of this feeling, some way to navigate the quagmire, because Keegain felt his path was now most precarious.

Part 4

Sapphires & Snow

30

*W*hy? Jane thought. Why after telling herself so many times that the earl was not the right man for her, did her heart have to insist otherwise? He had kissed her, and she had not protested. Oh no. She had felt transported. Bliss exploded across her tongue and filled her to bursting. She had clung to him feeling the strength of him corded beneath her hands. She had melted into his arms and wanted it to last forever, but of course, it could not.

It seemed to not matter what she told herself anymore, or even what her own eyes told her. Her traitorous heart insisted on a strange stutter when he was near. She lost the ability to think coherently, or even to breathe properly. And invariably, here she stood again, running away from what she knew she must. Tears began to collect in her eyes, and although she knew her mask would hide them, she blinked them back and sought a quiet corner.

Jane was so absurdly grateful that the house party

would end on the morrow. She could return home, and forget Lord Keegain and the heated emotions he raised in her. The thought brought a sharp pain to her breast. Her fingers rose to her lips. They still tingled with the earl's kiss. She could never forget him. She did not wish to. She would cherish the sensation of his lips on hers for as long as she lived.

Jane slipped to the back of the room, winding up in a small alcove, tucked away behind the drapes. She had found the spot quite by accident and disappeared into it now, looking for respite, for a chance to dry her tears and regain mastery of her emotions. Without the lights of the ballroom behind her, she could see outside if she pressed her forehead to the glass, she did so now, thankful for the icy chill that crept through her.

It was snowing outside, the wind not having abated in the least. Tiny icy flecks rattled against the glass, sounding for all the world like a patter of pebbles. The snow was not soft flakes then, but freezing rain.

A part of her longed to escape out into the storm, that she might lose herself forever in the swirl of ice and snow. Not that she wished for disaster to fall upon her. Rather, she was tired of the constant conflict, the way Lord Keegain had come into her life and somehow spoiled every other man just by his being in the world. Although not in her world, Jane reminded herself.

It was a foolish statement and made her smile. Maybe she did read too many romance novels. He was an earl; she was only plain Jane Bellevue. Somehow, she had gotten caught up in the idea of a love match, and convinced herself that there could be some future for the pair of them. Jane needed to be much more practical than that. She needed someone kind and solid. The earl was kind, her heart argued. Had not he seen her distress and come to collect her? He was certainly solid, she thought, remembering the feel of his arms beneath his coat when he wrapped her in his embrace.

Her heart still raced. He kissed her, she realized, but so had she kissed him. She certainly had not moved away or struck his face for such an offense. No, she had opened to him like a flower to the sun, and for one wonderful, breathless moment, there was only the two of them caught in the heat of passion. The thought startled Jane, for she had not thought herself one to be controlled by her desires in such a way.

A dance, a small amount of conversation, a single heated kiss, and she was lost. She realized that if Lord Keegain came to her chamber tonight, she would find it much harder to close the door than she had previously. It was as if the passion was much stronger than she. Did he feel the same?

"My lady," said one of the under footmen who was offering an assortment of drinks on a tray. She chose a glass of wine. White.

"Thank you, Mr. Hernon," she said.

He shot her a grin, recognizing her when she spoke. "You are most welcome, Miss Bellevue."

He moved on, serving other guests.

She sipped the wine and tried to calm her nerves. Her gaze returned to the window and the world outside. The storm had worsened. Ice clung to the trees, making them look like they were encased in glass. She wondered if there were guests who had come expecting to drive home later tonight. Surely not. They would have to stay as well. Possibly for more than one day. The land was a glittering expanse of ice. It looked quite beautiful, and dangerous.

Jane might have to stay as well, no matter that it was clear now that she must leave. She could no longer stay in his house. There might be more days in his company, more days to suffer seeing him and Lady Margret together. More days, and nights, where he might come to call upon her at her chamber door. Or days he would not.

Still, Jane stifled a sob. It was all so confusing. She could not stand anymore. She did not wish to meet other gentlemen. Had not that been clear when she had turned down the knight, and even more so when she had danced with the pirate? Her heart refused all but Lord Keegain.

She had even invented in her mind strange tensions and worked herself up to the point of a fright, all to find an excuse to leave, to not have to dance, only to find herself in the arms of the very man that had left her so overwrought in the first place.

She had no idea what to do. To return to the ball now seemed impossible. She untied her mask and wiped her tears before replacing it. She was sure her face was blotchy, but the mask would cover it. Still, she could not bear to return. Much as her father expected her to marry well, and her sister counted on her to do so, she would rather remain a spinster forever than to unite herself with someone, anyone who was not Lord Keegain.

Well, I cannot stay here, Jane thought. It was cold in the nook by the window and sooner or later she would be discovered. What then? *Am I a literal wallflower, perched here?*

Jane thought a moment. She could not return to her room, not without drawing attention to herself. Midnight would be the unmasking. *I will endure then, for a time longer, but I cannot...I absolutely cannot stay in this press of people until then.*

There had to be some small parlor or room nearby that would be less crowded, where she would be less likely to see *him* again. Jane remembered Lady Charlotte's tour. She would find a place where the conversation was quieter, where the expectations were less. No one could fault her for that.

Not the ladies' sitting room though. Her friends would only express concern, or press her to find a new dance partner. They would never understand. Not with the dowagers either. She noted the Dowager Lady Keegain had brought the older ladies all into her fold. There was nowhere to go to find privacy.

Thus decided, Jane slipped from her alcove and found a tray upon which to leave her glass. Then making a wide circle around the edges of the room, she found a back corridor and a series of doors that she had hitherto not explored. Frowning a little, she chose one at random, one that seemed tucked away, a little less unobtrusive than the rest.

Jane discovered her mistake almost immediately. The room was as chill as the alcove near the window. A cautious look inside showed furniture draped with sheets, towering forms, indistinct in the dim light from the hall. She was about to turn to go when she heard a voice behind her. Lord Keegain, talking with another man.

She could not endure another conversation with him. Not now. With a hasty glance behind her, she saw the earl, just outside the ballroom. That she had heard him above the noise from within was a miracle. That he had not seen her there, in the shadows of the open door a godsend.

Desperate to escape him, wondering why he seemed to be at every turn when there were so many other places he could be, Jane slipped into the empty room and shut the door behind her as quietly as she could. He would be gone in but a minute. She could escape then and find some other place to settle.

Oddly enough, the light did not fade once the door was closed. It took her a moment to realize that the flickering glow came from a candle somewhere on the other side of the furniture. Appalled that someone might have left an untended flame in what was clearly an unused room, Jane stepped further into the chamber, intent upon rescuing the flame before a fire started. Her thought went to that night in the library, when Keegain had rescued her candle. The burn was long healed. It was such a small thing, but the night had seared her heart. He had touched her that night, and kissed her hand. Now, he had held her in his arms and kissed her lips. She could not undo what was done. Worse, she did not wish to do so.

She was stopped a moment later by an unfamiliar voice, deep and masculine, from somewhere just to her left.

"You have chosen, then?"

The voice was one not known to her. Jane turned to go. Whatever conversation they were having was none of her concern. That someone else had thought to escape the ball for a moment of privacy was of no consequence to her.

"It was easy enough. In a ball of this nature it is a simple matter to determine quality. I am sure she is the one. I recognized the sapphires at once. The father dotes upon the girl. He will pay."

What?

Jane had turned to go but was stopped by the response from the first man.

"Good, then there should be no problem obtaining the gold. Not like last time."

Gold? Last time? The conversation had taken a sinister turn. Jane paused, reversing direction and creeping closer that she might hear more clearly.

"It was hardly my fault they had no means to pay. They hid it from society well enough. That the father had gambled away the bulk of the estate was not on me. Trust me on this one. There is no doubt as to her quality. In fact, someone so brazen deserves what she gets. She wears at her throat jewels enough to feed a country, and I have never seen a lady festooned with quite so many peacock feathers."

Feathers? Jane's hand went to her mask and then to Lady Amelia's jewels at her neck.

"When shall we take her?"

"Soon as the carriage is brought around."

Carriage? Take her? They were talking about her,

there was no doubt. Jane backed toward the door, her heart in her throat. She had stumbled upon something terrible. Something terrifying. It was all she could do to not scream, though she felt the sound, trapped in her throat, only waiting to be set free.

"Deuced bad weather..."

"Good. None will follow."

Jane backed carefully toward the door. She would run...fetch the earl. He must know that there were terrible people were within his house. Terrible people who planned...she could not finish the thought. Oh surely, this was not happening!

She knew she should not have borrowed Lady Amelia's jewels. She should have been demure and herself! Those feathers! Those terrible feathers! She longed to wrench the mask from her face and cast it away, but they would know then that she had been here. Oh why had she chosen something so gaudy, so ostentatious for her costume? And the jewels! What had seemed a good idea, to draw the attention of an eligible man, seemed so foolish now.

Biting her lip so hard it bled, Jane whirled to go, her hands already seeking for the doorknob and finding it with relief. Only the door opened under her questing hand and the man that entered was one she recognized. The pirate stood in the doorway, as startled by Jane's unexpected presence as she was by his. She was flooded with fear. She opened her mouth to speak, to beg him to take her to the earl that they might resolve this whole matter. Instead he grabbed her arm roughly, jerking her with him into the room, and shutting the door behind him.

"Here, now gentlemen, we have a spy in our midst," he called out as he dragged Jane into the light. "It looks as if our prey has come to us!"

⁓✦⁓

31

*L*ord Keegain had found Fitzwilliam, but now he turned away from the man in agitation, pacing the corridor.

"I do not believe that you have the right of it," Lord Keegain insisted.

"Or perhaps I do, and you simply do not care to listen?" Fitzwilliam retorted. He followed Keegain, speaking through his ridiculous mask which made all of his words blurred and muted. "Set aside any... outside influence at all. Your problem, old boy, is that you have found someone that you desire more than..." he looked around uncomfortably. "Well, more than your betrothed." It seemed near impossible to say even that much. "That tells me, and should tell you, that you are not certain of your chosen bride."

"I barely know her."

"Lady Margret? You have known her your entire life."

"Not Margret...."

Fitzwilliam caught at his arm. "Quietly, old boy," Fitz

said through the mask. "Remember, we are not discussing just any man. In point of fact, we are discussing you." He took a breath and tried to clarify. "She matters to you. Another woman matters to you so much so that you could forget you are already engaged."

Fitzwilliam turned to face Keegain, his tone for once solemn and serious, "An engagement, I might add, that has already many tongues set to wagging, wondering if you refuse to set a date because you simply do not wish to marry the lady."

His words hit the mark a little keener than the earl expected, but to agree would be to give credence to something he was not quite ready to accept. Keegain shook his head, he needed to justify his feeling, so that he might lie to himself a little bit longer. "I do not follow."

"Of course you do," Fitzwilliam said with no small amount of patience. "Do not be dense, man. I cannot wait to return home. I cannot wait to speak again with my beloved, to touch her, to kiss her, to hold her within my arms. If I could not touch her I would content myself to just sit across a table and gaze upon her."

Unbidden, the thought of Jane seated across the breakfast table came to him.

Fitz continued. "We set a date as soon as the banns could be announced, because I am anxious for her to be my wife. I long to take her into my home, my family, my bed."

"Ah, but you are blessed," Keegain said bitterly.

"And you are engaged." Fitzwilliam countered. "These two states do not have to be mutually exclusive. You can be wed *and* happy, my friend."

Keegain shook his head. "That is the exception, not the rule amongst the *Ton*. Most do not marry for love."

"Do you not think you could be that exception?" Fitz implored him.

The music swelled and swallowed Keegain's reply. He turned back toward the dancers, staring at them without seeing them. The music rose in a crescendo and he had to wait until the music evened out again, that he might speak without shouting. The moment gave him time to think. "Perhaps." He shrugged. "Let us even say I agree with you. That still leaves me in an awkward situation."

"However awkward, is better than the alternative, would you not say?"

"I gave my word to Lady Margret. If I break it..." He let the statement hang.

"No doubt her father will bring a lawsuit against you," Fitz finished. "Make no mistake, this will cost you, Keegain."

Keegain shuddered. Yes, Fitzwilliam was right. Margret's father would probably sue him for breach of promise. And he would be right to do so. When a couple was engaged as long as himself and Margret, they were as good as married. At least, certain assumptions were made as to the lady's virtue. Other suitors would be wary. Margret would have to wait nearly a year before accepting another offer, just to prove she was not with child. Even then, tongues would wag. Many would not think her pure, no matter that it was the truth. No matter how honorable he was, or she, it would not stop the talk.

"I truly have made a mess of things, Fitz." He muttered. "This is awful."

"Still better than a lifetime of regret," Fitz pressed.

Lord Keegain considered the utter indifference he felt towards Margret, interspaced with moments of annoyance and pure disgust. How had it come to that? And then, there was Jane...

"You are thinking loudly," Fitz said and Keegain sighed.

"I realized within these past weeks that my thoughts are on someone else. Not my intended bride and frankly, Fitz, I want what you have." Lord Keegain added that last under his breath.

The words came hard but with considerable relief. His friend was right. He did not love Lady Margret. He was entering a loveless marriage for the sake of what, wealth? He had enough of that. Power? He had his title and his estates; Margret's family was powerful, but her lineage would have done little to raise his position.

Was it just a matter of honor then? His word and his father's deathbed wish? Keegain's father made him promise to marry well, and he had so wished the families to be joined. His sentiments mirrored those of Margret's mother. So Keegain had contacted Margret's father. The man had agreed.

Keegain had known Margret from childhood, introductions were not thought to be necessary. However, it was also true that no one had consulted Margret, merely telling her the news when the declarations were made, and she was roundly congratulated for her engagement. She was so young. They both were. That was the year she had been sent to finishing school. She came home to a betrothed. It was possible that she did not love him. Probable even. Did she long for more as well?

"It is not the way things are done," Keegain lamented.

"True." Fitzwilliam nodded and then smiled.

The earl thought he now understood that smile. "No, not for you, Fitz. You would wed on your own terms. Tell me, my friend, how did you do so?"

"In defiance of convention?" Fitz scratched his chin. "I suppose it was easier that my parents are no longer with us, but I am sure my mother would have loved Mary. Though for you, my friend, you must know that your mother wants you to be happy? And there must be some advantage to lineage. What nattering the *Ton* goes through should have little enough effect in your case. Truth be told, the *Ton* has not been overly kind to either of us. Still, they do not matter. I simply did as I wished. You may do the same. Your father is gone, Keegain," Fitz said softly. "He would want you to be happy. Above all, he would want that for his son."

"Margret's father shall be livid."

"Yes, but in the end, the man wants her happiness too. Speak with her, Keegain. I would venture, that she is not pleased with this engagement either. You are an earl, and the title of countess shall be a hard loss, but Lady Margret knows you would make each other miserable. In fact, you are already well on your way toward that end."

"Gentlemen," Ted Reynolds approached them both from the direction of the door. Keegain looked at him and the entirety of the cloak and dagger plot came back to him in a rush. The earl stood ready as if some villain were to leap from behind a curtain.

Reynolds shook his head at Keegain's unspoken question. "No, nothing has happened as of yet, but I do have a rather dreadful feeling... as though I'd overlooked something. I cannot place my finger on it now, but something is not right."

"Have you seen any disturbance?" Fitz asked, but Reynolds again shook his head to the negative.

"There is not a single thing I can reveal; nothing I can point to, and I have just made the rounds, speaking to all my men," Reynolds explained, "but if my instinct is correct, something foul is afoot, and it seemed prudent to involve you gentlemen."

Ted was experienced in these matters, and there was much to be said for acting instinctively.

Lord Keegain stood a little straighter and scanned the crowd. The other two watched as his eyes searched over the revelers, but when he would have taken a chair to stand on, they both drew the line.

"I spoke to Lady Margret not ten minutes ago, and I see all of your sisters," Reynolds said as he continued to scan the crowd, his shoulders tense.

Lord Keegain shook his head. "I do not see her!" Keegain protested. Panicked, he turned to his friends. "Fitz, she's not here. Ted!"

He did not use her name. Not that he needed to do so, for Fitz would understand without lengthy explanation. Reynolds, on the other hand, was confused.

Still, both men understood the need for discretion; there were still people near, drinking punch, talking as though the world itself were not ending. Conversations were going on about other Christmas parties happening during the twelve days of Christmas, and gifts and services to come. Some spoke of who would be seated next to whom at certain dinners as though such a thing were important.

Lord Keegain felt Fitzwilliam's hand on his arm. The man's voice in his ear was both urgent and assured. "Calm yourself man. I am sure there is a logical reason."

"Be easy. I see Lady Margret," Reynolds said, relief evident in his own stance.

"No, not Margret," Keegain said.

"About whom are we speaking?" Reynolds looked from one man to the other in confusion.

"Miss Jane Bellevue." Fitzwilliam said, with a stern glance toward Lord Keegain.

He understood despite seeing so little of Fitz's eyes through the mask.

"I would not recognize her," Reynolds said, but he craned his head to look all the same. "What is she dressed as?"

"The girl with the peacock feathered mask and fan." Lord Keegain answered hurriedly, his eyes still scanning the crowd.

"Oh, yes, I did see her tonight, come to think of it. She entered the ball with your sister, Lady Charlotte." Ted turned toward the crowd surveying it and shaking his head. "Still, she is not the sort to be taken, Keegain. I would not worry. Previously, the abductees have all been ladies of worth."

"She is of worth to me," the earl spat.

Reynolds turned back to Keegain, confused by his sudden ire, and Fitz explained. "Keegain is enamored.

He went to speak to the girl in her room as I stood guard."

"You what?" Reynolds spun to Keegain. He looked for all the world as if he wanted to take a swing at the earl.

"The venerable Lord Keegain has slipped from his honorable perch," Fitz teased.

"Margret was cruel to her," the earl said miserably. "I wished to apologize. To assure her that we are not all so uncouth."

"Uncouth?" Reynolds repeated in a low tone. "Lady Margret is your intended."

"Not for long," Fitz said gaily. "Chin up, old boy." He patted Reynolds on the back. "You may have your chance."

"Fitz." Keegain hissed between his teeth, and his friend sensed his anger. With villains in the house there was no time for levity. "Not now!" Keegain admonished. He turned to Reynolds. "Could they have taken her?"

Reynold's jaw was clenched.

"Ted?" Keegain pressed, urging the man to think.

It took Reynolds a moment to change from friend to the King's man, but he made the switch. "I suppose they could have made a mistake, but I am sure she has come to no harm, Keegain. She is not worth..."

At Keegain's glare, he corrected himself. "I mean to say, they are looking for heiresses. Her family is distantly related to a lesser peerage and not greatly wealthy to hear your sisters speak of it. Why would they take *her*?"

"Because it is a masked ball," Keegain spat through clenched teeth. "No one can see who she is, and she wore a necklace of sapphires." He realized now that the jewelry could not have been her own. Even peacock feathers were expensive. "The jewels must have been borrowed."

His distress took up residence in his throat and roughened his tone. "Now that I think of it, they were far too expensive for her family to afford. They were a veritable cascade of diamonds and sapphires." As Keegain described the set, the Duke of Ely joined their conversation.

"Amelia's," he said, recognizing the description. "She must have loaned them to her friend."

"Blast it all," Keegain swore, feeling all the more helpless.

"Steady on," Fitzwilliam cautioned him. "Do not assume the worst. Miss Bellevue might have wandered off. Likely she's in the ladies' retiring room or returned to her own chamber."

"That is true," Reynolds said. "There are endless possibilities in a house this size."

"I suppose you are right," Keegain said to him, "but I have your uncertainty. You sensed something amiss."

"I do," Reynolds said. "My men shall keep watch on this crowd. I will go with you myself and search for the lady. Come. We shall find her."

"I shall tell Amelia," the duke said, "Perhaps she has seen her friend."

Reynolds nodded unobtrusively to a young man who made his way through the dancers to his side. The three conferred with one another for a moment before Reynolds sent the young agent back to his station and the duke also parted company. The musicians were winding down between songs as the three of them slipped out of the ballroom and gathered near the door to Keegain's study.

Keegain stripped off his mask and opened the door that he might toss it inside. "I will see if she has returned to her rooms." He looked to Reynolds who raised a brow. "I know you cannot be too far from your men, and I thank you for your contribution. I suggest you look in these immediate rooms."

The earl turned to his other friend. "Fitz, find Davies. He knows of the danger. If you would be so kind as to check with him. He will have the servants in hand. Find out if anyone saw Miss Bellevue, or noticed something amiss. Someone may have entered through the kitchen, although I believe Reynolds had a man stationed there."

Reynolds nodded and then the men dispersed.

The earl turned quickly, heading for the stairs.

Jane was in danger. He could feel it.

32

---

*P*ropriety be damned, Keegain thought. Miss Bellevue had not responded to his pounding on her door. First, thinking to ascertain that she was not dead, and then apologize for effrontery, he wrenched the door open and ran into the room calling her name.

The chamber was empty, save for a few odds and ends lying neatly folded. No sign of foul play, then. At first he wondered if the few things were all the luggage she brought. At first glance it was far sparser than the trunks with which his sisters would ever travel to another's home.

The wind lashed ice against the window, and looked to soon smash its way inside. From habit, he drew the heavy curtains closed against the storm.

Just to be sure, he looked under the bed and in the wardrobe. The dresses that hung there were pretty enough, but more sturdy than elegant. If the villains had taken Jane, what would they do when they found out that her father could ill-afford the handsome ransom they hoped for?

I shall pay it. He made the words a solemn vow. Propriety be damned. After all, she was his guest, was she not? He was responsible for her safety. It was rationalization at its best, and he chose to not examine it too closely. There were certainly more important matters at stake here. Wherever she was, she was not here.

He stood still for a moment to think. Rushing around in circles was not going to avail anyone of anything. The problem was, there was no other logical place for her to have gone.

It occurred to him that she might likely have already been found by one of the others. She might have stepped away from the dancing for a moment; for some air. She might have been in the retiring room. There were a dozen reasonable explanations, but somehow he knew the fiends had taken her.

The wind beat against the window as Keegain closed the door on the empty room. He hurried back downstairs to the entryway to see Fitzwilliam rush in from the kitchen area.

"She was not in her room," Keegain said. "Did anyone see anything at all?"

"No. One of the footmen saw her earlier, but no one since." Fitzwilliam shook his head. "You should see the chaos back there in the kitchen, Keegain. I never knew the amount of insanity that existed behind the scenes of a ball like this. White says no one came through the kitchens, but I doubt that anyone would have noticed an invasion of Huns through that calamitous mess."

"Then where the devil…"

"Keegain," Reynolds called. He came through the door from the ballroom, but he was not alone. As the music from the other room carried into the entrance, Reynolds led a distraught Lady Margret by the wrist. Keegain never remembered Reynolds laying a hand on Margret. He doubted she would have allowed it, but now Reynolds seemed quite in command of the situation.

"Repeat to them what you told me." Ted looked at her sternly and spoke so sharply that Keegain glanced at him in surprise.

"Please don't be angry with me," she said to Reynolds with a measure of softness that Lord Keegain had forgotten she had.

"What is it, Margret?" the earl demanded, and the girl quailed; even more so when she saw the look on his face, but she complied.

"That… that common girl, Jane." She swallowed and rushed on, "She left. At least I assume it was her, she was still wearing the peacock feathers. Where she got such an outfit…"

"Left?" Keegain was incredulous. In this weather? No one in their right mind would leave with the storm at its height. In fact, there was not a single guest who was not staying the night at this point. He had ordered every horse to be taken from the carriages, and brought into the stables and bedded down where they too could be warm and dry. "What do you mean left?"

"She… she had a riding cloak thrown over her and… and a man was with her. I did not know him, but I assumed he was a guest. He was in costume. A pirate. She may have been...struggling. I thought perhaps it was a lark."

"Struggling?" The earl's voice was a low growl. He did not have time for Margret. Her information was slow in coming and right now, time was all that mattered. He reached for her before he even realized he was about to do so. He grasped her shoulder and turned her to him. "Margret, what did you see?" he snapped.

"Easy, Keegain," Reynolds reached for Keegain to disengage his grasp. Keegain allowed it, but might not have if Margret had not answered.

"I do not know! Three men, all in masks. I mean, we all are, aren't we? But these were plain. Black masks. I had not expected to see anything so plain here, and so I noticed. I mean... I did not realize...how could I have? It seemed so odd for them to be taking her." She glanced at the men, looking from one face to another, her own face pale beneath her mask which she touched with trembling fingertips as though hiding behind it would protect her somehow. "Why do you look at me that way? I could not possibly know any more than that. I swear to it."

"How long ago?" Keegain was loud now, his voice carrying above the music in the other room. He was drawing attention from the guests in the ballroom. He saw several heads turn in his direction, but he was long past caring for civility. Margret seemed to wither under his glare.

"Keegain," Reynolds said with an irritating calm. He laid a hand on Keegain's shoulder and addressed

Margret. "When was this? I pray you think carefully. It is important."

"About... ten minutes? No more than a quarter hour." Reynolds put an arm around Lady Margret, drawing her away even as her hands came up to cover her mouth and tears welled in her eyes.

"Good," Reynolds said. "That is good. Thank you for telling us, Lady Margret."

She was crying, Keegain realized, and he did not care. Not now. Not after all her cruelties. She had seen Jane struggling and done nothing. In fact, she had waited to tell anyone. His heart grew cold within his breast, and if he had not already been debating the matter of their engagement, this would have ended it. He could never marry anyone who could act so callously. Then the realization hit him.

"A quarter hour is too long. They have a good head start on us." Lord Keegain began to turn, to initiate a pursuit regardless, but it occurred to him that he had no idea where to start. He spun back to Margret to ask. "Which way?"

"There." She pointed an accusing finger down a hallway that lead beneath the stairs.

Keegain turned to Reynolds. "That way leads to an external door and is close to the stables. If they had a carriage ready, they could be far from here."

"Didn't you have all the carriages unhitched and the horses bedded?" Fitz asked.

"Yes. Yes," Keegain said gaining some measure of hope.

"It is good that you ordered the stable lads to unhitch

all the horses and to take them out of the storm. Maybe that delayed them."

"Still, they will take a carriage," Reynolds said. "They could not keep a woman captive on horseback, and why should they. They have no notion that they will be followed so soon."

"We can catch them on horseback. Gather your men and follow," Keegain ordered. "I will take some men from the stables and initiate pursuit. Come, Fitz!"

"What shall I do?" Margret looked between them.

He turned on his heel, spitting one last comment over his shoulder at her. "You, madam, have already contributed much more than your fair share to this evening."

"I am sorry," she said.

"Are you?" Keegain spat. "Or are you just glad that she is gone?"

Margret seemed to wither under his gaze.

Keegain could barely look at her. He had never wanted to strike a woman, but longed to take his rage out on something. The villains were the proper outlet, he reminded himself. He would deal with Margret later. Right now, she did not matter. Only Jane mattered.

"I say, Keegain." Reynolds stepped between the two of them.

Keegain felt shame for his words, but he could not apologize. He would not. If Jane came to harm, he would never forgive her.

"Let's go," he said to Fitz. He left Margret standing shoulder to shoulder with Reynolds.

"We will follow as soon as we can," Reynolds said. "I

must inform the Duke of Ely, lest there be other brigands still in the house."

Keegain gave a short nod and spun, racing for the exit, ignoring a gasp from the small crowd who had gathered near the door and now knew something was afoot. Fitzwilliam called for their coats as he followed in his friend's wake.

Reynolds whispered a word to Lady Margret. She gathered herself and smiled at the nervous crowd. "Come," she said. "Christmas carols are to be sung. Lady Amelia promised to play a duet with me."

Reynolds slipped through the crowd.

The doors between Keegain and the stable were mere annoyances to be gotten through; each twisted open and slammed. The ice left little in the way of tracks. The world was glittering glass. At any other time, it would have been beautiful. Now, it was treacherous.

"Had we best allow Reynold's men time to join us?" Fitzwilliam shouted over the wind as they ran toward the stable.

Keegain was bent near double as he wrenched open the stable doors. The wind was howling across the mews. "I know this area, these roads. They do not. We will make twice the time they will. Reynolds can be there for the arrest, but I will not lose Jane."

Lord Keegain burst into the carriage house. "Everyone on your feet!" The earl shouted as the stablemen jumped at his intrusion. Cards scattered on the floor as the men abandoned their game. Startled exclamations followed him as Lord Keegain snagged a bridle from a nearby hook.

"My lord…" A grizzled man stepped forward. "What has happened?"

"Griswold. Saddle horses for me and Fitzwilliam and every man here who can ride or fight. Take along whatever you find to hand for a weapon. There are traitors afoot in the dark, and they have abducted Miss Bellevue. They will not defile my name or my house! We ride now and damn the men in our sights!"

The four men scrambled, shouting furious agreement with him, as they grabbed saddle blankets and tack and attempted to calm the beasts who borrowed Keegain's anxiety. They only had to quiet the animals long enough to get them outfitted.

Keegain's stallion was led to him first, followed by Fitz's nervous mount. They lead them out into the crisp feel of hard sleet propelled by the wind into a biting squall. They mounted, each horse catching the excitement of the men, and dancing in circles in their eagerness to run.

The footing was precarious with the ice against the cobblestones. Keegain felt his mounts unsteady footing and knew this pursuit for the folly that it was. If they did not break a leg, or worse, a neck, in this wild chase it would be a miracle.

"Keep your mounts to the sides of the road where the ice will be less treacherous," he shouted as he mounted up. "Follow at pace." At least he hoped the rutted ditch would be less slippery than the cobblestone road.

When the stable hands came out and mounted, Keegain looked to every man there and smiled. His people answered him, not from fear or some archaic notion of the noble class ruling the commons. Not even because he paid them. The looks on their faces were fierce and determined. His people genuinely respected him, and they would ride with him. Just then, his heart was full of admiration for these men.

"We look for a carriage with three men in black and a damsel to be fought and won. Come and let us teach these villains the name of Keegain is one that is respected and feared."

He spun his stallion and kicked the animal calling out "HAH!" The horse felt the eagerness of his rider and stretched, gathering powerful muscles under it and springing into a gallop; dashing into the night.

Fitzwilliam and the men followed like the very hounds of hell were after them.

Lord Keegain urged his mount onwards.

Danger meant nothing. Jane's life was in the balance. He pitied any who chose to stand in his way.

33

*J*ane fought. She never ceased her struggle. She had struggled as they'd dragged her from the room and into the entryway. She had tried to scream there, but her cries were muffled, stopped by the cloak and heavy hands that dared to touch her person. She bit at her assailant's fingers as he put his hand over her mouth, but his thick gloves protected him. She kicked at him as they walked her out of the house and into the cold. She had twisted and tried to lash out at them as they thrust her into the carriage. In short, she did everything she could to *not* be taken, and it was still not enough.

Finally, they threw her in the conveyance, her head striking the edge of the carriage, leaving her dazed, lying on the floor. She felt the carriage shift and rock as they climbed in after her. Two of them. The other would ride with the driver she supposed. Or for all she knew, he would return to the house, a devil in disguise, there to express shock and dismay when it turned up that one of the guests was missing. Why were they doing this?

Jane struggled to sit up, and they seemed only too glad to help her until she realized they used the opportunity to bind her hands in front of her. She shook with the cold, feeling the frigid tears upon her cheeks and she tried to stammer something coherent, but could not, for she had also come to realize something else. They were on the road, traveling swiftly down the long drive through the storm, through the ice that, by now, surely lay treacherous in the deep ruts of the road.

Her mother. Her mother had died traveling a road like this, going to the side of a dear friend who was experiencing difficulty lying in, who had begged her to come, to be with her through the birth of her first child. Her own mother had died. So too, had the woman she had been set to visit. Some said it was the guilt which had killed her, leaving her babe born, but motherless within hours of its birth, just as Jane and her sister had likewise been left motherless. But now, the icy road was her least worry. The villains at her side were the more pressing danger.

"Please. Please, I do not understand what is going on," she said, speaking through chattering teeth.

The men only looked at one another and laughed. "Cover her," one said gruffly to the pirate. The one with whom she had danced. "If she freezes to death, she will not be worth so much as a farthing to us."

The pirate nodded, bending to drape the heavy cloak about Jane's shoulders.

A farthing? Was she to be ransomed then? She had

heard of such things, but her father certainly never had the means for it. Not to the extent that any other lady at the ball had. Her mask...her mask was long since gone. Surely they knew by now who she was, and what she was worth. She opened her mouth to tell them. They would have to let her go. She was not worth the bother. She had never seen their faces after all.

Then two thoughts came to her. The first being that they would likely not believe her anyway. The second, that they would as likely kill her as let her go. What would her word matter to men such as these? She would offer nothing. Jane drew back against the seat, huddling into the warmth of the cloak, raising her bound hands to try and adjust the fabric to keep out the chill.

Besides, they would just kidnap another. *Would you let them treat another in such a way? Lady Charlotte?* Oh, how Keegain would suffer if his sister were to be lost, but would anyone else's sister be a better choice? What if it were Lady Amelia or Lady Patience? Should any lady be made to suffer like this?

No, Jane could not bear the thought.

She had to think, to find some solution, but she flinched at every jolt of the carriage. Already, she thought she might be ill. To be trapped thus was frightening, but to be forced to travel in this weather at such a breakneck speed was her nightmare. The carriage slid going around a corner. Jane held her breath, and wondered if it might be her last. What had been her mother's thoughts that fateful night, when she had been taken so cruelly from her daughters?

No. Stop it. You must think. You must find a way through this.

She had to breathe. Jane took one careful breath and then another. The men were not even watching her. They sat bent with heads together, conspiring no doubt, their blades at their sides. The blades should have alerted her. No gentleman would wear a sword to a social gathering, even if it went with his costume.

Such a display was considered in poor taste. Even for a masked ball it would have been deemed too much. Why had she not noticed when she danced with the pirate? Why had she not said something to someone then?

She moaned as the carriage slipped again. How could she possibly think when the carriage could overturn at any minute, and she would be dashed to her death? There was truly no help for it. They would take her somewhere...she had no idea where...and send a demand for ransom. When none came, they would kill her, and take someone else.

Their skill now spoke of experience. Jane realized they had done this on previous occasions. There would never be an end to it; ladies' reputations ruined and lives destroyed, for the sake of a few pounds. It was infuriating and wrong, and needed to be stopped. Yet what could she do?

The horses squealed. For a moment the carriage felt precarious, like it would topple. Jane shuddered. Even the men in the carriage gasped, grasping at the seat for balance. With her hands bound, Jane had no means to do likewise. As the carriage slid on two wheels for a moment and then crashed back to the ground, she fell, slamming hard against the side of the carriage and gasping in terror and outrage. "We will all die for this!" She shrieked.

"My dear lady, when a cause is just, there is no fear of death. If Napoleon desires it, then so it shall be!"

"*Vive l'Empereur!*" They both shouted.

They were fanatics; the same sort who beheaded the nobility in France. Jane saw it now in the whites of their eyes behind the masks. Fear clutched at her, and for a moment she thought she might indeed be sick.

She swallowed hard against the bile, and knew that for the sake of the ladies of England, nay, for the sake of England itself, she had to do something. Not to save herself, for surely she could not, but for the others that would suffer if she would not.

These men would die for Napoleon if need be. Am I willing to die for a greater cause as well? How can my resolve be any less, when theirs is so badly misplaced?

Jane would have no time to think, only to act. Nor would she be afforded more than one opportunity. Jane considered the road. There was another hairpin turn ahead. She remembered the road as she was driving into the estate, the turn, around which she and Mrs. Poppy had first seen Kennett Park.

Jane braced herself against the carriage and closed her eyes. Praying. Praying that whatever happened, this would be over quickly...that she would not suffer long. Perhaps her act would be seen as courageous someday, and the earl would know that even if Jane had not been a true lady, she had at least been brave.

She felt it: the curving of the road. The horses

squealed. Something was wrong. There were shouts outside. This was it, her only opportunity. Jane felt the carriage rocking, slipping on the icy curve. She only needed to wait.

Then it came, the very chance she needed. The carriage rocked, sinking dangerously into a rut, sliding on the ice. They were leaning and off balance. In that instant Jane sprang from her seat, ignoring the men's cries of alarm. She threw herself against the side of the vehicle that already was leaning too far. For a moment they hung like that, and she heard shouts, so many shouts.

Then they were tipping, so slowly that it seemed they could have hung there forever. The men in the carriage scrambled to grab at her, but their weight only added to her own, tipping the carriage further. Jane felt a hand close painfully around her arm and she threw her weight back and away, as the carriage fell, taking forever, crashing hard into the road. The horses screamed. No... she was screaming. The world shattered around her, and she felt the wind and sleet upon her face.

In the distance, Jane could have sworn she heard Lord Keegain calling her name. She smiled, and thought she must look as crazy as the fanatics. Providence had given her the sound of his voice at the moment of her death.

I have done it, she thought, as she tried to open her eyes, wanting to see. The world had stopped moving, painfully so. *I have done it and they are stopped.* She could die now and be content, for they would likely perish as she had, ending this. Ending whatever terrible conspiracy they had concocted. They would never hurt another again.

She stared up at the sky, seeing for the first time that the sleet had turned to snow, thick heavy flakes that caught at her lashes. The flakes would cover her like a blanket. It was a cold blanket, but a blanket nonetheless and she would die warm. Content, Jane lay twisted in the wreckage making no move, unable to feel her limbs in the cold except to know that she ached. She could accept it though. She had stopped them, or so she thought, until impossibly, the pirate rose from the wreckage.

Jane turned her head, opening her mouth to scream as he pulled himself up out of the debris. One arm hung uselessly at his side, but the other held a gun. A dark pistol that he aimed with one hand, pointing back the way they had come.

For the first time Jane became aware of hoof beats. Then she saw him. Keegain. The pirate would shoot Keegain.

Jane struggled from the debris. Nothing else mattered anymore. She had failed and she would pay for that failure with Keegain's life. She must rectify the mistake, now, quickly, before she lost the man she loved more than any other in the entire world. She leapt at the pirate.

34

————

The earl sighted them first. The carriage was ahead, careening wildly in the muddy slush. It fishtailed, all four wheels sliding sideways as the horses strained to keep the thing moving on the icy ground. That was the sole reason that he had been able to catch them.

Well, that, and the fact that he had run his horse into a lather. Behind him, Lord Keegain heard the others. The men were shouting, urging their horses onward. He had outstripped them all in his mad race.

The poor beast under him would run itself to death from exhaustion if he did not soon stop. He hated using an animal in this way, but his quarry was close enough to touch and he could not slow. The driver of the coach was whipping his horses to greater and greater speed, but there were only two and their burden was considerably greater than a single mounted man.

The carriage rose for a moment on two wheels, the strain of that much weight on the axles was telling, one of the wheels no longer ran true, and wobbled dangerously. There was no telling what would happen to Jane if the carriage went over. His heart in his throat, Keegain shouted to his horse.

"Hah!" He leaned into his mount's neck with his knuckles, urging it faster, begging for the animal to give everything it had. He sent a silent apology to the horse. It was cruel, but necessary. Jane's life hung in the balance.

Maybe the horse understood his master's urgency on some level. The beast seemed to rally and give a final burst of speed. Fitzwilliam and the stable hands fell behind as Keegain's stallion churned up the mud and slush, spraying wings of water around them in an icy cascade as he narrowed the gap between him and Jane.

The carriage again rose on two wheels, as the driver anticipated the turn. Icy sleet turned to snow even as the storm intensified. The wind swirled the flakes. It would have been wildly beautiful on any other night. Here, it made things that much more treacherous. Keegain's horse slipped on hidden ice now, before his hooves dug in. The road was more dangerous by the minute.

And then it happened. The carriage rounded the perilous turn at the riverbank, where the spray made the road a solid sheet of ice.

The carriage balanced for a long moment on one side, tipping further and further on two wheels until eventually, it fell with a horrible crash and the screaming of men and horses.

"JANE!" The name tore from the earl's throat. He urged his mount forward. The stallion pulled strength from some hidden reserve. The carriage smashed against the fence. The driver was thrown over the bank into the icy waters.

Keegain searched for Jane, seeing her body lying still in the wreckage, illuminated by a bright moon reflecting against the glittering ice and snow. His heart pounded in his chest until he saw her move and shout his name. His eyes were only for her.

"Keegain!"

The earl never saw the man or the gun until Jane moved. She leapt at the man, a dark shadow really, but surely a man.

Keegain heard the sharp report of a pistol. For a moment his heart stopped. When he heard the sound of the ball whiz past his own ear, he felt relief. At least the man was not shooting at Jane.

Jane clung to the villain's arm and he pushed her aside. The man climbed out of the fallen carriage, favoring his right side. He dragged himself through the ruined door and fell heavily to the ground. He was close now. The earl could see him clearly. The fiend was dressed as a pirate and Keegain remembered seeing him at the ball.

The pirate pulled a blade from his side, a serviceable weapon, no costume prop. He turned to face the earl's charging mount, weapon raised. Keegain leaned back as far as he could, pulling the reins savagely to keep the horse from the weapon.

The exhausted horse, now commanded to stop and seeing a threat, reared. His sharp hooves flashed. The pirate tried to duck and run, but one flailing hoof connected behind his head. He fell into the icy mud, looking up at a half-ton of frightened stallion with hooves the size of dinner platters stamping the frozen ground around him.

"Stop! Mercy!" the pirate screamed. He curled into a ball covering his head to protect it from the flashing hooves.

Keegain turned the horse away and dismounted. The animal danced sideways, wrought up by the run, eyes rolling, showing the whites. Foam and sweat dripped off his heaving sides, steaming in the cold night air. The animal stood blowing as if brightening a forge.

Keegain ran to the wreckage, crawling over what should have been the underside of the carriage. He flung open the door where Jane had scrambled to hide when the pirate flung her away.

Jane was huddled in one corner; in her bound hands, she held a pistol, aimed straight at his heart.

"Jane." Keegain spoke quietly, almost reverently. "Jane."

She stared at him as though not comprehending what she saw. "My lord?" The words choked on a sob. Jane threw the pistol down and rose to meet him. She grabbed his proffered hand and he brought her to her feet. He pulled his lady from the wreckage just as Fitzwilliam and the men thundered to the scene. They drew up as Keegain freed Jane from the ropes that held her wrists together.

Two of his men continued past the carriage, wielding cudgels. The other two checked on the villains thrown from the wreckage.

"Good God!" Fitzwilliam stopped his horse beside Keegain's. "Are you injured, Miss?"

Jane was incapable of speech. She seemed to be laughing and crying all at once. Keegain held her head in his hands as they stood within the open door in the side of the overturned carriage.

"Jane..." he said as quietly as if he were trying to calm a nervous horse. "Jane, look at me. Look at me." Her wide, frantic eyes were everywhere, and then they fixed upon his urgent hazel gaze.

"I would like that," she said on a gasping sob, "to look upon you." She colored very prettily in his hands.

His left hand stayed on her cheek but the right hand slid behind her and pulled her to his chest. She came, unresisting. He saw nothing but her, as he clasped her softness to him. She fit as no other. "Jane," he whispered against her hair. "Oh, Jane."

He had almost lost her. She turned her head up to his and he kissed her, a gentle kiss of love between them. She was so sweet in his arms, he never wanted to let go. She clung to him desperately, molding her body against his, and he was lost.

"I no longer have to worry about you, old boy," Fitzwilliam said with a smile Keegain could hear without glancing at the man. "You can have a marriage and happiness both."

At the word 'marriage' Keegain felt Jane pull away. For a moment he could not understand it, for she had been there in his arms, kissing him back as though she meant it, and felt the same. Now her eyes were troubled and full of pain.

"I am sorry," she said softly, for his ears alone. "I have forgotten myself in the moment."

With that she turned away looking for a way down from the broken carriage.

"Come, now, before that thing disintegrates beneath your feet!" Fitzwilliam called. He had given over his horse and Keegain's to Griswold, who had caught up with them. Others had cut loose the terrified horses from the fallen carriage. The animals stood, heads down, sides heaving. One limped badly and the other was bloodied from the harness workings when the carriage had overturned. Between the stablemen and Fitzwilliam, Keegain and Jane were gently lowered to the ground.

Jane immediately sank into the mud.

"My lady." One of the stablemen said and draped what looked suspiciously like the cloak of a pirate's costume on the ground in front of her. She smiled in gratitude and stepped on it. Although it did nothing for the water, it did keep the mud from pulling at her ruined slippers.

"We need to get out of the storm," Fitzwilliam said looking at the sky. Snowflakes danced around his face.

"Beggin' pardon," Griswold interrupted. The master of horse stepped up and pulled his hat. He bowed to Jane as though she were royally born and continued. "My lord, that horse of yours shan't be fit to ride for a fortnight after this. I fear that riding him back to the house will damage the poor thing, and the others aren't faring much better."

"You, your men, and these valiant steeds, have done me a great service this evening, Griswold. I thank you.

How are the horses from the carriage?" the earl asked with concern.

"They're blown, my lord, though not as bad as these. The scoundrels had a head start, and I guess they saw no reason to push the team 'afore they saw us barreling down upon them."

"And the villains?" Fitzwilliam questioned the older man.

"Tied up and secured sir." Griswold grinned, his leathery face folding into a great smile. "Both of 'em over there, 'course, now, they may not wake up for a while and when they do, they'll have a great blooming headache."

"Both?" Jane turned to the stable master for confirmation and then back to Keegain. "There were three of them, and a driver."

Griswold shook his head and shrugged. "I'm sorry, but we only found the two. Didn't see no third."

"Griswold," Keegain looked at the sky. "I think that this storm is going to bring more snow down upon us, and soon. We need to get the lady back to the house. Find me the least winded horse and walk the rest back at pace. It is most cold and miserable. I'll be sure that a few bottles of my best port end up in the stable for celebration."

Griswold's face lit up. "Aye sir! I will at that!"

Keegain raised his voice so that all could hear. "A bonus for every man here tonight and my heartfelt thanks."

A thin but heartfelt cheer rose from five throats.

"Why are you cheering, Fitz? You've wealth enough."

"It is the principle of the thing, Keegain," he said with wink to Jane.

Hoofbeats in the distance caused the company to reach for their cudgels. "Easy men." Keegain called out. "It is likely Reynold's men arriving to take charge of your prisoners."

Indeed, it was Reynold's men, but Ted was not with them. Their horses were determined to be the freshest as they had come at a brisk pace without the break-neck speed of someone trying to save his love. They gave up two horses so that Keegain, Fitzwilliam and Jane would be able to make their way back. Keegain rode back to the manor with Jane held firmly in his arms.

Upon their return, a young servant explained Reynolds' absence from the rescue. Lady Margret had identified a member of her staff as an imposter, and the man had attempted to escape on foot through the kitchens, although he did not get far.

"No, my lord," said young Jack, the kitchen boy. "He was accosted by baked goods and a breadknife," he confessed, laughing aloud.

Keegain was confused. "Whatever do you mean?" he asked, and Jack explained.

The man came through just as Mrs. Muir was taking a batch of cinnamon rolls from the oven and somehow ran directly into the hot pan of sticky buns. While he was yowling with burns and sugar stuck to his skin, Mr. White came forth with one of the bread knives and pinned the rogue against the stove.

"Gilly was terrified. Of course, Mr. Reynolds came in directly and took charge of the situation." Jack concluded.

"And you, Jack?" Keegain asked. "What were you doing?"

"My job, my lord. Assistin' Mr. White."

Keegain sized the boy up for a moment, realizing that he was much too old to be considered a kitchen boy any longer, and the fact that he stepped up to help was telling too.

"Thank you," Keegain said to Jack, making a mental note to promote the lad. He hoped that Reynolds had all under control and the guests were not traumatized. The earl still felt shaken.

When Jane was taken struggling for her life, his heart had near shattered. He loved the woman dearly. He did not know what he would have done had she perished in the crash, but Jane was safe. She was here beside him now and he intended to never again let her go.

35

It was a somber early morning breakfast. The partygoers had yet to wake. Breakfast would come later, no sooner than ten after a night such as they had. Even then many would be staggering half-blind and with aching heads until well past midday. By arrangement, Keegain met Margret and Reynolds at the table before the guests arrived. Lady Margret was silent, but her head was unbowed, and her eyes met his straight on.

"Thank you for coming here first." Keegain said, pouring himself a cup of coffee. It was a habit he had never broken and the staff, over the years, had given up on training him to wait to be served. He had given Mr. White a generous purse and the day off for his part in last night's activities. His staff indulged his foibles with the long-suffering grace of an overindulgent parent. He was their lord and they were loyal to him, no matter his eccentricities.

Reynolds and Margret were served coffee and tea and

then at a wave from the earl, the servants vanished as unobtrusively as they had come. Reynolds rose to leave as well, but Margret put her hand on his arm, and Keegain shook his head.

"No. Stay, Reynolds. I think this concerns you too."

"I would never dishonor your name, or your lady's," Reynolds said stiffly.

"Of course not," Keegain said. Whatever was the man on about?

He turned to Margret. "Our marriage," Keegain said to his fiancée, "would strengthen our coffers and make the resulting union one of the most powerful in the country. It would not, however, bring either of us any joy."

"I am sorry," Margret said with unaccustomed softness.

"Don't be." Margret looked down at the table for a moment as Keegain continued. "I have funds enough and if I am far down on the list of influential families, so be it. I choose contentment."

Lady Margret's eyes again strayed to Reynolds, who stood so stiff and unyielding. Keegain wondered how he never saw it, the light in her eyes when she looked at his friend. As she looked back at him, her eyes hardened.

"You said some things last night." Margret bit her lip. For a moment he wondered if she might cry, but Margret had always been made of sterner stuff. "And I discussed them with Mr. Reynolds..." She flushed with color. "At length, as he was trying to get me to remember small details about... about the incident." She swallowed. "I have to say, in my own defense, I have never treated another living soul the shameful way I treated Miss Bellevue. I do not know what came over me." She hesitated. "I suppose I was angry."

That Lord Keegain could well believe. He had known Lady Margret for years and had never seen such cruelty from her.

Her voice dropped to a whisper. "I never wanted her injured and certainly not...." Margret shook her head. Keegan could see the brightness of unshed tears in her eyes. "I went too far, I know that, I... I am sorry, indeed. My behavior was not that of a lady."

"And I also. I did not act, nor speak as a gentleman. I apologize as well," Keegain said.

"But what I did was unconscionable. Please, believe me, I wanted no harm to come to her, I only wanted her gone." Margret broke off.

"Why?" Keegain asked. The question was without malice. He was more curious than anything. "Why, if you are generous to all and sundry, should you choose Miss Bellevue to vent your cruelty upon?"

"Because." Lady Margret said in a rush. "Because of the way she looked at you. And the way that you looked back at her. That she could have what I could not...I suppose I envied her."

This was perhaps the last thing he had expected Margret to say. Keegain shook his head incredulous. "You expect me to believe you were jealous? Of Miss Bellevue?"

"Yes and no." Margret winced and took a deep breath. "I envied love itself," she said. "Love I would never have."

Keegain was confused. "You do not love me, surely. I

have known you throughout my life, but there has never been such feeling between us."

Margret sighed, and the earl did not understand. She held up a hand to stay his further protests.

"I was to be your wife. I was *commanded* to be your wife. After a time, I came to realize that my fate was not such an onerous thing, better than most, in fact. You are a good and decent man, but I never..." Margret stared at her hands. "I never looked at you the way she did. I never felt that draw as she does. Nor, if you are honest, did you ever look at me the way you look at her. I was not afraid of losing you. I never had you and knew then I never would. I think I was afraid that I would live the rest of my life never knowing what it was to look at someone in that manner, only then..." Her eyes drifted to Reynolds and pulled away again. "Only then, I suddenly knew, and that made it so much worse," she whispered.

Lord Keegain looked at Ted. The man was watching Lady Margret with an expression on his face that was the perfect illustration to underscore her meaning. Keegain now knew the look for what it was. It was the same expression he wore whenever he looked at Jane. He would move heaven and earth to see to her happiness.

Lord Keegain leaned back in his chair and closed his eyes. When had that happened? While the man was making witty comments over dinner, or while he was running down culprits in the kitchen? Or even before that, considering Margret's familiarity with Reynolds. If it was before, Keegain knew he should be angry, with her and with Ted, but all the anger had left him now. It did not matter.

When Margret looked at him again, she met his eyes, unflinching and unafraid. This was the Lady Margret he knew. "I had nothing to do with the kidnapping, I hope you believe that. I would never..." She paused a moment and cleared her throat delicately. "I know I waited an unconscionably long time to say anything, but if the truth of it be known..." She looked up again, but not to him. It was Reynold's solemn nod she sought out.

"I hoped to find Mr. Reynolds," she finished finally. "At first, I was confused. I did not credit that I was witness to something so dire in this house of all places. I could not believe what I had seen. When they were gone and I was alone in the entryway, I realized that... that I had seen a terrible thing. I do not know how long I stood there, I really do not. I froze, like a frightened child."

"I then thought to seek out Mr. Reynolds. I knew he was a King's Man. I have known him almost as long as you have, and he seemed... the wisest choice. I know now that he was off searching for her, for Jane, but his men did not know where he had gone and...." Margret's eyes fell again, color rushed to her cheeks. "After the horrible things I said to her, I know it must look as though I had something to do with it, especially considering that I harbored such a villain on my staff, but I never wished her harm, Keegain. Truly, I did not."

The earl sat back with his coffee and looked at the both of them. When he spoke it was his friend's name. "Ted."

Reynold's head shot up with the familiar use of his first name. It was not a look of defiance, but he was more alert than before. Lady Margret looked at Keegain too, concern on her face. The earl pretended not to notice her hand gripping Ted's under the table.

"Do you love her?" he asked his friend suddenly.

Reynolds never let a bit of emotion show on his face, but he said the words with all seriousness. "I do, more than anything. I have no prospects fitting for…"

"I do not care," Margret burst in. "I would live in a hovel, if it were with you." She gazed up at Reynolds adoringly.

"I hardly think that will be necessary," Keegain said. "We will find a way around this, Ted." Keegain took a deep breath. "In the meantime, have you questioned the prisoners?" he asked.

"Yes, they enjoyed the hospitality of your cellar last night. They were cold enough and miserable enough to talk rather freely this morning."

"So who was the fourth man? The one that got away?"

Reynolds shook his head. "They do not know his name, or they wouldn't say for fear of repercussions. I do not know if they are lying, but they said all contact with the man was done with him in a mask or cowl, they had no good description except to say he was a gentleman, by the sounds of the power he commanded, someone pretty high up."

"So there is a maniacal kidnapper working for Napoleon loose not only in my area, but has infiltrated the gentry as well. And is quite likely still in the house, because the roads are too much of a mess for anyone to leave."

"He will give himself away somehow." Of this Reynolds seemed certain. "And then we shall catch him.

The Duke of Ely seems to have some inkling of the man's identity regardless of the near useless description. We will find him."

Keegain had his doubts. They had not found him in the days leading up to the ball. They had less chance now that it was over. Soon the guests would start finding their way home. It was very likely he would slip out with the rest and justice would go unserved. "If I find out who it was, I shall put a ball into his head." Keegain made the words a solemn vow.

Margret chuckled, though with a tinge of regret despite the smile upon her face. "You speak as a protective husband."

"I do not know how this will end, Margret. For my part, I believe that you are innocent of these things, but I cannot offer you forgiveness, as I am not the injured party. Know that I have no grudge against you. As for whether or not you will ever be welcomed into this house again..." Margret raised hopeful eyes, and the earl did not want to hurt her more than he had already done. "That depends greatly on the disposition of the future Lady Keegain." he said. He let her take that in for a moment.

When Lady Margret nodded, it was with a grim sort of resignation, coupled with the relief that she had tried so hard to hide. "As it should be," she whispered.

"In the meantime, I will hold you blameless for the dissolution of our banns. I am given to understand that the length of our betrothal has some wondering at our sincerity, so it should come as little surprise that we are not marrying after all. I will, however, not see your reputation impugned, and I see no need to mention any part of your witnessing the abduction, nor your hesitation in reporting it, nor the fact that one of the scoundrels had wheedled his way into your employ."

"Thank you." Margret said.

"I will explain our decision to your father. He will not be happy, but I will make him understand."

"*I* will speak to Father," Lady Margret said authoritatively. In that moment, Keegain saw the girl he once knew, the one that had once seemed free and kind and regal. She was lovely then, a trait she had lost and traded for a coldness. Now that gentle authority had returned. He thought he approved of this new Lady Margret.

"If your parents give you difficulty, just let me know. I will speak with your father, if you so wish."

"I will speak with her father," Reynolds interrupted and then flushed. "I am sorry, my lord," he blurted.

"What's with this formality, Ted?" Keegain smiled, nudging the man. "We are friends, are we not?"

Reynolds returned Keegain's grin with his own small smile.

Lord Keegain did not know when he had ever felt so free and happy. He was free to court Jane, and apparently, Reynolds was free to court Margret, even though the man had no money. Her father would hate that she was giving up an earl for the second son of a baron, but Keegain had faith that Lady Margret would bring him round. Perhaps, the Duke of Ely could speak to the Regent about giving Reynolds a bit more prestige after his work here tonight. After all, they did catch three of the four traitors.

"So then." Keegain said. "I wish you both the best of each other, and a long and happy life."

Reynolds looked startled. Keegain smiled at him. "I know that look," he said, by way of explanation. "The look you give her. I know it from the inside out." The servants returned, opening the doors again. "To a long and happy life." Keegain raised his cup in a toast.

"You cannot toast with coffee, old boy!" Fitzwilliam said as he strode into the room, "Have I taught you nothing? And why are your servants jealously guarding the food from your guests? We are all out in the hallway suffering from various hangovers."

"I'm sure you shall survive." Keegain grinned at his old friend.

"Oh, I might, yes, but judging from the sounds coming from the stable last night, you shall not have groomsmen for a fortnight!"

"Nor horses," Keegain ventured.

The other guests began walking in, smiles and greeting all around, even if some did so rather quietly.

"Oh my!" A young lady Keegain did not know exclaimed, as she looked out the large window. The storm last night had dropped a large amount of snow and ice, and it turned the landscape into an unbroken white vista. "It is lovely."

"It is," agreed her male companion, "but a terrible thing in which to travel."

"The invitation has been extended to you all to please stay another day or two, or a fortnight." The earl offered. "We shall enjoy Christmas together. In any case, you all must wait until the roads are passable again."

There was a ragged chorus of thanks.

The man who had spoken about the ills of travel continued. "I appreciate, that my lord." He bowed slightly. "But I was thinking of that poor girl, the one from last night. Still, she showed a lot of good old English backbone throughout that whole affair. I am sure a little ice and snow shall not dissuade her."

"What are you saying?"

"Ruddy." Alice piped up. "You do not know? Jane is leaving. Jacqueline just told me."

"What? When?"

"Even now, her trunk is loaded, she's out in...." but Alice spoke to an empty chair. The earl was already on his feet and through the door before his sister could finish.

"To a long and happy life!" Lady Margret called behind him.

36

---

*J*ane knew she had to leave.

She had spent the night in Lady Amelia's room. The gown was ruined, but she returned the jewels with shaking hands and recounted the whole dreadful story.

Lady Amelia was horrified. "They thought you were me," she whispered. "Because of the sapphires."

"I doubt that," Jane began, but then she remembered the men saying her father doted on her, and wondered if Lady Amelia could be right.

"Oh Jane, I feel awful. I am so sorry," Amelia said reaching out to hug Jane. Lady Amelia had never seemed to be a demonstrative person, and the embrace shocked Jane, but held close, she felt a true friendship blooming.

"You could not have known," Jane said. "You were being kind."

"And I might have gotten you killed," Lady Amelia lamented. "Oh, Jane, I never would have forgiven myself."

"No harm was done," Jane said.

Lady Amelia moved over in her bed and patted the spot beside her. She declared that Jane should not leave her side. Lady Patience joined them, and then Lady Charlotte and Alice. There was not room enough in the bed for all of them, but none of the girls could sleep. They talked until nearly dawn, sharing stories and confidences. Only Alice seemed to really get a good night's sleep, curled up between the others while they talked.

They spoke of love, and swore that they all would be married to gentlemen of their choosing and no other. Eventually, they all started to doze from sheer exhaustion. It was just breaking dawn when Lady Helen found them. She knocked on the door and peeked in.

"Did you all sleep in here?" she inquired as the others rose in various stages of wakefulness.

"We did not want to leave Jane alone," Lady Charlotte said as she stretched and rubbed her eyes.

Lady Helen nodded her understanding. "I am sorry, Jane," she said. "I was not a good hostess to you, or a good friend. In fact, I was quite rude."

"Lady Margret is your friend," Jane said.

Helen nodded. "She is, but she is not right for my brother, and she does not love him."

"Ruddy doesn't love her either," Alice chimed in.

"We have all known for some time that it was far from a love match," Lady Charlotte agreed. "You and he suit much better, Jane." The comment was said in an off-handed way, and Jane caught her breath. In a moment, she realized that Charlotte had no idea of what had transpired between Jane and Keegain. Jane could not allow the statement to stand.

"No," Jane said shaking her head. "I am no one. He deserves a lady."

"Poppycock," Lady Patience said. "You are as much a lady as any of us here."

"Lady Jane," Charlotte said. "Isn't that what your father calls you?"

"He does, but only when I am being pretentious."

"I have never seen you act so," Lady Patience declared.

"He may call me Lady Jane, but I am not," Jane disagreed. "It does not matter so much to me now. I am who I am meant to be."

"Some are born to nobility," Lady Amelia said. "And some earn it with fortitude and poise. You are the later, Jane. It is no wonder the brigands saw a lady when they looked at you. I am sorry that my jewels put you at risk, but I think they would have seen a lady no matter what you wore."

The ladies nodded all around, making Jane feel quite special. For the first time since she'd arrived, Jane sensed that she had someone to confide in. The girls felt like family, all of them, even Lady Helen. Jane knew that she had true friends.

Although they had talked for well into the night, the ladies once again asked Jane for her rendition of the harrowing tale so that Lady Helen could know the truth. All shivered with the thought as Jane retold the story.

"You must have been terrified," Lady Helen said.

"Yes," Lady Charlotte added "I would have been so frightened, I probably would have swooned."

"You would have fought them just the same as I," Jane assured her friend.

"Oh no! You are a heroine, Jane," Lady Charlotte said. "Without you the gentlemen would not have caught the brigands."

"I hardly think that is so."

"Nonetheless, I am glad you are staying with us," Lady Charlotte said.

"I do not think I should stay."

"Oh, no!" Charlotte cried. "But, you must."

Jane shook her head uncertainly.

"You may stay with me for the season," Lady Patience offered. "Mother will not mind."

"Or me," Lady Amelia added. "Father will agree, I am sure of it, and my Aunt Ebba will chaperone once the weather breaks. You will put this awful night behind you and think of it no more."

"No," Charlotte argued. "You already agreed you would stay with us."

"Yes. Please, stay with us." Alice put out her lip in a pout. "You know I always get my way," she said, eyes twinkling, and Jane had to laugh. For once, she had someone to laugh with, and if she cried, they would be here to cheer her.

She lay back against the pillows as outside, the sun came up for the first time in days, lighting up bright frost patterns on the glass panes of the window. The snow had stopped, but the world was aglitter. Still, she had to leave. She could not see Keegain day in and day out. She could not see him and know every day that he would not be hers.

Jane considered the carriage ride home in the snow. It no longer frightened her. She felt as if she could conquer the world. Perhaps, Charlotte was right. She was a heroine. There was a fear that she had always carried, that she was not good enough, that someone would see through her and always find her wanting. Last night, that fear had left her. In its place was a certainty that no one could take away her own self-worth. Perhaps she was Lady Jane. She smiled at the thought, but she was also plain Miss Jane Bellevue, and that was fine as well.

"Well," Lady Helen said standing and straightening her night clothes. "We should all be awake and dressed. It looks to be a lovely day. It is a winter wonderland."

"Cold, but lovely," Lady Charlotte agreed. She paused at the door. "Perhaps after breakfast we can go for a ride," she said, "If there are any fit horses in the stable. I do love making tracks in the snow, and it rarely stays long enough to make them."

Jane smiled but said nothing. The sisters left to go to their rooms and only Lady Patience and Lady Amelia lingered.

"I have to leave," Jane said finally. "I do not see how it can be any other way."

"Why?" Lady Amelia demanded.

"I cannot see him every day," Jane whispered.

Amelia nodded her understanding.

"But what about the roads? I am sure they are all ice!" Lady Patience protested.

Jane could only smile a little as she answered, "Truly,

I am not bothered by it. I trust the coachman to take me through. I am in no hurry, and if some caution is warranted, I shall respect that. But I expect that I shall be fine. I find I want to be home in time for Christmas."

The girls hugged Jane and went to dress with promises to see her at breakfast.

It was a strange feeling, having faced down her worst fear, only to find it not so terrifying anymore. Nothing could scare her, it seemed, save seeing the earl marry someone else.

The invitation had been issued to everyone who had attended the ball to stay until tomorrow or the next day to recover from the event. Odd how she was the one who truly needed to recover, and here she was, ready to leave. Jane's fingertips traced a bruise upon her cheek, and when she sat up she moved stiffly, but she would be all right. If it would pain her to travel, then so be it. The physical aches would match her broken heart.

She called in the maid to help her dress, and Jacqueline exclaimed over the bruise upon her shoulder. The maid scolded her anew for being so careless in the first place leaving the ball, but it was a gentle chiding, covering how much Jacqueline had grown to care for her. Still, Jane was ready to return home to her father and sister. Her mind was made up.

Jane thought she would leave while the others were preoccupied with breakfast. She told Jacqueline to call for the footman and the man came for her trunk as the others drifted downstairs.

"I do not think you should go, *Mademoiselle*," Jacqueline said.

But Jane was adamant. She told no one, not even Lady Charlotte, that she was going. When the girls left her room, they thought she would follow them down the stairs to breakfast. She slipped away when they were caught in the crowd heading into the dining room. Jane watched them go, seeing the happiness on the faces of those around her as they relived their favorite memories of the ball.

Jane knew her story would be passed around and become gossip for the *Ton* for a while, but eventually the rumors would fade. She was glad that she was leaving; that she need not be part of the gossip. Jane suspected that her friends would let the story slip about what she had done to stop the carriage. They had thought it incredibly brave. In retrospect, she saw how foolish she had been.

Still, the villains were caught. At least three of them were. The other...the other was still out there somewhere.

She had told Keegain last night, and he said he would discuss it with the others. That there were King's Men in the household had surprised her not a little. They would find him then, she was sure, but the news that the man had not yet been caught made it easier to leave. It just felt safer that way. Safer on all accounts; mostly, safer for her heart.

"The carriage is ready, my lady," the footman said, and bowed as he helped her with her cloak. She flushed, and corrected him gently. "*Miss* will do fine," she said softly, as she stepped past him into the bright glare of the new day.

The trees were coated in ice, giving the lane the look

329

of an enchanted winter fairyland. She stood a moment upon the steps, caught up in the wonder of the bright and glittering world. The footman came forward to help her, and she carefully made her way down the steps, pausing to touch a branch of a frozen bush near the door. Jane smiled and tilted back her head to gaze up at the impossible blue depths of the sky. What an absolutely beautiful day it truly was, with the sun shining off the newly fallen snow, and the ice dripping from the trees.

Why then was she crying?

"Mademoiselle!" It was Jacqueline on the stair. "If you must go, it is not seemly that you go..." She paused, struggling for the word. *"Tout seul,"* she said. "If you will have me, I shall ride with you."

Jane was surprised, but happy. She liked the young French girl displaced by Napoleon's rampages. She could have been in much the same position if she were French instead of English.

"What of your mistress?" Jane asked.

"Lady Charlotte will understand," she said, and Jane nodded.

"Thank you," she said, and the coachman handed Jacqueline into the carriage, but Jane paused looking back at the manor.

She dashed at her tears with a gloved hand and turned toward the carriage, steeling herself for the inevitable fear that she usually felt when about to step into any conveyance, but her body was at peace on this fine and beautiful day. For the first time in years, she thought nothing of the simple act of going somewhere. She laughed in shy wonder, drawing looks of confusion from the coachmen, which in turn only caused her to laugh harder.

"Miss Bellevue?" She knew that voice. It was his gentle baritone, the same voice that had calmed her when she was at her worst. Lord Keegain.

She paused in the act of placing one foot upon the step up into the carriage. She stiffened and had to remind herself how to breathe. Her body seemed to have forgotten how. Would he always have that effect upon her?

"Lord Keegain," she said softly and turned to face him.

He stood on the steps, without hat or coat though the air was cold enough that his breath formed white clouds as he spoke.

"You would leave us so soon?" he asked, and her heart wrenched at the pain that lay within his tone.

"I do not belong here. I think that has been made abundantly clear."

"You are still my guest," he said, reaching her side, and then reaching for her, as though to draw her away from the carriage.

"I think it is time I went home." She replied, trying to make the words gentle, for one of them had to say it. "I find I want to be with my family for Christmas and you should be with yours."

The earl swallowed hard, and for the first time she saw how pale his face was, how urgent his expression. His voice was so soft she barely heard it. "And what if I told you that I am no longer engaged?" he asked suddenly, and she gasped, stepping away until her back was against the carriage itself.

"No. You cannot do that!" she said, though the protest was automatic. In truth, she was remembering being in his arms, feeling his lips pressed against hers. Her heart throbbed within her breast, each beat painful in her ears. "Tell me you have not been so foolish! Lady Margret is a fine lady."

"*You* are a fine lady, and the foolish thing would have been to let you go."

Jane shook her head, denying his words. "No. Please, stop. This is not right. You have a commitment to Lady Margret..."

"Who never wanted to marry me any more than I wanted to marry her. My father wanted me settled. He never wanted to trap me in a loveless marriage. I see that now. You have made me see how untenable that would be. You have helped me to find my strength."

"I?" Jane questioned looking at him with wonder.

"Jane, please. Darling, listen to me." The earl took both her hands in his.

The endearment stopped her in her tracks.

"I have loved you since I first saw you."

She had felt the same. Was there truly such a thing as love at first sight?

"And last night, when I thought you would die, I wished to die myself. When I came upon the wreckage, I never saw that man rising up to shoot me. I saw only you. I saw your body, still and lifeless among the debris. Never have I felt so helpless, so terribly useless in my life. If I could not save you, then what value could I possibly have as a man? Then, when I saw you rise, when I heard your shout, I realized that God himself had given me a second chance, an opportunity to make things right." He brought her gloved hand to his lips that he might kiss it. "Let me make this right. Please."

Tears were streaming down her face. "I do not know how...."

"It is the simplest of things." He knelt in the wet snow at her feet and she was stunned.

"I know I must speak to your father first, but say you will entertain my suit. Nay. Say you will marry me, Miss Bellevue. Here, now, today if we could. I know this is sudden. I am not an impulsive man, but please understand the thought of losing you has made me bold. The thought of losing you is too much to bear. Miss Jane Bellevue, will you be my Lady Keegain, as you are already the lady of my heart?"

Jane had never heard poetry more beautiful than those few words honestly spoken. Never could there be a partner who would be a better fit for her than the man who knelt before her in the snow and asked her to be his. Truly, there was nothing left to say, but what was in her heart.

"I love you," Jane admitted shyly, as he looked up at her with adoration shining in his eyes. She felt the emotion reflected in her own gaze, proof of her affection laid bare for him to see. "I would be honored to become your wife."

"My lady, my love, my dearest Jane, it is I who am honored." The earl stood, and whether he reached for her, or she for him, it was hard to say.

He kissed her with a gentle passion and Jane was transported. He held her in the cradle of his arms. "This is what my father wished for me," he whispered against her lips. "Love and true happiness."

Jane smiled. "I wish my Mother was here," she said softly. "She would love to see our wedding day. At last I shall be a lady."

"Oh, Jane," Keegain said. "You have always been a lady," he said. "Only soon, you shall be *my* lady."

His lips claimed hers again and she knew that truly she had come home. Keegain was everything she had wished for, and more.

Jacqueline leaned out of the carriage window. "I shall have your things brought back into the house, *Mademoiselle*, yes?"

"Yes," Jane said, laughing through tears, and Keegain himself helped Jacqueline from the carriage, and the footmen began untying her bags.

"Has the other villain been found?" Jane asked Keegain as he started to escort her into the house.

He frowned. "Not yet, but I promise you, I will keep you safe. I swear by my life that it will be so." A smile touched his lips. "Though I daresay you are well equal to the task of managing any villain entirely on your own."

She blushed, biting her lip and looking away. "You heard about that?"

"My love, I was there. But you told Charlotte. Which means by now, I believe everyone at breakfast will have heard about your heroism. It shall be the talk of the *Ton*," Lord Keegain said and lifted her chin with his forefinger. "Now let us go in before I must steal more of your kisses to keep myself warm." He gathered her close and kissed her fingers, her forehead, the tip of her nose, and then her lips, first gently and then with more passion.

"*We* shall be the talk of the *Ton*," she said, with an impish smile.

Keegain caught Jane's hands in his. "So long as they remember the most important part of the story," he said.

"And what would that be?" she asked, looking up at him with a sort of shy wonder.

"They lived happily ever after," he said, and kissed her again to prove that they would.

❦

EPILOGUE

A few days later, when the snow melted, Jane and the earl, along with a suitable entourage, went to bring Mr. Bellevue and Julia to Kennett Park for the Christmas holiday. Jane was not sure her father would make the trip, but Keegain promised to stay with her family for the holiday if her father did not want to travel. Jane knew what a sacrifice that would be for him.

"But you so love Christmas and your house is all decorated," Jane said. "Besides, the Christmas choir would miss your voice at the service."

"They shall have to do without me," the earl said. "I belong at your side." Keegain assured her that he would have a happy Christmas anywhere, as long as they were together.

As it happened, when Lord Keegain asked for Jane's father's permission to marry her, Mr. Bellevue decided he should meet the whole family. They packed posthaste to arrive back at Kennett Park in time for Christmas.

"Christmas!" Julia cried. "I shall not have to have

337

Christmas without you!" She threw herself into her sister's arms and hugged her fiercely.

"You shall not, little sister," Keegain said. "And you shall forever be welcome at Christmas and any other time."

Christmas Day dawned, and at last Jane's soon to be sisters found out what their presents were. Apparently, the Keening family often made one another gifts. Jane humbly passed out the small tokens she had chosen for Lady Charlotte and her sisters and Keegain's mother. That of course, was before she realized that they would one day be her own sisters, but the girls did not seem to mind the humble gifts.

Jane was surprised that Helen had a gift for her as well as her own sisters.

It was a lovely embroidered handkerchief, and Jane had to exchange a glance with Keegain. The best handkerchief belonged to her gentleman and was still wrapped around her mother's pearls, but the violets embroidered on this handkerchief would always remind her of the violet dress that had changed her life. Perhaps in some small way, even the villains had played their part in bringing Lord Keegain to the realization that he loved her. Jane could not hold any malice in her heart on this holy day.

After various handcrafted items were exchanged, her father said, "My own best Christmas gift has always been and always will be your happiness." He looked from one daughter to the other and then toasted Lord Keegain. "I am glad to be certain that my eldest daughter will be in good hands."

"I wish only to devote myself to her safety and happiness," the earl promised.

They raised a glass of Christmas cheer and toasted each other wishing all the joy of the season.

Today there were no traitors in the house, only friends and family and Jane was content. It seemed that nothing could be better than this moment. Eyes sparkling, Jane looked at Keegain.

"I do have a gift for you," Jane told him and he wondered aloud what it might be. In the tradition of the family, she led him to the kitchen where a pan of his favorite cinnamon rolls was kept warm. "I baked them myself," she confessed.

"I do believe these are better than Mrs. Muir's," he said dutifully and when everyone begged for a taste, he flatly refused. "These are all mine," he said.

"If you eat them all, you shall be fat as Father Christmas," Helen teased, and while they were still laughing, Charlotte came dancing into the room.

"It's snowing," she cried, just as they had all just settled in to enjoy the peace of a family Christmas. Without another word, she turned towards the staircase. She took the stairs two at a time in her hurry to get her riding outfit. "Come on, Jane. Let's make tracks!"

"Charlotte. Walk," her mother said in a long-suffering voice.

"It's Christmas, Mother," Keegain said with a kiss to his mother's forehead. "Do not scold her."

Alice hurried to follow her sister, but turned at the bottom of the stairs. "Are you coming riding?" she asked Julia.

Jane's little sister frowned. "I'd rather not," Julia admitted.

"Perhaps you would like a tour of the house," Helen offered. "Jane said you like to paint. We have several paintings by Johann Winckelmann and another by his student, Angelica Kauffmann. Have you heard of her?"

"The lady painter?" Julia questioned, and Helen nodded. "I would like to see that."

Comforted that Julia was in good hands, Jane hurried after her friend, Charlotte, to don her new riding outfit.

The snow was falling softly, turning the lane into a fairy land, and Keegain caught her hand and tucked it into the crook of his elbow as they walked to the stable, where Keegain introduced her to her very own mare. "Happy Christmas," he said.

"She's mine?"

"She is. Now, you must ride with me every morning," he said.

"For every day of my life," Jane said as she turned her face up for his kiss.

"And every night," he whispered, making her blush as he lifted her up onto her mare, and Jane, with her intended and her new sisters, rode out to make new tracks across the park.

CONTINUE READING FOR A SNEAK PEEK OF...

The Duke's Daughter ~ Lady Amelia Atherton
by Isabella Thorne

1

With a few lines of black ink scrawled on cream parchment, her life had changed forever. Lady Amelia had to say goodbye, but she could not bear to. She sat alone in the music room contemplating her future. Outside the others gathered, but here it was quiet. The room was empty apart from the piano, a lacquered ash cabinet she had received as a gift from her father on her twelfth birthday. She touched a key and the middle C echoed like the voice of a dear friend. The bench beneath her was the same one she had used when she begun learning, some ten years ago, and was as familiar to her as her father's armchair was to him.

Lighter patches on the wood floor marked where the room's other furniture had sat for years, perhaps for as long as she had been alive. New furnishings would arrive, sit in different places, make new marks, but she would not be here to see it. Amelia ran her fingers across the keys, not firmly enough to make a sound, but she heard the notes in her head regardless. When all her world was turmoil, music had been a constant comforting presence. Turmoil. Upheaval. Chaos. What was the proper word for her life now?

She breathed in a calming breath, and smoothed her dark skirt, settling it into order. She would survive; she would smile again, but first, she thought, she would play. She would lose herself in the music, this one last time.

∽⊙⧼⧽⊙∼

Two Weeks Earlier

LADY AMELIA LOOKED the gentleman over. Wealthy, yes, but not enough to make up for his horrid appearance. *That* would take considerably more than mere wealth. He leered at her as though she were a pudding he would like to sample. Though it was obvious he was approaching to ask her to dance, she turned on her heel in an unmistakable gesture and pretended to be in deep conversation with her friends. Refusing the man a dance outright would be gauche, but if her aversion was apparent enough before the man ever asked, it would save them both an embarrassment. She smoothed her rich crimson gown attempting to project disinterest. It was a truly beautiful garment; silk brocade with a lush velvet bodice ornamented with gold and pearl accents.

Lady Charity, one of Amelia's friends in London, smiled, revealing overly large teeth. The expression exaggerated the flaw, but Charity had other attributes.

"That is an earl you just snubbed," said Charity, wide-eyed. It both galled and delighted Lady Charity the way

344

Amelia dismissed gentlemen. Lady Amelia did not approve of the latter, she did not take joy in causing others discomfort. It was a necessity, not a sport.

"Is he still standing there looking surprised?" Amelia asked, twirling one of her golden ringlets back into place with the tip of a slender gloved finger. Looking over her shoulder to see for herself would only confuse the man into thinking she was playing coy. "I am the daughter of a duke, Charity. I need not throw myself at every earl that comes along."

"Thank goodness, or you would have no time for anything else." Charity's comment bore more than a tinge of jealousy.

Lady Amelia's debut earlier this Season had drawn the attention of numerous suitors, and the cards still arrived at her London townhouse in droves. Each time she went out, whether to a ball or to the Park, she was inundated with tireless gentlemen. If she were a less patient woman, it would have become tedious. Gracious as she was, Amelia managed to turn them all down with poise. Lady Amelia's father, the Duke of Ely, was a kind man who doted on his only daughter but paid as little mind to her suitors as Amelia herself; always saying there was plenty of time for such things. Her debut like most aspects of her upbringing was left to the professionals. What do I pay tutors for? He had said, when a younger Amelia had asked him a question on the French verbs. There had been many tutors. Amelia had learned the languages, the arts, the histories, music and needlepoint until she was, by Society's standards, everything a young woman should be. She glanced across the hall to that same father, and found him deep in conversation with several white haired men, no doubt some of the older lords talking politics as they were wont to do. She flashed him a quick smile and he toasted her with his glass.

Father had even indulged her by hiring a composer to teach her the piano, after she proven herself adept and eager to learn. If any of these flapping popinjays were half the man her father was... she thought with irritation.

Lady Patience, the less forward of Lady Amelia's friends, piped in, "Men are drawn to your beauty like moths to a flame." Her voice had a sad quality to it.

"I'm sure you will find the perfect beau, Patience." Amelia replied.

"Yes, well, you might at least toss them our way, when you have decided against them." Charity said. She peeked wide eyed over her slivered fan which covered her bosom with tantalizing art. Amelia's eyes were brought back to her friends and she smiled.

While Charity was blonde and buxom, Patience was diminutive, yet cursed with garish red hair. The wiry, unruly locks had the habit of escaping whatever style her maid attempted, leaving the girl looking a bit like a waif, frazzled and misplaced at an elegant ball like the one they were attending. Though her dress was a lovely celestial blue frock trimmed round the bottom with lace and a white gossamer polonaise long robe joined at the front with rows of satin beading.

Charity's flaws were more obvious, apart from her wide mouth. She had a jarring laugh, and wore necklines so low they barely contained her ample bosom. The gown she was wearing extenuated this feature with many row of white scalloped lace and a rosy pink bodice clasped just underneath. It bordered on vulgar. Amelia intended to make the polite suggestion on their next shopping trip that Lady Charity perhaps should purchase an extra yard of fabric so she might have enough for an *entire* dress.

"Do not be foolish, Patience. You deserve someone wonderful. If we must be married, it should be to someone that... excites us," Amelia said, rising up onto her toes and clasping her hands in front of her breast.

Her comment caused Patience to flush with embarrassment. It was easy to forget Patience was two years older than Amelia and a year older than Charity, for her naivety gave her a childlike demeanor.

"Not all of us are beautiful enough to hold out for someone handsome," said Patience. When she blushed, her freckles blended with the rosiness of her cheeks. Her eyes alighted with hope, and she was pretty in a shy sort of way.

Charity nodded her agreement, but Amelia frowned and clasped Patience's hands. "You are sweet and bright and caring. Any man would be lucky to have you for his wife. Do not settle because you feel you have no choice. The right man will come along. Just you wait and see."

Tears swelled in Patience's bright blue eyes. Amelia hoped she would not begin to cry; the girl was prone to hysterics and leaps of emotion. Charity was only a notch better, and if one girl began the other was certain to follow. Two crying girls was not the spectacle Amelia hoped to make at a ball. She clapped her hands together and twirled around, so her skirts fanned out around her feet.

"Come now; let us find some of those handsome men to dance with. It should not be hard for three young ladies like us." Amelia glanced back.

Patience was wiping at her eyes and fidgeting with her dress— no matter how many times Amelia scolded her for it, the girl could not quit the nervous and irritating gesture—which generally wrinkled her dress with two fist sized wads on either side of her waist. Meanwhile Charity was puffing out her chest like a seabird. One more deep breath and she was sure to burst her seams.

It would be up to Amelia, then. In a matter of minutes she had snagged two gentlemen and placed one with Charity and one with Patience on the promise that she herself would dance with them afterward. Though men waited around her, looking hopefully in her direction, none dared approach until she gave them a sign of interest. She had already earned a reputation of being discerning with whom she favored, and no man wanted the stigma of having been turned away. Amelia perused the ballroom at her leisure, silently wishing for something more than doters and flatterers after her father's influence.

❧

SAMUEL BERESFORD DID NOT WANT to be here. He found balls a tremendous waste of time, the dancing and the flirting and, thinly veiled beneath it all, the bargaining.

For that was what marriage boiled down to, a bargain. It was all about striking a deal where each person involved believed they had the advantage over the other. If it were not for his brother's pleading, he would never been seen at a fancy affair like this. Dressed in his naval uniform, a blue coat with gold epaulets and trimmings and white waistcoat and breeches, he attracted more attention than he wished.

"Stop scowling, Samuel," said Percival as he returned to his brother's side from a brief sojourn with a group of lords. "You look positively dour."

"Did you find the man?" Samuel inquired.

Percival sipped his wine and shook his head. "It is no matter. Let us concentrate on the women. We should be enjoying their company and you seem intent on scaring them all off with your sour expression."

Unlike himself, Samuel's older brother Percival loved the frivolity of these occasions. As the eldest son of an earl it was very nearly an obligation of his office to enjoy them, so Samuel could not begrudge his brother doing his duty.

"You think it my expression and not our looks that are to blame?" Samuel asked, only half in jest. To appease his brother he hid his scowl behind the rim of his wine glass.

The Beresford brothers were not of disagreeable appearance, but they lacked the boyish looks so favored at the moment. They did not look gentlemanly, the brothers were too large, their features too distinctly masculine, for the women to fawn and coo over. Additionally Samuel had been sent to the Royal Naval Academy at the age of twelve, a life that had led him to be solidly built, broad across the chest and shoulders. He felt a giant amongst the gentry.

"Smile a bit brother, and let us find out." Percy elbowed Samuel in the side.

CONTINUE READING....
The Duke's Daughter ~ Lady Amelia Atherton

or

**Download the Entire
Ladies of Bath Collection**

WANT EVEN MORE REGENCY ROMANCE...

Follow Isabella Thorne on BookBub
https://www.bookbub.com/profile/isabella-thorne

Sign up for my VIP Reader List!

at

https://isabellathorne.com/

Receive weekly updates from Isabella and an
EXCLUSIVE FREE STORY

Like Isabella Thorne on Facebook
https://www.facebook.com/isabellathorneauthor/

Manufactured by Amazon.ca
Bolton, ON